D0047799

That Certain Summer

Books by Irene Hannon

Heroes of Quantico

Against All Odds

An Eye for an Eye

In Harm's Way

Guardians of Justice

Fatal Judgment

Deadly Pursuit

Lethal Legacy

Private Justice

Vanished

That Certain Summer

A Novel

IRENE HANNON

a division of Baker Publishing Group
Grand Rapids, Michigan

© 2013 by Irene Hannon

Published by Revell
a division of Baker Publishing Group
P.O. Box 6287, Grand Rapids, MI 49516-6287
www.revellbooks.com

Printed in the United States of America

All rights reserved. No part of this publication may be reproduced, stored in a retrieval system, or transmitted in any form or by any means—for example, electronic, photocopy, recording—without the prior written permission of the publisher. The only exception is brief quotations in printed reviews.

Library of Congress Cataloging-in-Publication Data

Hannon, Irene.
That certain summer : a novel / Irene Hannon.
pages cm
ISBN 978-0-8007-2249-4 (pbk.)
1. Sisters—Fiction. 2. Homecoming—Fiction. 3. Mothers and daughters—Fiction. 4. Love stories. 5. Christian fiction. I. Title.
PS3558.A4793T48 2013
813′.54—dc23 2013000138

This book is a work of fiction. Names, characters, places, and incidents are the product of the author's imagination or are used fictitiously. Any resemblance to actual events, locales, or persons, living or dead, is coincidental.

The internet addresses, email addresses, and phone numbers in this book are accurate at the time of publication. They are provided as a resource. Baker Publishing Group does not endorse them or vouch for their content or permanence.

13 14 15 16 17 18 19 7 6 5 4 3 2 1

To my dear nieces,
Catherine and Maureen Hannon—
may you always be sisters *and* friends.

And to Janice McCreary—
a treasured friend . . .
and a sister of the heart.

Prologue

—— Karen ——

Storms, she could handle.

This, however, was a tsunami.

As the nurse adjusted the drip on her mother's IV, Karen Butler fought back a wave of panic and shifted in her chair to stare out the window. In the distance, a solitary oak tree reached toward the sky, its bare limbs devoid of life despite the lush growth of a Missouri spring all around it. A casualty of the harsh winter.

She could relate.

"Your mother's doing very well. She's lucky it was a mild stroke. How are *you* holding up?" The nurse moved toward the door.

"Fine."

Liar, liar.

"Well, if you'd like some coffee or a soft drink, there's a small kitchen next to the nurses' station. Help yourself."

"Thanks."

Giving up the futile attempt to find a comfortable position, Karen rose, stretched the kinks out of her back, and began to pace.

No matter how mild the stroke, her mother was still going to need lots of help for the foreseeable future.

And guess who was expected to provide it?

Good old reliable Karen.

A weight settled on her chest, squeezing the breath from her lungs. So far, she'd kept all her balls in the air, but how many more could she juggle? Didn't a shattered marriage, a job outside the home for the first time in more than a dozen years, and a rebellious daughter whose transition to teenager had been complicated by her parents' split provide enough challenges?

Pausing at the foot of the bed, Karen watched the steady rise and fall of the white sheet over Margaret's prone form. Her mother had looked the same for as long as she could remember. Iron gray hair, rigidly coiffed in a style twenty years out-of-date. Thin lips that turned down at the corners in a perennially disapproving expression that remained unyielding even in repose. An angular bone structure, softened neither by the extra weight she carried nor by a charitable, tolerant disposition.

In the best of times, she wasn't easy to please. While dealing with a stroke? She'd be impossible.

The knot in Karen's stomach tightened, and she crossed her arms, squeezing the flesh above her elbows. All her life, she'd tried to please Margaret. To accept family obligations without complaint. And what had it brought her? Nothing except criticism.

Yet what choice had there been after Val abdicated all family responsibilities and ran off to pursue a career in theater?

Her gaze fell on the small silver roses in her mother's pierced ears—a gift from her sister on some long-ago birthday—and the familiar resentment bubbled up inside her . . . followed, as usual, by annoyance.

Good grief, would she never grow up? She was too old for such petty nonsense. So what if Val was the golden girl with the charmed life? So what if she was Mom's favorite? She ought to get over it.

But she couldn't.

Because it still hurt.

Huffing out a breath, Karen turned her back on the bed. Enough.

She had more important things to worry about at the moment than her messy tangle of emotions—like figuring out how she was going to deal with this latest complication. It didn't help that Kristen was hobbling around on a broken leg or that the busy season at work, with its requisite longer hours, was kicking in, either.

Face it, Karen. You need help.

No!

She clenched her teeth and straightened her shoulders. Maybe she wasn't as pretty or popular or confident or talented as Val, but she'd always been organized and competent and able to cope with whatever life threw at her.

She'd get through this, like she always did.

A garbled sound came from behind her, and she turned. Her mother jabbed at the air with her good hand.

Karen crossed to the side of the bed. "What do you need, Mom?"

Margaret grabbed her arm with surprising strength and uttered more gibberish as she shook it, her face contorted with frustration.

The heart monitor began to beep.

Her own pulse tripping into double time, Karen grabbed the call button and pressed it.

"Hang on, Mom. I'll get the nurse."

Two minutes later, as the woman calmed her mother down and retrieved a bedpan, Karen backed away.

She couldn't do this alone.

Everyone had their limit, and she'd just hit hers.

Gritting her teeth, she pulled her cell out of her purse. Like it or not, Val needed to come home.

Not being the operative word—for both of them.

—— Val ——

Hand on the door of her condo, Val Montgomery hesitated as the phone began to ring. Her teenage cast was going to freak if she was late for the dress rehearsal, and spending the first hour trying to calm a gym full of hyper adolescents held zero appeal.

Hitching her purse higher on her shoulder, she dug through her oversize tote bag for her keys. Let the caller leave a message.

"Val, it's Karen." Her sister's voice echoed through the condo as the answering machine kicked in, and her hand froze. "I need to talk to you as soon as possible. Please call me on my cell when you get this message. I have a new phone, and I jotted the number down somewhere. Give me a sec . . ."

In the silence that followed, a tingle of apprehension zipped through her.

If Karen was calling, there must be a serious problem.

Hand still on the knob, she chewed on her lower lip. A crisis wasn't in her plans for tonight . . . but if she left without talking to her sister, she'd be distracted all evening—and adrenaline-pumped teens required her full attention.

With a resigned sigh, she walked over to the phone and lifted it out of its cradle. "Karen? I was walking out the door. What's up?"

"Thank goodness I caught you! I'm at the hospital. Mom had a stroke."

Stroke.

As the word ricocheted through her mind, Val tried to process that bombshell.

It didn't compute.

Their mother had a lot of problems, but despite her myriad complaints, she'd always been healthy as a horse.

Combing her fingers through her hair, she stared out the window at the gray clouds gathering on the horizon. "How bad is it?"

"Mild, according to the doctors. They're still doing tests, but it's clear she's going to need some help for a while."

And I expect you to pitch in.

Though the words were unspoken, the message came through loud and clear.

Clamping her lips together, Val tightened her grip on the phone. Not going to happen. The very notion of spending an extended period with her manipulative, self-centered mother turned her stomach. How Karen had managed to live in such close proximity to her all these years without going crazy was beyond comprehension.

As the silence lengthened and she struggled to fabricate an excuse that would absolve her of the implied obligation, Karen spoke again.

"Look, I'm sorry to dump this on you." A thread of desperation wove through her sister's words. "I'd deal with it on my own if I could, but Kristen broke her leg a couple of days ago in gymnastics, and things are hectic at work. I can't manage two patients without some help. With your school year ending soon, I thought maybe you could come down for a few weeks, just to get us over the hump."

A few weeks!?

As she tried to wrap her mind around that nauseating notion, the second part of Karen's comment suddenly registered.

"Why didn't you tell me about Kristen?"

"I didn't see any reason to bother you. It's not like you're close enough to help out."

Val let the inferred criticism pass. "Is she okay?"

"Not to hear her talk. She missed the final gymnastics meet, the pool's off-limits, and she's out of commission for her typical summer activities. In her mind, the world is ending. But according to the doctor, she'll be fine."

Val's lips quirked. "Being a teenager is tough."

"Trust me, I'm reminded of that every day."

"Me too. As a matter of fact, I've got a bunch of high school thespians waiting for me, and if I don't show up pronto, the drama won't all be on the stage. Can I get back to you later tonight to talk about this?"

A slight hesitation, followed by a terse reply, told her Karen recognized the request for the stall tactic it was. "Yeah. I'll probably still be at the hospital. Let me give you the numbers for Mom's room and my cell phone."

As Val jotted them down, she checked her watch. "I'll call you in a couple of hours."

"Fine."

The line went dead—and based on her sister's resigned tone, it was clear Karen expected her to bail.

But as she shoved the phone numbers into her tote, guilt niggled at her conscience. When had Karen ever asked for help—with anything? Never, as far as she could remember. Meaning her sister must be at the end of her rope. And it wasn't as if her own plans for the summer were all that pressing, other than two modeling commitments she could commute to fulfill. Plus, she knew how to handle their mother—a skill Karen had never mastered.

She could go.

But as she toyed with the idea of returning to the Missouri river town of her childhood, a wave of panic swept over her.

Tightening her fingers on her keys, she closed her eyes and fought back a surge of painful memories—the same ones that had been cropping up more and more often during the past few months, battling their way out of the dark prison where she'd banished them, clamoring for release. So far, she'd managed to corral them. But they were growing more unruly and insistent, and her control over them was slipping.

One of these days, she was going to lose the battle to contain them.

Then what?

She swallowed. It was time to face the hard truth she'd been dodging for months.

The only way to free herself from the mistakes that haunted her was to confront them and deal with them once and for all.

And maybe she'd just been handed an opportunity to do that.

Her hand began to throb, and she loosened her grip on the keys, eying the angry red imprint they'd left on her fingers. If she'd continued to hold on to them, the ridges would have become deeper, numbness would have set in, and function would have become more and more limited. Letting go was the only way to restore normalcy.

To her fingers.

And perhaps to her life.

Val closed her eyes.

It was time to go home to Washington.

—— Scott ——

"Come on, guys, pick up the pace. I'm ready to crash."

Scott Walker shot Mark a weary grin and transferred his saxophone case to his other hand as they exited the jazz club. "Maybe you're getting too old for this life."

"Maybe we all are." Joe led the way to their van. "What city are we in again?"

"Philadelphia." Their publicist hit the remote for the locks. "After the honky-tonk dives you guys played for ten years, you should be grateful Prestige booked you in some class places to promote your debut album."

"We are." Scott opened the door of the van and climbed in. "But we've been doing one-night gigs for six weeks. It takes a toll." He stifled a yawn. "We'll be fine after some z's."

He hoped.

But the constant travel and disrupted sleep and incessant demands of the recording company for more radio and TV interviews, more social media visibility, more PR appearances and glad-handing were wearing. They hadn't pursued careers in music to schmooze.

Funny how their big break had given them less time to do what they loved best.

Silence fell as they all settled in and their publicist took the wheel. Joe and Mark fell asleep within minutes. Lulled by the motion of the van, Scott began to drift too—until a rough jolt jarred him awake.

As he struggled to jump-start his brain, he heard a sudden squeal of brakes. His shoulder slammed against the side of the van. Headlights that seemed mere inches away blinded him. A screeching cacophony of ripping metal ricocheted in his ears, and he raised his hand to shield his face.

There were screams.

Shouts.

Pain that was sharp and intense and suffocating.

Confusion.

But in the moments before blackness engulfed him, Scott knew one thing with absolute clarity.

Their promotional tour was over.

And even if he survived, his life would never be the same.

—— David ——

"Why are we moving, Daddy?"

David Phelps set aside the stack of plates he was packing and looked down at his daughter. How many times had he answered that question over the past few weeks? Dozens, for sure. But five-year-olds didn't retain information long—especially information that didn't make sense to them. And no matter how he explained it, Victoria couldn't understand why they were leaving the condo that had been her home since she was born.

"Because I have a new job in a different place called Washington, Missouri, and because I want us to live in a house with a yard for you to play in." David dropped down to balance on the balls of his feet beside her, brushing a stray strand of silky blonde hair off her forehead.

She frowned, planted her hands on her hips, and tilted her head. The stance, so reminiscent of Natalie, clogged his throat.

"I can play in the park at the corner. It has swings and a slide."

"But it's not your very own yard. And you'll have a much bigger room too. We can paint it pink."

"I like purple better."

"Then purple it is."

All at once her shoulders drooped and she hung her head. "I still don't want to move. I like St. Louis."

So did he. But prayer had led him to this decision. To the acceptance that certain dreams had died and that it was time to let go of the past.

But how to explain that to a five-year-old? All Victoria knew was that her world was about to be turned upside down. Again.

He pulled her into his arms and gave her a hug. "St. Louis is nice, honey, but I think we'll like Washington too, once we get there."

"What if we don't?" Her tear-laced words were muffled against his shirt.

"Then we'll move somewhere else."

She backed up and scrutinized him. "Solemn promise?"

Their private version of "cross my heart and hope to die," reserved for only the most serious matters.

David's gaze didn't waver. "Solemn promise."

She fingered a button on his shirt. "Okay. But we won't know anybody there. We'll be all by ourselves."

"No, we won't. Remember, Jesus is always with us, no matter where we go."

"When you can't see someone, though, it's hard to remember they're there."

Pulling her close again, David cradled her head against his chest. No argument there. During the past few years, there had been many occasions when God had seemed far away to him too. But he had to keep believing that even on his most challenging days, when he felt most alone, God wouldn't desert him.

Because he had a feeling moving to Washington would bring a whole new set of daunting challenges.

1

"Karen? Put the food out. We've waited long enough. Just leave some for Val in the oven. She can eat when she gets here if she's hungry."

At her mother's annoyed call from the living room, Karen leaned on the kitchen counter and counted to ten.

Slowly.

All the while battling the temptation to snatch her purse, walk out the door, and tackle the bills and the laundry waiting for her at home instead of fetching, carrying, and cooking for her mother after her demanding day at work.

"Karen? Did you hear me?"

As the shrill question reverberated through the house, she squelched the impulse to flee. She was the responsible daughter, after all. But was it uncharitable to wish her mother's speech hadn't returned to normal with quite such alacrity?

On the threshold of the living room, she paused as her mother flipped through the TV channels. "I heard you, Mom. But it might be nice to wait for Val. I'm sure she'll be ready for some food after the long drive."

"The theater business is unpredictable. She probably got tied up."

Her blood pressure edged up another notch. "She teaches high school drama. She's not on Broadway."

"She could have been. I never understood why she didn't try harder to make a name for herself. Help me into the kitchen."

In silence, Karen moved beside her. By the time she managed to hoist her mother out of the easy chair, she was breathing hard.

"You need to get in shape. A young woman like you shouldn't be winded from a little exercise."

Compressing her lips, Karen counted to three; she didn't have the luxury of ten this time. "I don't have a spare minute to go to the gym." *And you're not exactly a lightweight.*

"Val never went to the gym, and she was always thin."

Sure. Rub it in.

"Maybe her metabolism is different." The comment came out sharper than she intended.

"You don't have to get huffy about it."

Biting back another retort, Karen handed her mother her cane. Too bad she hadn't insisted Margaret take the walker or wheelchair that had been offered, despite her mother's protest that she didn't want to look like an invalid.

But the assertive gene seemed to have passed her by.

At least physical therapy should restore full function to her mother's left arm and leg—and the sooner the better; her shoulder screamed in protest as they inched toward the kitchen, Margaret's weight dragging her down.

"What's for dinner?" Margaret settled into her chair and re-adjusted her cutlery, straightening the knife and spoon, putting a more precise crease in the napkin, moving her water glass two inches to the right.

Her stomach knotted. She couldn't even set a table to her mother's satisfaction.

Let it go, Karen.

She tried, even managing to infuse her voice with a dash of animation. "One of your favorites. Shepherd's pie. And since there's nothing to cut, you should be able to manage on your own."

"You didn't use canned carrots, did you?"

Karen turned her back to retrieve the casserole from the oven. *Lord, give me patience and strength.* "No. I followed your recipe."

She set the casserole on the table. It was a little crisp around the edges, but it had held up well despite the delay. The mashed potato crust was golden and the aroma enticing. "Smells good, doesn't it?" Karen dished out two generous servings.

"The test is in the tasting." Margaret gave the crust a prim, exploratory poke with her fork.

No thanks for going to the trouble of making the involved dish. No comment about how appetizing it looked. No enthusiasm.

Typical.

Shaking her head, Karen covered the rest of the casserole with foil and put it back in the oven. After sliding into her seat at the table, she bowed her head.

"Lord, we thank you for this food and for the many gifts you give us. We ask you to keep us in your care and continue to provide for all of our needs, both physical and spiritual. Nourish our souls with your love, as you nourish our bodies with this food. Amen."

Margaret scooped up a forkful of potato. "It's too bad some of your faith didn't rub off on your daughter."

So much for any hope of a pleasant dinner conversation.

"Kristen's just going through the usual teenage rebellious stage. She'll find her way back to God."

"Hmph. God isn't the only one she's deserted. I haven't had more than a glimpse of her since my stroke."

"It's hard for her to get around with the broken leg."

"It wouldn't kill her to make a little effort to see her grandmother."

"How's the shepherd's pie?"

The question came out before Karen could stop it. Prompted in part by a need to change the subject, but more by the need to win her mother's approval about *something.*

"Too much salt." Despite that critique, her mother continued to eat with gusto.

The last vestige of Karen's appetite vanished, and pressure built behind her eyes.

No! Don't you dare cry! Just hang on a few more minutes. As soon as Val gets here, you can escape.

Two minutes later, after she managed to choke down a couple more bites, she heard the crunch of gravel in the driveway.

Yes!

She was already pulling open the back door as Val lifted her arm to knock.

As her sister's hand froze, Karen did a quick inventory. In the year since she'd seen her younger sibling, Val hadn't changed much. Same sleek blonde hair. Same perfect figure. Same chic taste in clothes. Same aura of glamour.

In other words, her polar opposite.

Karen smoothed down her crumpled khaki skirt and rubbed at a spatter of grease on her blouse. She already knew she was a slightly overweight woman approaching middle age, with dull brown hair, drab clothes, and a mundane life—but standing next to Val, she felt downright dowdy.

Then again, what else was new?

Val inclined her head toward the table and spoke softly. "A little anxious for relief, are we?"

Karen stiffened. "You're late."

"There was major road construction an hour north of here. My cell was dead or I'd have called. I didn't think it would be a big deal."

"Kristen's waiting for me at home. She hasn't eaten yet. I held dinner as long as I could, but Mom was hungry. I left you some in the oven."

"Close the door! You're letting all the cool air out. My electric bill will be sky high." Margaret waved a fork in their direction.

"It shouldn't be this hot in the middle of May. Must be that global warming they keep talking about. The world is going to pot, if you ask me."

A humorless smile twisted Val's lips. "I see she hasn't changed."

"She's sick."

"She's always been like this, sick or well." Val took a deep breath. "Okay, I guess I have to face the lion." She resettled her purse on her shoulder, stood up straighter, and stepped past Karen. "Hi, Mom. Your prodigal daughter has returned."

"It's about time." Margaret looked her up and down and sniffed.

"It's good to see you too."

"Hmph." Margaret pushed her glasses higher on her nose. "Well, of course I'm glad you're home. Karen can't keep up, and I need help."

"That's true." Val's reply sounded innocuous, but Karen caught the double meaning.

Margaret didn't.

"We'll have to talk in the morning." Margaret chased the last minuscule morsel of ground beef around her plate and forked it into her mouth. "I need to lie down. Karen, help me into the bedroom."

"I'm here now, Mom. I can take over those kinds of chores." Val dropped her purse on the table and moved to Margaret's side.

"You're too thin to have any strength. Let Karen help. She has more meat on her bones."

A warm flush suffused Karen's cheeks.

That's right, Mom, just keep rubbing it in.

"We'll both help." Val flexed one of her arms. "I've been doing weight training. You might be surprised how strong I am." She motioned Karen to the other side of Margaret's chair.

Karen moved into position, and between the two of them they had Margaret into her room and ready for bed in fifteen minutes flat. Once she was settled, they returned to the kitchen.

"I made shepherd's pie." Karen picked up a pot holder. "There's enough for you and Kristen. I thought you might be hungry after the long drive."

"I appreciate that, but I stopped and got a salad along the way."

"That's all you're eating for dinner? Lettuce?"

"There was chicken in it."

"That's not much of a dinner. This is a lot heartier."

Without comment, Val moved toward the counter as Karen peeled back the foil.

Unfortunately, the dish hadn't held up as well the second time around. The filling had spread over the bottom of the casserole, and small pools of grease dotted the surface. The once-fluffy potato topping had caved in and dried out, and the carrots were tired and limp.

Karen caught the curl of distaste on Val's lips before her sister masked it.

Her blood pressure moved into the danger range.

"It looked a lot better an hour or two ago, when you were supposed to be here." Hot spots burned in her cheeks.

"Hey, I appreciate the thought. But the salad was all I needed."

Turning away, Karen recrimped the foil over the casserole and shoved the dish into a thermal tote. "I have a daughter at home who's probably starving. I'm sure she'll be happy to eat your share."

"Look, I'm sorry. I know you went to a lot of trouble. This is one of Mom's favorites, isn't it? I bet she enjoyed it."

"Not that you'd notice. She said it was too salty." Once more, tears pushed against the back of her eyes. Once more, she fought them into submission.

"That sounds like Mom."

"Sometimes I wonder why I even try." Karen zipped the tote with more force than necessary.

"So do I."

She fisted her hands and faced her sister. "Look, I don't need any more criticism tonight, okay? I try because I have no choice. I live here. I have to make an effort to get along with her."

For a moment, Val regarded her in silence. "You do have a choice, you know. And maybe you try too hard."

"That's easy for you to say. You don't deal with her every day."

"By choice."

"I couldn't walk away."

"Why not?"

"My life was here. I was married."

"Also a choice."

And not a good one.

Although Val didn't say the words, the message resonated.

Karen picked up the casserole. "I need to leave."

"I did too."

There was an odd undertone in her sister's quiet response, but she was too angry to dwell on it. "That didn't absolve you of family obligations. I've had to do everything around here since you went off to college seventeen years ago and never came back. Didn't you ever feel guilty?"

A shadow crossed Val's eyes. "Why don't we leave this discussion for another day? I'm tired and you're stressed."

"Fine with me." Karen hoisted the casserole into the crook of her arm and grabbed her purse. "Call me tomorrow and I'll fill you in on Mom's therapy schedule and medications. Do you need any help bringing your stuff in from the car?"

"I can manage."

"I made up your old room for you. There are fresh towels in the guest bath."

"Thanks."

At the door, Karen paused. Val was leaning against the nicked Formica countertop that had been in the kitchen for as long as she could remember. Not much had changed in the house since they were kids.

In any way.

But walking out in a huff wasn't going to improve things.

"I don't know how we got into all that stuff tonight, but I do appreciate your willingness to help." Her words came out stiff. Grudging instead of grateful. But she'd been at her mother's beck and call for years. This was only fair.

Val lifted one shoulder. "It was my turn."

"Don't let Mom get to you."

"I'll cope."

"I'm sure you will." Being their mother's favorite hadn't spared Val from Margaret's acerbic tongue, but she hadn't let the criticism bother her. "I'll talk to you tomorrow. Welcome home."

"Thanks."

The response was perfunctory—but from Val's tone and expression, Karen knew that home was the last place her sister wanted to be.

The TV was blaring when Karen stepped through her own kitchen door ten minutes later, and the pounding in her temples went from easy-listening bass to heavy metal.

"Kristen? I'm home!"

No response as she set the casserole on the counter. Given the volume on the TV, that didn't surprise her.

Girding herself for the onslaught, she waded into the noise.

She found Kristen in the family room, angled away from the door, her thigh-high cast propped on an ottoman while she typed on her laptop. She wore headphones and was tapping her uninjured foot to a beat only she could hear.

Shaking her head, Karen picked up the TV remote and punched the off button. Blessed silence descended.

With a frown, Kristen pulled the buds from her ears. "I was watching that."

"It's impossible to do three things at once."

Kristen scowled at her. "It's called multitasking. Kids do it all the time."

"So do adults. But you constantly have to switch back and forth. That takes a lot of effort and it's not very efficient." She motioned toward the blank TV screen. "And that particular program wasn't worth the effort."

"You don't like anything on TV."

"Not much. Are you hungry?"

"I had some chips earlier. I thought you were going to be home sooner."

"Val was late. I tried to call twice, but the line was busy."

"I was talking to Gary." Kristen gave her a defiant look.

Karen resisted the bait. She might not care for Kristen's latest heartthrob, but she wasn't up to another argument tonight. "I brought you dinner. Come on. I'll help you up."

Far lighter and much more agile than Margaret, Kristen didn't need much assistance. Once her daughter was on her feet, Karen picked up the crutches from the floor and handed them to her.

"This broken leg stinks." Kristen grimaced at the cast as she fitted the crutches under her arms.

"It could have been worse."

Kristen rolled her eyes and expelled a noisy breath. "Are you going to bring up Steven again?"

"You did it for me. Thinking about him should give you some perspective. Being forced to use a pair of crutches for a few weeks is a lot better than spending the rest of your life as a paraplegic. He's got a tough road ahead."

"Yeah." Kristen furrowed her brow. "The accident was awful. I feel bad for him."

"I hope you also pray for him."

"It won't do any good." Her daughter's features hardened. "He isn't going to get better. And why did God let him get hurt in the first place?"

"I don't know. Only God has that answer. That's where faith—and trust—come in."

"That doesn't make bad stuff any easier to accept." Kristen

stared down at the iridescent purple toenails sticking out of the bottom of the cast. "Erin said she heard from her boyfriend, who's Steven's cousin, that he tried to kill himself."

Karen's heart stuttered. "When?"

"After he came home from the hospital."

"Then we need to pray harder."

"God doesn't listen to my prayers." Kristen's jaw firmed. "I prayed you and Dad would get back together, but you got divorced instead."

The pounding in Karen's head intensified. "There were problems in our marriage that couldn't be overcome."

"You didn't even try! You sat back and let Stephanie take Dad away from you! Why didn't you stand up to him? Tell him to stay with us, where he belonged? You always let him walk all over you, just like you let Grandma boss you around!"

Karen drew in a sharp breath. "Kristen! That's enough!"

"It's true!"

Instead of responding, she turned on her heel and spoke over her shoulder. "I'll put your dinner out."

Thirty seconds later, the zipper balking under her shaky fingers, she opened the thermal tote. She shouldn't let Kristen get away with that kind of disrespectful behavior, but she hated confrontations—especially with her daughter.

Besides, Kristen was right.

She *had* let Michael walk all over her. She'd put up with his moodiness, his demeaning comments, his autocratic manner. Had deferred to his opinion and his judgment, hoping her acquiescence would keep peace in the household. She'd done the same with her mother, convinced that if she was docile, if she did what she was told, the relationship would improve.

But that approach hadn't worked with either of them. Margaret continued to fault-find and Michael had left for greener pastures. Namely, Stephanie.

The creak of crutches signaled Kristen's arrival, and Karen lifted the foil off the casserole. The food was in worse shape than it had been earlier, and Kristen's reaction mirrored Val's. In fact, with her long blonde hair and vivid blue eyes, her daughter bore a striking resemblance to her aunt at the same age.

"What is it?" Kristen wrinkled her nose in disgust.

"Shepherd's pie."

"Gross." With one more glance at the sorry casserole, she turned away. "Can I order Chinese?"

Swallowing past the tightness in her throat, she choked out a single-word response. "Fine."

As Kristen clumped away, Karen surveyed the pie and blinked back tears. Her daughter was right. It was a mess.

Just like her life.

Even through the thick plaster walls of the solid brick bungalow she'd called home for the first eighteen years of her life, Val could hear her mother snoring.

At least someone was sleeping.

Rising on one elbow, she peered at the bedside clock. Two in the morning.

There wasn't going to be much sleep this night—but her mother's snoring wasn't to blame.

She flopped back on the pillow and stared at the dark ceiling. Nights were the pits. In her idle mind, the unwanted memories crept from the darkness and swooped like hawks stalking their prey.

After twenty more minutes of tossing, Val gave up the battle and swung her legs over the edge of the bed. The mattress creaked in protest when she rose, then the room fell silent again as she moved through the shadows, letting her fingers brush over a beauty pageant trophy, a framed program from a school play, a blue ribbon for a dramatic reading she'd done while on the speech team.

Those represented the good memories.

She paused in front of the bureau, where the object representing her worst one was hidden, and wiped her palms down her gym shorts. She hadn't opened the top drawer in years. And maybe it was a mistake to take this step on her first night home.

But she had to look inside sooner or later—and it might be easier to take this first step under cover of darkness. In the shadows, perhaps she could hide from herself . . . and God.

Grasping the handles on the top drawer, she gave a tentative tug.

It didn't budge.

She tried again, with more force.

This time, it shifted a little. But it was clear no one had opened it in a long while.

Val hesitated. Maybe this was a sign. Maybe she wasn't supposed to stir up the ashes of the long-ago fire that had consumed her soul and left her heart in tatters.

But if she didn't, would she ever vanquish the nightmares that were growing more intense as she approached the anniversary of the day that had changed her life forever?

No.

She had to do this. Now.

Val grasped the handles again and pulled with more force. After a squeal of protest, the drawer gave way. She paused, but Margaret's snoring continued unabated. That figured. Her mother was as oblivious to her younger daughter's nocturnal activities now as she had been eighteen years ago.

Once the drawer was half open, she reached inside, feeling her way into the farthest corner.

For a brief second she thought it was gone, and she groped with more urgency. Then her hand grazed the familiar cylinder, and she closed her eyes.

All these years it had lain undisturbed. Hidden. In the dark. Seen only by her since the long-ago day she'd tucked it here.

But maybe it would have been better if someone had discovered her secret, had called her to task for her terrible mistake. Perhaps if she'd been caught and punished, she would have found her way to absolution years ago. Been freed from the yoke of guilt that had weighed her down far too long.

But she couldn't change the past. She could only deal with the present.

Fighting down her dread, Val withdrew the innocuous brown cardboard cylinder that had once held waxed paper.

Now it contained something far more precious.

Clutching it to her chest, she groped her way to the window seat. Her hands trembled as she fitted her fingers inside the tube and eased out the single sheet of paper. It was curled into a tight scroll, and as she carefully spread it out next to her on the faded floral upholstery, the yellowed paper crinkled in protest.

For several minutes, Val stared at the brittle sheet, heart pounding as silent tears ran down her cheeks. One splashed onto the paper, forming a damp, dark circle. Once dry, it would leave a spot with ragged edges. Like all the others scattered over the sheet.

This was why she'd come back to Washington. Across the miles and across the years, her tragic mistake had hung like a shadow over her life, awaiting her return. It was time to confront it. Make peace with her past. Move on.

The destination was clear.

Figuring out how to get there, however, was far more murky.

And even though caring for her mother wasn't going to be easy, it would be a piece of cake compared to her quest for redemption.

2

"Are you telling me the paralysis is all in my head?" Scott stared at the white-coated figure seated behind the impressive walnut desk. His fingers itched to yank the cord on the blinds behind the man and shut out the glare of the mid-May sun seeping between the half-closed slats, but he resisted.

"No. Your hand suffered serious nerve damage. In time, if you continue to do the exercises the physical therapist prescribed, you should see significant improvement. And complete recovery isn't out of the question—if that's what you want."

Scott narrowed his eyes. "What's that supposed to mean? Do you think I want to spend the rest of my life like this?" He lifted his left hand and tried to flex his unresponsive fingers.

"Not on a conscious level, perhaps, but the trauma you sustained in the accident was psychological as well as physical." The gray-haired doctor leaned forward. "You lost more than the use of your left hand, Scott. You lost two friends. You lost the future you'd prepared for. You lost the dream that had been your focus for what . . . ten, fifteen years? After your hand heals, you'll have to rebuild your life. You'll have to make decisions about your future and move on. And you may not be ready to do that yet."

"I didn't know you were a psychologist, Doctor."

If the man was insulted by his sarcastic tone, he didn't let on. Settling back in his leather chair, he steepled his fingers. "You learn a lot about what makes people tick in this business. But someone trained in psychology could offer you a lot more insights than I can."

Scott let several beats of silence tick by. "Are you saying I should see a shrink?"

"You've been through a lot. Professional counseling could be helpful."

"What about the headaches? Are they all in my head too? Pardon the pun."

"No. You had a severe concussion. The headaches will diminish over time, but it could take months. How often are you getting them?"

"Every day."

"On a scale of one to ten, with ten being debilitating, how bad are the worst ones?"

"Eight. Sometimes nine."

The doctor leaned forward and pulled a prescription pad toward him. He scribbled a few words, tore off the sheet, and handed it to Scott. "This should help." Then he wrote on a second sheet and handed that over too. "If you change your mind about seeing a psychologist, here's the name of a good man."

After a brief hesitation, Scott took the sheet and stuck it in his pocket. "Thanks."

The doctor tapped his pen against his palm as he assessed Scott. "You're not going to call him, are you?"

"I'd prefer to get through this on my own."

"It's not a sign of weakness to admit we sometimes need help coping with the challenges life throws our way."

"I'll keep that in mind."

With a sigh, the doctor rose and extended his hand. "Call me if you need anything before our next appointment."

Scott returned the handshake. "Thanks."

As he exited the office and walked toward the elevator, every step sent a reverberating ripple of pain to his temples. An attractive twentysomething woman in a lab coat gave him a discreet once-over as he passed, but he kept moving. Entered the elevator. Closed the door. Once upon a time, he'd enjoyed that kind of attention. Had worked hard to get it, in fact. Thanks to a strict regime of exercise and diet, few people would put his age at thirty-eight. All he would have had to do to encourage that lab assistant was smile and strike up a conversation.

But he just didn't care about the dating game anymore.

Or much else.

Stepping out of the elevator, he scanned the lobby.

It didn't take long to locate his mother. Dorothy Walker always stood out in a crowd. She looked like no other sixty-year-old woman he knew. With her slender build, short, stylish salt-and-pepper hair, propensity to jeans—plus her youthful attitude—she could pass for someone twenty years younger.

He watched her animated face as she sipped a cup of coffee and spoke with a young mother who was bouncing a baby on her knee. When the infant grabbed her finger, a tender yearning softened her features—and sent a pang through his heart. She'd have been a wonderful grandmother. But his passion had always been music, and his nomadic lifestyle wasn't conducive to marriage.

If she'd been disappointed by his choice, however, she'd never let on. In her typical style, she'd filled the void by volunteering as a foster grandparent at a local day care center. That was how his mom was. Always making lemonade out of lemons.

Too bad he hadn't inherited that ability.

He started toward her, placing each step with care to avoid any unnecessary jostling, struggling to swallow past the bitter taste of the lemons life had handed him. Maybe, in time, sweetness would return to his world. Maybe the shadows would clear and the hollow, empty, nothing-matters-anymore feelings would go away.

But he wasn't holding his breath.

His mother spotted him, and with a parting word to the young mother, she rose and met him halfway.

"Everything okay?" She laid a hand on his arm, a trace of anxiety playing counterpoint to her mild tone.

"Yeah. He said to keep doing the exercises, and that the headaches were normal. He gave me this for the pain." Scott withdrew a sheet of paper from the pocket of his jeans and handed it to her.

She read it, a puzzled frown creasing her brow. "All it says is Dr. Lawrence Matthews."

Great.

He'd given her the name of the shrink.

"Sorry." He plucked it from her fingers and fished in his pocket again. "Do you think we could get this filled here?"

Sharp pinpoints were beginning to prickle along his scalp, and he knew that within minutes they would ricochet with piercing intensity through his skull. The bright lights of the lobby were accelerating the process.

"Sure. There's a pharmacy down the hall." She took the script and urged him toward a chair. "Wait here." He reached for his wallet, but she stilled him with a touch. "We'll settle up at home. Sit."

Her ten-minute absence passed in a haze of pain, and when she rejoined him she had both a bottle of pills and a paper cup of water. By then, his headache was in full throttle, and even the simple motion of shaking out the pills was painful. After he downed them in one gulp, his mother took the cup out of his unsteady hand.

"Must be a bad one." At his silent, almost imperceptible nod, she took his arm. "Come on. I'll get the car."

He didn't argue. The pain was approaching ten on the scale his doctor had referenced, throbbing through every capillary in his head. All he wanted to do was lie down.

Instead, he had to endure the long drive back to Washington from St. Louis.

They didn't talk much during the trip. His mother asked only one question as they left the city traffic behind.

"Scott, who's Dr. Matthews?"

He didn't lift his head or open his eyes. "A psychologist."

He felt her silent scrutiny.

"You might want to consider talking to him."

"I'm not crazy."

"No, but life can be. Sometimes it's difficult to cope without help."

"You've always managed alone. Even after Dad died."

"I wasn't alone. God was with me every step of the way."

Lucky her. But even if his relationship with the Almighty hadn't faltered somewhere along the road to success, he doubted it would have held up in the face of the senseless tragedy that had taken three lives and destroyed his dreams.

"Are you saying people of faith never need human help?" He didn't really care about her answer, but neither did he want to be rude. Not after all she'd done for him.

"No. God often uses third parties to show us the way when we're lost."

"It wouldn't help, Mom. Trust me."

A few beats of silence passed. "I know your world seems dark now, but I also know the sun will shine for you again. And I have faith that one day you'll play the saxophone with every bit of the skill you had before the accident. Maybe more."

Instead of responding, he once more closed his eyes.

He wasn't in the mood for any more lemonade.

One hand on the refrigerator door, Val sighed as she perused the contents. How could a house contain so little food of nutritional value? Everything was either high carb, high fat, or loaded with sugar. Her mother's eating habits had never been very sound, but they'd bottomed out with age.

A quick trip to the grocery store to stock up on some essentials jumped to the top of her Thursday priority list—right after her mother's first physical therapy session.

Val closed the refrigerator and opened the freezer. A sausage and egg biscuit would have to do for Margaret. For herself, she'd settle for a whole-wheat anything—bagel, muffin, slice of bread.

No such luck. Processed white bread was the only option.

And the pineapple juice in the fridge was far too sweet.

So much for breakfast.

By the time she got her mother up and settled at the table, she felt as if she'd already put in a full day. Then again, her restless night could have something to do with her fatigue. She might not need eight hours of sleep, but three didn't cut it.

She retrieved the sausage/egg entrée from the microwave, set it in front of her mother, and poured herself a cup of coffee. Maybe a strong shot of caffeine would help.

"Is that all you're having?" Margaret peered at the coffee in disapproval.

"I'm not a breakfast person."

"You're too thin. There's plenty of food in the house. Eat something."

"This is all I want." Val propped a hip against the counter and checked her watch. "According to the schedule Karen left, you have your first physical therapy session at nine o'clock. We'd better get you dressed."

Her mother's jaw locked into a stubborn line. "I don't want to go."

"Sorry. Doctor's orders."

"It's a waste of time. I've been doing the exercises they gave me in the hospital. I'll eventually get better on my own."

"Eventually isn't good enough. Physical therapy will speed up the process."

"So you can go back to Chicago sooner?"

Val took a sip of coffee and kept her tone neutral. "I have the summer off except for a couple of modeling commitments. I plan to stay as long as I'm needed, but you should be well on the road to recovery long before I have to leave."

"And I suppose we won't see you again for another year or two." Margaret poked at her food, a sulky pout dragging down the corners of her mouth.

"Maybe. I lead a busy life." She took another unhurried drink of her coffee. Thank goodness she'd learned long ago to give no visible evidence that her mother was getting under her skin. It helped preserve her own sanity. Too bad Karen hadn't developed the same skill.

"Your sister's busy too, but she finds time for me."

She would. Karen had always been the perfect daughter. No sense trying to compete with that kind of ideal.

Pushing off from the counter, she changed the subject. "Let's pick out a comfortable outfit for you to wear."

With very little assistance from her mother, Val got the older woman dressed, into the car, and delivered to the physical therapy center with minutes to spare. Less than two days into her caretaker role, she was already wearing out. How did her sister manage to cope with their high-maintenance mother while dealing with the demands of her job, an adolescent, and the stresses of post-divorce life?

Then again, she'd always been the type to dig in her heels and get the job done, whatever it took. No shirking of responsibilities for her.

Val quashed a niggle of guilt as they entered the waiting room. She was already full up on that particular emotion, thank you very much.

Once seated, Margaret kept her busy retrieving a glass of water and scrounging up a selection of magazines after rejecting the first two Val offered as "trashy."

She'd just dropped into a chair when a sandy-haired man came to the door, clipboard in hand.

"Margaret Montgomery?"

No rest for the weary.

"Here." Val lifted her hand and stood to help her mother up. Despite her weight training and fitness regime, it had been much easier to get her mother up working in tandem with Karen.

Val was still struggling when the man in the doorway moved to Margaret's other side to assist.

"Let me help." He glanced at her with a smile over the top of her mother's head.

She stared at him.

He had the greenest eyes.

And that little dimple in his right cheek . . .

"On three, okay?"

Val dipped her head to hide the telltale flush creeping across her cheeks. "Okay."

Although she gave the effort her all, the man across from her did the lion's share of lifting, based on the impressive bulge of muscles below the sleeves of his T-shirt.

Once Margaret was on her feet, he gave Val an engaging grin. "Mission accomplished."

"Thanks."

"Not a problem." He turned his attention to her mother and held out his hand. "Margaret, I'm David Phelps. I'll be working with you for the next few weeks."

"How do you do?" Margaret took his hand. "This is my daughter, Val."

The man smiled at her again. "Nice to meet you. Will you be staying for the session?"

"I can, but I'd hoped to do some grocery shopping."

"There's plenty of food at the house." Margaret scowled at her over the top of her glasses.

"I want to pick up a few other things."

"No problem. Margaret and I will be fine by ourselves. Right, Margaret?" The man fixed his charming smile on the older woman.

Soft color suffused her mother's cheeks and she patted her hair. "Yes, I expect we will. You go along, Val. I can see I'm in good hands."

Reprieved!

She grabbed her purse. "I'll be back in an hour, if that's okay."

"That will be fine." David took her mother's arm. "Once Margaret and I are finished, I'd like to spend a few minutes with both of you to go over her therapy routine." He directed his next question to Margaret. "Do you have a walker?"

"No. I'm not an invalid. I just have this cane—and not for very long, I hope."

"That's the spirit. If I had more patients like you, I'd be out of a job."

Preen was the word that came to mind as Val watched her mother flutter her eyes at David.

Amazing.

Chalk one up for the therapist's boy-next-door good looks and easy charm.

"You run along." Margaret gave a regal, dismissive wave with her good hand. "We'll see you later."

Val was out the door before her mother had a chance to have second thoughts.

And she took full advantage of her hour break. She downed a container of yogurt as she waited in the checkout lane, indulged in a latte at the coffee shop next door to the grocery store, and picked up enough fresh fruit, vegetables, whole-grain bread, and lean meat to last until the weekend.

By the time she returned to the therapy center with five minutes to spare, she was feeling much more relaxed.

No sooner had she settled in with a magazine, however, than David summoned her from the door of the waiting room.

"How did it go?" Val edged past as he moved aside to let her precede him.

The man had nice manners.

"We had a productive session. Your mother was very cooperative, and she has a lot of spunk."

Val could think of many adjectives to describe her mother. "Cooperative" and "spunky" weren't among them.

"Mom can be pretty determined about going after what she wants." It was the kindest thing she could come up with short of lying.

"That's a good quality—under these circumstances, at least." He closed the door behind him.

"True. But to be honest, I'm a little surprised. I almost had to drag her here."

"A lot of patients feel that way. Part of our job is to help them see the value of therapy, persuade them it will speed up their recovery."

That argument might work with most people, but she was surprised it had swayed her mother. Speeding up her recovery meant less dependency. It meant her daughters wouldn't have to care for her with quite the same level of attention—and Margaret liked to be taken care of, sick or well. Why else would she have sold the car twenty years ago, after Dad died? She could have learned to drive, become more independent. She'd only been fifty. But no. She preferred relying on other people to take her places, then felt sorry for herself if they couldn't—or wouldn't. It fed into the long-suffering martyr complex she nurtured.

"You seem skeptical." David cocked his head as he regarded her.

The man was perceptive too.

"On the contrary. I'm admiring your powers of persuasion."

"And don't forget my charm."

His comment might have been made in jest, but he *was* charming. She could see why her mother had fallen under his spell. Not that he was Val's type, of course. He was too wholesome, too all-American for someone like her.

Besides, she wasn't in the market for romance.

"Shall we join your mother? Third door on the right."

He motioned down the hall, and Val preceded him, slipping into a chair beside her mother once they entered the tiny office. David took a seat behind a small desk.

"I did very well," Margaret told her.

"That's what I heard."

"Margaret certainly helped me get my new job off to a good start." David flashed the older woman a smile. "I hope it's an omen."

"You'll do fine." Margaret leaned over and patted his hand. "David just moved here from St. Louis. I was his very first patient in Washington. He decided to leave the big city behind." She arched her eyebrows at Val. "Some people appreciate the charms of small-town life."

David looked from mother to daughter and changed the subject. "I'm going to give you some sheets that describe the exercises we did today, Margaret. Val, I want to be sure you understand them too, since you'll be supervising the program at home."

For the next few minutes, he explained the exercise regime he'd developed. When he finished, he put the sheets in a folder and handed it to her. "Any questions?"

"It sounds straightforward."

"Margaret? How about you?"

"I just hope Val won't be a hard taskmaster." She sniffed and shot a dark look in her direction.

"A good coach pushes his or her players to the limit. That's their job. You thought you couldn't do one more rep today, yet you managed to pull it off with a little encouragement. You'll do fine with Val too. And I'll want a full report on Tuesday."

"Could you go over that finger exercise once more? I think I may be doing it wrong."

"Sure."

While David worked with Margaret, Val looked around his office. Diplomas hung on the walls, and a shelf behind his desk was filled with medical and exercise books bookended by two framed photos. One showed David with a beautiful blonde-haired woman who was holding a baby. The other was of a blonde girl about four or five years old who had David's merry green eyes and a captivating smile. She was the kind of little girl meant for tea parties, bedtime stories, and snuggling on your lap during a summer thunderstorm.

The kind of little girl Val would never have.

"Val! I'm ready."

With a start, Val shifted gears. "Sorry. I-I was admiring the photo of the little girl. Your daughter?"

"Yes. Victoria. She's five."

"Oh, such a lovely child!" Margaret leaned forward and adjusted her glasses. "What an angelic face!"

One corner of David's mouth hitched up. "Don't let the face fool you. She can be a handful."

"Don't I know it." Margaret gave a long-suffering sigh. "I raised two daughters of my own."

"But I wouldn't change a thing, would you? Victoria's been such a blessing in my life—as I'm sure your daughters have been in yours." Without giving her mother a chance to respond, he rose. "Well, my next patient awaits." He came around the desk, and together they helped Margaret to her feet. "Don't hesitate to call if you have any questions between now and our next session." His last comment was directed to both of them as he opened the door.

"We won't." Margaret took a firm grip on her arm.

Val held out her hand. "Thank you again."

As David's perceptive gaze connected with hers, the oddest feeling swept over her. It was almost as if he were looking straight into her heart, past her veneer of sophistication, and seeing far more than she wanted him to see. Stranger still, when his lean fingers closed around hers, his sure, steady grip seemed to say, *I care. You can trust me. I'm here for you.*

Talk about off-the-wall. What had gotten into her today?

Still, the impression lingered . . . and added to his charisma. Perhaps others picked up on it too. If so, it was a great skill to have in a profession that required him to motivate patients and push them beyond their comfort level.

Too bad he was married.

Not that it mattered, of course. Even if he was available, she wasn't.

With an effort, Val retrieved her hand and took her mother's arm. The trek down the hall was slow, but as she opened the waiting room door to usher Margaret through, she caught sight of David. He was still standing by his office, watching them. Raising a hand in farewell, he stepped back inside and shut the door.

The symbolism resonated with her.

Closed doors were the story of her life.

And she had no one to blame but herself.

David leaned against the door and took a deep breath. He did have another patient waiting. That had been the truth. But first he needed to jot down some notes about his session with Margaret—and collect his thoughts.

Because these past few minutes had been interesting . . . and intriguing.

Not so much in terms of Margaret. She was easy to read. The woman was a master manipulator—but he'd dealt with enough patients like her to know how to elicit cooperation.

Her daughter was another story. There were layers there, and deep, turbulent pools beneath the placid surface. Complexities and shadows and hidden corners, all safely concealed behind a beautiful face and great body.

And *safely* was the appropriate word. He'd be willing to bet most people never got past Val's physical beauty. Never delved deeper. Including her mother.

Pushing off from the door, he walked over to his desk, sat, picked up his pen—and turned it end-to-end on his desk instead of writing his session notes.

Margaret had referenced Val's theater and modeling background, so it wasn't surprising her daughter moved with grace and poise. Or that her body language suggested confidence, conveying the message that she was in control of her destiny and certain of her place in the world.

Yet her melancholy eyes told a different story—especially when she'd looked at the photos on the shelf behind him.

Swiveling in his chair, he studied the family photo, a familiar heaviness tugging at his heart. He might not understand Val's reaction, but he did understand the sadness of wishing for something that would never be. They'd looked like a perfect family, he and Natalie and Victoria. Yet something had been missing. When Natalie had held Victoria in her arms back in those early days, she'd never worn the soft, special expression he'd seen on Val's face a few minutes ago.

Of course Natalie had loved Victoria, in her own way. He'd never doubted that. It just hadn't been the way he'd always hoped his wife would feel about their child. And it certainly wasn't the way he felt. He cherished each day with his precious daughter.

His gaze shifted to the shot of Victoria. His daughter was adorable, and few people were immune to her charms. He'd often had patients and co-workers tell him he was a lucky man to have such a lovely daughter.

Though Val had left the words to Margaret, her eyes had spoken volumes. As she'd gazed at the photo, they'd been filled with longing. Easy to understand, since Victoria would appeal to the maternal instincts in any woman. But what was the story behind the sadness in their depths? The wistfulness?

It was as if what she longed for was beyond her grasp.

Why?

Sighing, he pivoted back to his desk and opened Margaret's

file. He couldn't take on the burdens of the world, solve everyone's problems, as Natalie had always reminded him when he'd made one too many commitments at church or to some worthy project in need of volunteers. And she'd been right.

Whatever Val's issues, he needed to steer clear of them.

Because he had more than enough challenges of his own trying to settle into a new life and a new job, all the while doing his best to play both mother and father to a little girl who had plenty of adjustments of her own to make.

3

At the sound of a car in the driveway Saturday afternoon, Karen lifted the living room curtain to peer outside. "Kristen, your father's here."

"I'll be right out."

"You're going to be late."

"I said I'll be out in a minute!"

Karen rolled her eyes. After eighteen months, you'd think Kristen would give up on this ploy. Did she really think that by hanging back in her room whenever Michael came by—thereby forcing her parents to engage in small talk—she might prod them into a reconciliation?

Good luck with that. Michael had no interest, and she found the whole thing awkward.

The bell chimed, and she headed toward the foyer. Straightening her shoulders, she tucked her hair behind her ear and pulled the door open. "Hello, Michael."

"Hi." He gave her his usual dismissive, distracted glance. "Is Kristen ready?"

"Almost. She'll need a little help getting to the car."

"Oh. Right." He looked toward his late-model sports car, then stepped inside.

She gave him a quick once-over. As usual, his attire was impeccable. The crease in his khaki slacks was razor sharp, the starch in his Oxford shirt crisp. It didn't matter where he was—in the classroom at the university, on the golf course, or attending today's school picnic with his daughter. He was Mr. GQ.

He was also in great shape, even if he was thirteen years her senior. Regular visits to the gym and a diligent exercise routine had kept him looking far younger than his fifty-one years. Only the touch of gray in the dark brown hair at his temples hinted at his age. But instead of making him look older, it gave him a distinguished appearance.

Maybe that's why he still attracted younger women.

Good looks, stylish clothes, and firm abs were no excuse for infidelity, however. Even if your wife was a little overweight and more plain Jane than Jane Russell.

She lifted her chin a fraction and shut the door with more force than necessary. "I'll check on Kristen."

Her daughter chose that moment to appear. What a coincidence.

Not.

"Hi, Dad." Kristen's voice was a little too bright, and she refused to meet Karen's gaze.

"Hi, sweetie." He moved forward and gave her a hug. "I see you've been collecting some autographs on that cast."

"Yeah. Most of the kids stopped by in the beginning, but they don't come around as much anymore."

"You'll see them all today, though. Are you ready?"

"Uh-huh. Mom, where are the brownies?"

"In the kitchen. I'll get them."

"Were we supposed to bring something?" Michael directed his question to Kristen as Karen passed by.

"Yeah. But Mom makes great brownies."

"Stephanie could have picked up a cake at the bakery."

Meaning his cute little love interest didn't frequent the kitchen. Karen stifled a smirk. No wonder Michael's waistline was so trim. He probably hadn't had a home-cooked meal since they separated.

"Homemade stuff is better. And Mom's a great cook."

Misplaced though it was, Karen had to admire her daughter's tenacity.

"Could you hurry it up, Karen?" Michael called. "I don't want to keep Stephanie waiting."

Not even a thank-you.

How typical.

Their voices carried into the kitchen as Karen retrieved the brownies, and she didn't feel one iota of guilt about listening in.

"Why did you bring her?"

"We're a couple, Kristen. We do things together."

"But this was supposed to be just us. Father-daughter time."

"I thought the end-of-school picnic was a family event?"

"It is. But Stephanie's not family."

"She may be."

"She isn't yet."

"Look, do you want to call the whole thing off?"

Karen stepped back into the room to find them glaring at each other.

Shoulders slumping, Kristen ended the standoff. "I've been looking forward to this for weeks."

"Then let's go and enjoy ourselves."

"It would be better without Stephanie."

Smiling sweetly, Karen handed the plate of brownies to Michael. "Have fun."

His lips tightened into a thin line. "Yeah. Thanks."

Karen's smile faded as she regarded her daughter. Kristen had been so excited about spending the day with her dad. He hadn't given her a lot of attention in the past few months—thanks to Stephanie, Karen assumed. Now she was fighting back tears.

Karen reached over to hug her, whispering as Michael opened the door, "I'm sorry, honey."

"It won't be the same." Kristen sniffled in her ear. "Nothing's the same."

What could she say?

After giving her one more squeeze, Karen backed away. Michael and Kristen left the house in silence, and a few minutes later she heard the car start. From behind the sheer curtain in the living room, she watched as Michael pulled out of the driveway.

Stephanie was in the passenger seat, looking out the window—away from Michael. Michael was staring straight ahead, both hands gripping the wheel. Kristen was sitting in the back, her leg propped on the seat, her arms folded tight across her chest.

Looked like they were all in for a jolly afternoon.

"Karen? Val. Can I ask a favor?"

A caution sign flashed in Karen's mind, and she shifted the phone to a more comfortable position as she pulled plates out of the dishwasher. "What is it?"

"My car was making a funny noise on the way down from Chicago, so I took it to the shop this morning. I couldn't believe Fred was still there. He must be eighty-five! Anyway, he says I need a new timing belt—whatever that is. He gave me a ride home, because the car won't be ready until late in the day. I was planning to go to the grocery store while Mom naps, and I wondered if you might be able to run me over there. I grabbed a few quick things on Thursday during her therapy session, but the whole kitchen needs to be restocked."

Turning toward the window, she considered the request as she watched the sun play hide-and-seek with the branches of the maple tree. Her first inclination was to say no. She'd much rather stay home and enjoy the rare treat of uninterrupted personal time on a

Saturday afternoon. On the other hand, she did need some things herself. If she took Val, she should still have plenty of time to herself before Michael brought Kristen home from the picnic.

"Okay. When do you want to go?"

"ASAP. I just got Mom settled for her nap. I should be able to escape for a couple of hours."

"I'll be there in ten minutes."

"Thanks. I'll be ready."

Not likely. Val had always run late for everything.

But nine and a half minutes later, when she pulled into the driveway, her sister was already on the porch—looking chic as always, of course. Her loose blonde hair shimmered in the sun, her long legs were tanned and trim beneath her white shorts, and her black-and-white-striped knit top showed off her curves to perfection.

Karen squirmed in her seat and smoothed a hand down the denim on her thigh. Would it have killed her to take five minutes to freshen up? Brush her hair, apply some lipstick, change clothes instead of pulling her long hair back with a rubber band, going au naturel in the makeup department, and settling for too-tight jeans and baggy T-shirt that emphasized her extra pounds instead of disguising them.

Then again, why even try to compete with Val?

"Hey, I appreciate this." Her sister slid in beside her. "Sorry for the short notice."

"I need some stuff too." She put the car in gear and backed out of the driveway. "Shopping today will save me a trip early in the week. Work is busy this time of year, and I hate having to stop at the grocery store after a long day."

"How's the job going?"

"Okay. It took me a while to adjust to the nine-to-five routine, but the construction business is interesting, and I like the steady paycheck as well as the feeling of independence. I even got a promotion a few months ago. I'm an administrative assistant now."

If she couldn't compete with her sister on looks, at least she could point to her success in the business world.

To her surprise, Val's pleasure seemed sincere. "That's great! But you always were smart. With your business degree, I was amazed you didn't shoot for a higher position than secretary to begin with."

"I had very little experience, and the degree was fourteen years old. I assumed that was the best I could do."

"I'm glad they're recognizing your intellect. If our places were reversed, I'd still be a secretary."

Karen shot her a skeptical look. "I don't think so."

"Trust me. People see me and think 'dumb blonde.' Including Mom. As far as she was concerned, my appearance was my only asset. She always told me you were the one who got the brains."

Her mother had praised her to Val?

That was news.

She flexed her fingers on the wheel. "Well, she always told me you were the one who got the looks."

"She's a piece of work, that's for sure."

They lapsed into silence for the remainder of the drive, but for once it was companionable rather than strained.

After circling the crowded lot twice to find a parking spot, Karen led the way into the store. Pulling a cart free for Val and another for herself, she followed her sister toward the produce section.

"How did Mom do with her first therapy session?" Karen picked up a bag of Fritos from a table of snack-food specials near the entrance. "When I asked her, all she said was that it went fine."

"It did. Mom's therapist had her wrapped around his finger in sixty seconds flat. It was amazing. Can you imagine Mom being docile? Or flirty?"

She almost choked on the sample of gooey butter cake she'd snagged from a display as they passed. "What!"

"Yeah. It's a kick, isn't it? David knows just how to handle her. And I'm not having any trouble at home, either, since she doesn't want to disappoint him on Tuesday."

"You're kidding!"

"Cross my heart."

"I'll have to take some lessons from him."

"Wouldn't help. It's that male charm thing. Though I would have thought Mom would be immune."

Karen wiped the powdered sugar off her fingers with a napkin. "How old is this guy?"

"I don't know. He's got a five-year-old . . . maybe midthirties."

"Handsome?"

"In a boy-next-door sort of way."

"How about that?" She shook her head. "But let's not look a gift horse in the mouth. I was afraid it might take both of us to drag Mom to therapy."

"Nope. I think she'll go like a lamb." After examining a head of broccoli, Val put it in her cart. "But I get plenty of resistance on other fronts. Like food. She doesn't like anything I make."

"So I've heard a time or two."

"Now why do I think that's a gross understatement?" Val snagged a bunch of green onions. "I hear complaints every day, but her eating habits are atrocious. I'm trying to remedy that."

As Val regaled her with stories about the healthy menus she'd been preparing—and their mother's reaction—Karen's lips quivered. "I'm surprised she hasn't had another stroke."

"Not yet. And not only is her diet healthier, she's bound to lose a few pounds. A good thing, if you ask me. She's gained a lot of weight. So tell me how Kristen's progressing."

As Karen gave her an update, they trundled up and down the aisles, heading at last for the meat and seafood section. While Val perused a selection of tilapia, Karen scanned her sister's cart. Val had focused on natural foods like whole-grain breads and fruits and vegetables, while her own basket was full of microwave dinners, salty snacks, cereal, and sweets.

"I guess those dishes you're making for Mom are the reason you stay so slender. Maybe I should adjust my diet too."

"Are you trying to lose weight?"

"No." Karen picked up a package of ground beef. "But I should be. I've put on twenty-five pounds over the past two years."

Leaning over, Val did a quick survey of Karen's cart. "It couldn't hurt to modify your eating habits a little. A lot of that frozen stuff is high in salt and carbs."

"But it's easy to fix." Her defenses rose. "And I don't have time to prepare elaborate dinners."

"I don't either, but I have a repertoire of quick, healthy meals, including some stir-frys that are out of this world. I'd be happy to share the recipes if you want to try them."

Karen weighed the pack of ground beef in her hand and put it in her cart. "You know, I don't recall you cooking very much when we were growing up."

"I didn't. Mom never taught me the domestic stuff. I think she expected me to be a Broadway star and have servants running around at my beck and call." Val pushed her cart toward the front of the store.

"I did too. You have the looks and the talent."

Karen only had a side view, but she caught a sudden, subtle tightening in Val's features. "Good looks aren't all they're cracked up to be. I'd have traded them for your brains any day."

As Val guided her cart into the checkout lane and started unloading it, Karen glanced at her watch. This outing hadn't been half bad. She couldn't remember the last time the two of them had had a congenial, relaxed conversation.

Maybe never.

On impulse, she touched Val's arm. "Do you want to stop for a quick cup of coffee? There's a shop next door, and we have time to spare before your two-hour reprieve is up."

"A Saturday treat." A soft smile played at Val's lips. "That makes me think of our trips with Dad to the ice-cream parlor on summer Saturdays."

"Yeah. Those are some of my happiest memories. Mom could

never understand why we wanted to go with him to the hardware store every week. I don't think she ever figured out our little secret."

"Me, neither." Chuckling, Val grabbed the head of broccoli and put it on the conveyor belt. "Okay. Let's do it. Maybe we can start a new tradition."

Five minutes later, as they sipped their lattes at a small café table tucked into the corner of the shop, Val's expression grew wistful. "It's not ice cream, but it does remind me of our outings with Dad."

"Even after all these years, I still miss him a lot." Karen played with the edge of her lid.

"Me too. He was such a great guy. Kind and encouraging and supportive. He always made me feel special. Like I had a lot to offer."

"He made me feel the same way." Karen took a sip of her drink. "You know, I've often wondered why he was attracted to Mom."

"Beats me."

"Maybe she was different in her younger days."

"People don't change that much. But she might have softened during the courtship. People do a lot of things that may be out of character when they're in love, if they think it will make the other person love them back."

Sadness nipped at the edges of her voice, and a question sprang to Karen's lips. But she bit it back. They'd never been confidantes. Better to stick to a subject that was comfortable for both of them.

"Dad never complained, though." Karen swirled her drink. "I can't remember him ever saying one negative word about Mom."

"That wasn't his style. Whenever I criticized her, he'd say that was just how she was, but it didn't mean she loved us any less."

"He told me the same thing. And he did a good job tempering her. He even knew how to make me feel pretty." Karen dipped her head as she made the admission.

"Why was that so hard?"

She shot her a get-real look. "Come on, Val. Mom was right. You got all the looks in this family."

Val gave an unladylike snort. "That's a bunch of rubbish."

"It's true."

"Not."

"Look . . . I appreciate what you're trying to do. But if you put the two of us next to each other and gave a man a choice, who do you think he'd pick?"

Her sister's eyes narrowed. "Men can be very superficial."

"It isn't just men who notice beautiful women first."

"Okay, I might be the first one people notice. Blonde hair does have a tendency to attract attention. But you have great eyes—which a little makeup could enhance, by the way. And wonderful hair. I wish mine had a natural wave like yours. Plus you have cheekbones to die for."

"Nice try."

Val put her elbow on the table and rested her chin in her palm. "I never knew you felt so . . . so . . ."

"Dowdy? Try living in the shadow of a glamorous sister."

Val traced a thin trail of coffee across the café table with one perfect, polished nail. "I know I got the flashy looks, but it never occurred to me that you felt unattractive. Believe it or not, I was always jealous of you."

"You've got to be kidding. Why in the world would you be jealous of me?"

"Because you were Mom's favorite. The smart sister. The one who always did the right thing."

Karen's mouth dropped open. "Mom told you that?"

"Yes. With annoying regularity."

"But . . . but I thought *you* were her favorite! She always bragged about how pretty and talented you were. How you would go places someday. Maybe as far as Broadway. And she always talked about how the boys were knocking down the door to take you out. I never even had a date till college. I felt like a loser."

Val exhaled and shook her head. "I knew she was manipulative, but I never realized how much she played us off each other—and how much it affected our relationship."

"Me neither."

After checking her watch, Val reached for her purse. "Speak of the . . . well, *devil* may be too strong a word. I don't want to imply there was any diabolical intent. I think Mom just likes to control people. In any case, she'll be getting up soon, and if I'm not there when she wakes up, I'll have to listen to her complain for the rest of the day. I can take it—but I'd rather not."

"I hear you." Karen rose, but as she started for the door, Val touched her arm.

"You're not dowdy, by the way."

"And you're not a dumb blonde."

For a moment they regarded each other in silence.

"What do you say we do this again?" Val hoisted her shoulder purse into position.

"How does a week from Saturday sound? I have to help with month-end closing next week."

Her sister grinned. "I'll pencil it in."

Karen cranked up the oldies radio station, reached into the refrigerator for the leftover spaghetti from last night . . . and stopped as she pictured Val's shopping cart from this morning. There had been nary a noodle in sight.

Switching gears, she chose the deli turkey instead. A whole-wheat sandwich would be much healthier . . . and better for her waistline.

As Karen spread mustard on the bread, Bette Midler began to sing. Ah . . . "Wind Beneath My Wings." Now there was a song. They didn't write them like that anymore. And since no one was home, why not join in—even if she usually confined her musical efforts to the church choir, where she could anonymously blend into the group?

It was a sing-along kind of day.

Halfway through the first verse, however, she stopped mid-phrase at the sudden bang of the front door. "Kristen? Is that you?"

"Yeah."

Uh-oh. She was home far too early. They were supposed to stay for the fireworks.

But perhaps there'd been fireworks of a different kind.

Karen wiped her hands on a dish towel and walked into the living room. Kristen was slumped on the couch, arms crossed, face stormy.

"Aren't you home a little early?"

"Yeah."

"What happened?"

"Stephanie wasn't feeling well." Sarcasm dripped from her words.

Karen moved to the couch and perched on the arm. "People do get sick."

"Oh, please!" Kristen rolled her eyes.

"It's possible."

"She was sick all right. Sick of spending her Saturday at a school picnic. I heard her tell that to Dad. And she's so young! It's embarrassing. She looks more like his daughter than his . . . whatever."

No arguments there. Michael liked his women young. She'd been a student herself when she'd caught his eye. At least his current love was in graduate school. That would put her at twenty-three or twenty-four. Better than eighteen or nineteen, but she was still too young for a fifty-one-year-old man.

"I don't know what Dad sees in her, anyway." Kristen's words were laced with disgust. "She didn't talk much, but what she did say was all about herself. What movie she went to last week, what clothes she bought, what classes she was taking next semester. She never asked one single thing about me. Not even about my leg. She is, like, so shallow."

"I'm sorry your day didn't turn out the way you hoped." Karen draped her arm around her daughter's stiff shoulders.

"I should have gone to the picnic with you."

Karen tried not to let her second-choice status hurt. "You wanted some father-daughter time."

"That didn't happen anyway." She reached for her crutches and struggled to her feet. "I'll be in my room."

"Do you want some dinner?"

"I had a hamburger at the picnic. Stephanie didn't want to bother, but Dad insisted he owed me a meal." Kristen stopped on the threshold. "I guess there was one good thing about today, though."

"What was that?"

"There was something wrong between Dad and Stephanie. I mean, it was obvious she didn't want to be at the picnic. But it was more than that. It was like . . . I don't know. Like there wasn't a . . . a connection between them anymore. She wasn't focused on him at all, and she wouldn't let him hold her hand. It was . . . different. Maybe they'll break up."

And maybe you and Dad will get back together.

At the hope in Kristen's eyes, her throat tightened. How was it possible so many years had passed since the fierce grip of her newborn's tiny fingers had sealed the bond between them? And wasn't it just yesterday she'd run behind the bike as her daughter learned to ride, heart in throat, afraid her precious little girl would fall and get hurt? And it seemed like a week rather than a year ago that she'd sat in the audience, filled with pride and trepidation, as the poised young woman her daughter had become executed a flawless routine on the balance beam and walked away with a blue ribbon, her face filled with joy.

If going back to Michael would help restore that joy, she'd almost consider it.

Except even without Stephanie, Michael had no interest in her. And she, too, had moved on.

"Your dad isn't going to come back, Kristen." Her words were quiet but firm. "If he and Stephanie break up, he'll find someone else like her. Thin and pretty and young."

"You could be thin and pretty if you made an effort." Kristen's eyes filled with tears.

"It wouldn't work, honey."

"How do you know? You won't even try!"

"There's more to it than that."

"I just want us to be a family again. I don't know why that's too much to ask."

The first faint hum of a headache began to throb behind her temples. "I wish things could have been different too. But your dad and I weren't a great match from the beginning. We have very different—and incompatible—priorities. That doesn't mean you and he can't have a great relationship, though."

"It's not the same." As Kristen choked out the words, her face crumpled. With a strangled sob, she clumped down the hall to her room and slammed the door.

Hard enough to rattle the pictures on the walls.

As well as the resolve in a mother's heart.

4

Scott stood at the window of his mother's guest room and clenched his right hand into a fist. Neither the view of the colorful gardens Dorothy tended with such care nor the brilliant light of the May Saturday penetrated the darkness within him that had stolen his appetite, his energy, his interest in life. Every day was the same. Get up. Get dressed. Sit around his room. Go to bed. Stare at the ceiling.

What was the point of it all?

He fingered the dog-eared paper in his pocket. The one he'd been carrying around since his last trip to St. Louis.

Maybe he should give the shrink a call.

But the man couldn't bring back his friends or his career. Nor erase the fact that his years of training and practice and work had been wiped out in an instant by a truck driver who had fallen asleep at the wheel.

All the psychologist could do was listen as he vented his rage and frustration and despair.

And he didn't need to pay big bucks for a sounding board.

Lifting his left hand, he examined the once-nimble fingers, now stiff and numb. He'd done all the exercises, but there'd been minuscule improvement. At this pace, it would be years before full function returned and he could think about performing again.

And what was he supposed to do in the meantime?

He didn't have a clue.

"Scott?" His mother's muted query came through the door. "Everything okay?"

Taking a deep breath, he struggled to pull off the lie. "Yes. You can come in."

The door opened, and Dorothy stepped inside. "It's a beautiful day out. Perfect for a walk."

Another plea for exercise, thanks to that library book about depression he'd stumbled across in a kitchen drawer. Physical activity had been near the top of the "helpful suggestions" list. She'd stuck a slip of paper on that page to mark the spot.

"I'll think about it."

She hesitated, but to his relief she didn't push.

"I left salad and a piece of quiche in the fridge for your lunch. I also made those chocolate chip pecan cookies you like."

"Thanks, Mom." A healthy diet and regular eating schedule had been on the list too.

"I'm going to run a casserole over to the Ramseys'. Their son was injured in March, and they've been having a rough time. I'm also going to stop in and check on Margaret Montgomery from church. She had a stroke last month. Do you want to ride along? It might be nice to get out of the house for a while."

The names of her friends meant nothing to him, and he had zero interest in venturing back into the world. Or hearing about other people's problems.

"No."

Instead of responding, Dorothy walked into the room and leaned over to kiss his forehead. At close proximity, he could see new, fine lines on her face—put there by him, no doubt. Guilt gnawed at his gut. He ought to expend some effort for her sake, if nothing else.

"Maybe I'll take that walk instead."

"That would be good." Despite her upbeat tone, the strain around her mouth didn't ease much. "By the way, we're having a social after services tomorrow. Would you like to come?"

Making some concessions to please his mother was one thing. Going back to church was another. "I don't think so. I'm not ready yet to be around a lot of people." *Or anywhere close to the God who abandoned me.*

"Okay. I'll see you in a couple of hours." It was clear she hadn't expected him to embrace her suggestion.

A few minutes later, Scott heard the automatic garage door kick into gear as his mother pulled out. It rumbled again as she closed it. Then the house fell silent.

Summoning up the reserves of his ebbing energy, Scott reached over to close the mini blinds and shut out the sunshine that often triggered headaches.

Besides, darkness better suited his mood.

As the room grew dim, the outlines of the furniture became indistinct. Feeling his way, he crossed to the bed and stretched out. Not that he held out much hope of sleep. Insomnia had been his constant companion since the accident. Yet he craved the blackness of slumber, where he could escape from the torment of his memories.

In fact, blackness in general held a certain appeal. A promise of release that beckoned to him. Tempted him.

But that decision was so final . . .

No. He wasn't ready to take that step.

Yet.

"You must be Val. I'm Dorothy Walker, from church. I just stopped in to see how your mother is doing."

At the lively eyes and open manner of the jeans-clad, salt-and-pepper-haired woman on the other side of the door, Val smiled and extended her hand. "Nice to meet you. Won't you come in?"

"I don't want to intrude."

"To be honest, I'd appreciate the company. I haven't had a chance to talk with anyone but Mom since Karen and I went grocery shopping last weekend. I know Mom would enjoy a visitor too." Okay, that might be a stretch. Margaret wasn't the most sociable person even on her better days. But it wouldn't hurt her to practice her social graces once in a while. "She should be getting up from her nap soon."

"All right. I'll stay for a few minutes." Dorothy held out a bouquet of roses, peonies, and daylilies. "I thought Margaret might enjoy these. They're from my garden."

"Those are gorgeous!" Val took the tissue-wrapped blossoms and motioned the older woman into the living room. Lifting the flowers, she inhaled an old-fashioned, heady scent that evoked images of white picket fences and garden parties and lazy summer afternoons. Of an era when the pace of life was slower, and neighbors met for lemonade and a chat on wide front porches. Of a time when families sat in the deepening dusk of a garden, sharing laughter and stories as the fireflies flickered to life.

A time she'd never known but had always longed to experience.

With an effort, she managed to hang on to her smile. "Have a seat while I find a vase. Can I get you something to drink?"

"No, I'm fine. Thank you."

It took Val a few minutes to scrounge up a suitable container from the recesses of her mother's pantry. Rejoining Dorothy, she placed the bouquet on the coffee table. "You must have quite a garden."

"It is nice. And digging in the soil, helping things grow . . . it soothes my soul." She settled back on the sofa. "Are you a gardener?"

Val gave a wry shake of her head as she perched on the arm of a chair. "Not even close. I live in a high-rise condo in Chicago. My horticultural efforts are confined to growing a few herbs in pots. But I know what you mean about finding satisfaction in helping things grow. I teach drama at a high school, and working with young people, watching them develop, can be an amazing experience."

"I've heard Margaret talk about her theatrical daughter, but I didn't realize you were a teacher."

No surprise there. Her mother had always been more impressed by her stage work than her teaching. "You said you know Mom from church?"

"That's right. My husband and I moved to Washington three years ago, after he retired, and we joined the congregation. It's a very close-knit faith community, and I feel guilty it's taken me this long to get over to see your mother."

"People lead busy lives these days."

"I'm afraid mine's been busier than usual in recent weeks. My son was in a serious car accident a few weeks ago, and he's come home to recover. My husband died two years ago, and at emotionally taxing times like this I feel his loss very deeply."

"I'm sorry."

"Thank you. I guess we all have our crosses to bear. Fortunately, God walks with us on our journey."

As Val tried to think of a diplomatic response, her mother's strident voice rang through the house.

"Val? I'm ready to get up."

Saved by the yell.

"Coming, Mom." She rose. "Give me a few minutes and I'll bring Mom out for a visit. Do you mind waiting?"

"Not at all."

As Val had suspected, however, Margaret wasn't the least bit happy about entertaining an uninvited guest.

"I look a sight." Margaret peered into the mirror over her dresser and patted her hair, twin crevices etched in her brow. "You'd think a person would call before dropping in unexpectedly when someone is ill."

"I think it was very thoughtful." Val handed Margaret her cane.

"That's because good manners are about as rare today as piecrust made with lard. And the world is a worse place because of it."

"But a lot healthier."

"Hmph." Margaret peered at her over her glasses and took her arm. "We might as well get this over with."

As Val helped her mother into the living room, Dorothy rose and held out her hands. "Margaret, it's good to see you."

Her mother extended her good hand in an excellent imitation of a queen condescending to meet with a peasant. "Thank you."

"Look at the beautiful flowers Dorothy brought." Val motioned to the coffee table.

Margaret adjusted her glasses and scrutinized the table. "You better put a saucer under that vase. I don't want it to leave a water ring."

So much for graciousness.

"I checked. It's dry." She nudged her mother. "Aren't they lovely?"

Margaret glared at her but got the hint. "Very pretty. You always were quite the gardener, Dorothy, though it seems a waste to put that much effort into something that has such a brief life."

"But the flowers give such pleasure while they're here." Dorothy smiled. "I'm glad to see you looking better."

As Margaret gave a long-suffering sigh, Val decided her mother was the family member with the real dramatic talent. "I suppose I'm improving, but illness is a trial."

"That's true. On the plus side, you're lucky to have such good care from your two daughters."

"Yes, well, families should help each other."

"I agree. But young people are busy these days."

"I know. I haven't seen much of Karen since Val arrived."

Val resisted the urge to roll her eyes. Leave it to her mother to gloss over all the years of Karen's diligent care.

The chime of the doorbell interrupted the conversation, and Val eased Margaret into a chair. "I'll get it."

Glancing out the sidelight before she released the lock, she stifled a chuckle.

Perfect timing.

She called over her shoulder as she opened the door. "Look who's here, Mom."

Karen walked in, juggling packages in one arm while a load of clothing in clear plastic dry cleaning bags was draped over the other.

"Why, Karen, we were just talking about you." Dorothy gave her a welcoming smile.

A ruddy hue suffused Margaret's cheeks, but she masked her chagrin with annoyance. "Why aren't you at the office? I thought you always worked the last Saturday of the month for closure, or whatever you call it?"

Karen sent Val a questioning glance.

"Mom was just saying how she hasn't seen much of you lately." Val did her best to tamp down the curve of her lips.

Understanding dawned in Karen's eyes. "We finished the closing early this month, so I stopped to get your prescription and a few other odds and ends you needed on my way home. I also picked up the things you left at the cleaner before your stroke. I thought I'd save Val a trip."

"Hmph." Her mother inspected Karen. "I see you still have that pink blouse. It's not your color, you know. You ought to get rid of it. Too bad some of Val's style sense didn't rub off on you."

A few seconds of awkward silence crawled by, and Dorothy checked her watch. "I'm afraid I have to be running along. But I must say I wish I was staying for dinner. Whatever you're cooking smells delicious."

Margaret sniffed and sent Val a suspicious look. "What is that?"

"Ratatouille."

"Rat a what?"

"Ratatouille. It's a vegetarian dish made with eggplant, tomatoes, green peppers, and squash—you'll love it."

"More of that health food stuff."

"It's good for you."

"But I'm losing weight."

"Also good for you."

"As far as I'm concerned, you could take a few culinary lessons from your sister. She knows how to cook real food."

Dorothy picked up her purse. "Well, I'd better be on my way. I'm going to stop by the Ramseys' with a pan of lasagna."

In light of all the negativity pinging around the room, Val didn't blame their guest for making a fast exit.

Too bad she couldn't join her.

"Lasagna. Now that's real food." Margaret directed the comment her way.

Before she could respond, Dorothy jumped in. "I make it with turkey."

Margaret's jaw dropped. "You put turkey in lasagna?"

"You can't tell the difference, and it's much healthier than ground beef."

For once, Margaret was speechless.

Val was tempted to give their guest a high five.

"How's your son doing, Dorothy?" Karen draped the clothing over the back of a wing chair.

A shadow passed over the older woman's face. "Thank you for asking. It's been tough for him. His physical progress is slow, and the accident left a lot of invisible scars I suspect will take even longer to heal."

"I'll keep him in my prayers."

"Maybe we'll see him at church." Margaret folded her hands in her lap—meaning she was about to issue one of her platitudes. "The Lord gives great comfort in times of trial."

"Yes, he does." Dorothy pulled her keys out of her purse.

Margaret shifted her attention to Karen. "Are you planning to go with me next Wednesday to that travelogue Mary Nissan is doing at the library, about her trip to Africa? I have to call in a reservation."

"No, Mom. I have choir practice that night, remember?"

She huffed out a breath. "I don't know why you bother. Val got all the vocal talent in the family. I'm sure you wouldn't be missed if you took the night off to spend a few hours with your mother."

As a flush rose on Karen's cheeks, Val's blood pressure spiked. That crack had been downright mean.

She opened her mouth to speak, but her sister beat her to it.

"There may not be many more practices, anyway. Marilyn told us at the last practice that her husband has been transferred. They're moving in two weeks."

"Really?" Dorothy sent Karen a surprised look. "I hadn't heard that."

"There hasn't been an official announcement yet. I think Reverend Richards is planning to let everyone know at services tomorrow."

"Does he have anyone in mind for the music director job?"

"Not that I know of."

"I hope he finds a replacement soon." Margaret leaned over to the coffee table and wiped up a nonexistent speck of water with a tissue from her pocket. "Services won't be the same without music."

"That's true." Dorothy stood.

Val took the hint, leading the way toward the foyer as she fought the temptation to walk the woman to her car—and keep walking.

"I'll keep you on my prayer list." Dorothy paused on the threshold and spoke once more to Margaret.

"Thank you. I can always use a prayer or two."

Val lifted her eyes to the heavens as she closed the door behind their guest.

Amen to that.

At the sound of a key in the kitchen door, Scott set his empty water glass on the counter and turned to greet his mother. "You're late. I was getting a little worried."

Dorothy closed the door behind her, crossed the room, and dropped her purse on the table. "I stayed a little longer than usual to talk with Reverend Richards after the service. Did you eat anything yet?"

"I wasn't hungry."

"I could make some pancakes. Remember how we used to have them every Sunday after church?"

"Sure. That would be fine." Though he tried to put some enthusiasm in his voice, the words came out flat.

She opened a drawer and withdrew a mixing spoon. Dropped it on the floor. A moment later, a plastic bowl met the same fate.

At her uncharacteristic jumpiness, Scott frowned. "Is everything okay?"

"Of course."

"You seem a little on edge."

She measured the flour. "I suppose it's related to my conversation with Reverend Richards. You'd like him, Scott. His sermons always offer practical advice about how to put faith to work in everyday life."

"What did you two talk about?" Scott homed in on her first comment and dismissed the rest as he began to set the table.

For a brief second his mother's hands stilled. Then she resumed beating the eggs she'd cracked into a bowl. "You."

He froze. "What about me?"

"About how you'd be the perfect temporary replacement for our music director, who just resigned." She said the words fast, in one rush of breath.

Scott stared at her back as she added milk to the mix and stirred with more force than necessary. "You're kidding, right?"

"No. I'm dead serious. He is too. The job is yours if you want it." She cut a slab of butter to melt on the griddle.

"I'm not ready to even *think* about going back to work yet."

"It's not like digging ditches. I doubt your doctors would have any issue with this, but you could check with them if you're concerned."

"Doesn't the music director have to play the organ?"

The griddle was beginning to sizzle, and Dorothy spooned batter onto the surface. "We don't have an organ. Just a piano."

"Okay. A piano."

"Yes. And direct the choir."

"What about my hand? The one that doesn't work right, remember? I can't play the piano."

"I'll bet you play better with one hand than most people do with two. You were always good on the keyboard. Besides, the congregation doesn't expect concert quality, and playing might help restore some dexterity to your fingers."

A one-handed church music director—who didn't attend church. The whole thing was ludicrous.

"Does your pastor know I'm not the most religious guy around?"

"I discussed it with him." Dorothy flipped the pancakes. "He said the Bible is filled with stories about how the Lord sought out those who had fallen away."

Checkmate.

But even if that description fit him to a T, he had no interest in being a music director.

"It wouldn't work out, Mom." He placed the utensils on the table and retrieved the orange juice from the fridge. "Besides, I'm not ready for anything like that."

"Consider it from a practical perspective, then." She slid the pancakes onto plates and joined him at the table.

"What do you mean?" He upended the syrup container and squirted a generous amount on top of his pancakes.

"The job will provide some income until you decide what you want to do. I know the truck driver's insurance company is taking care of all your medical bills, but it might be nice for you to have some discretionary income."

That was a harder argument to fight. He'd done okay when he was playing full-time, but music wasn't the kind of career that made you rich unless you hit it big. His meager savings were already taking a hit.

Only the faint ticktock of the clock on the wall broke the silence as he watched the widening pool of syrup reach the edge of his golden pancakes and ease over the sides. His mother had always made good pancakes—and given good advice. Often over meals like this one.

The truth was, he could use the money. And after all her support, it wouldn't kill him to do something that made her happy.

He raised his head to find her watching him, her own food untouched.

"Okay. I'll fill in until they find someone else."

Her smile was gratifying . . . but it didn't counter the sudden panic that swept over him.

Because he wasn't ready to take this step yet. To venture back into the world. To interact with people. To act as if everything was normal when it wasn't, and never would be again.

But she'd pushed him into a corner.

And he couldn't think of a way to back out.

5

"Val? Could I speak with you for a moment?"

At David's summons, Val set aside the Hollywood gossip magazine she'd been flipping through. "Sure. Is everything okay?"

"Yes. I just wanted to discuss a few updates to your mother's program while she works on one of the pieces of equipment." He stepped aside to let her pass, gesturing toward his office. "Can I get you a cup of coffee?"

"That would be nice, thanks."

"Cream or sugar?"

"Black."

"A woman after my own heart—straight and strong. Sit tight. I'll be right back."

They parted at the door to his office, but in less than sixty seconds he was back with two steaming disposable cups. After handing her one, he picked up a folder from the top of a file cabinet and dropped into the chair beside her. "I added two more exercises to your mother's routine, and I wanted to run over them with you. How's she been doing with the program at home?"

"She doesn't like the exercises, and she's very vocal about letting me know it. But I have a secret weapon that always deflects the complaints."

"What?"

"You." When he tipped his head and sent her a questioning look, she smiled. "All I have to say is that you'll be disappointed if she slacks off, and she buckles down. You must have the magic touch."

He gave a self-deprecating laugh. "Hardly. I have plenty of patients who grumble at me."

"None of them women, I bet."

Much to Val's surprise, a flush rose on his neck. How endearing was that? A man who was actually embarrassed by a compliment.

Instead of responding, David leaned forward to put his coffee cup on the edge of the desk. To hide the blush, perhaps?

Even more endearing.

As he changed position, a loose sheet of paper on top of the folder slipped to the floor. They both bent to retrieve it, their heads colliding with a jarring bump.

"Ow!" Val jerked back and clapped a hand to her forehead.

"Sorry about that. Are you okay?" David touched her shoulder.

One side of her mouth hitched up as she rubbed her temple. "I have a hard head. I'll live."

"Let me see."

"It's fine."

"Let me have a look anyway."

He leaned over to move her hand aside, and the warmth of his fingers against her cool skin sent a bolt of heat ricocheting through her.

What in the world . . . ?

Val stared at him. At this proximity, she could see tiny flecks of gold in his vivid green eyes and faint lines etched at the corners that told her he smiled often. As for those supple lips that looked eminently kissable . . .

Don't go there!

With a supreme effort, she lowered her gaze.

Big mistake.

His taut T-shirt was stretched across his muscular chest, and those impressive biceps she'd noticed at their first meeting were now mere inches from her face.

All at once, she had to fight the urge to fan herself.

Had someone turned on the heat in here?

He tugged at her hand, his touch gentle. "Come on, Val. Let me see. You might need some ice on that."

She looked into his eyes again, and his hand stilled. A mere fraction of a second passed . . . but long enough for her to suspect he was experiencing a reaction to their nearness that was very similar to hers.

Her suspicion was confirmed when he abruptly dropped his hand and cleared his throat.

In the charged silence that followed, Val searched for something . . . anything . . . to say. Drew a blank.

What was wrong with her, anyway? Vocal Val, as her high school yearbook had pegged her, was never at a loss for words—except the moniker wasn't fitting so well at the moment.

Shifting in her seat, she tucked her hair behind her ear, leaving her forehead exposed.

"Wow!" David's eyes widened. "You do have a bump! Let me get some ice."

"I'm fine."

"It'll just take a minute." He was already half out of his chair.

She opened her mouth to protest. Closed it. A brief time-out would give her a chance to regain control of her emotions.

As he disappeared through the door, she collapsed back in her seat and let out a long, shaky breath.

Talk about being blindsided.

Sure, David was attractive—but she'd been around plenty of attractive men in her theater work and had long ago learned to steel herself against their charms.

Trouble was, her mother's physical therapist had launched a sneak attack.

Except attack wasn't quite accurate. There had been nothing deliberate in his actions. No intent to make her hormones go haywire, even if that had been the outcome.

So why had his closeness had such a dramatic effect on her?

Frowning, Val tapped a polished nail against the arm of her chair. Could it be that she'd simply been unprepared? After all, she hadn't expected to have to protect her heart from anyone in Washington—especially her mother's therapist. A man with a wife and child.

Yeah, that had to be it. He'd caught her off guard.

But why? With his boy-next-door looks, David was 180 degrees away from the dark, brooding sort of man she'd always found appealing. Plus, he seemed grounded, certain of his place in the world, a man whose values were solid and who had a clear sense of direction.

In other words, he was her polar opposite.

So what was the appeal?

The answer eluded her.

All she knew was that she needed to get her reaction under control. Fast.

Wrapping her fingers around the disposable cup, Val took a fortifying sip of the strong brew and gave herself a pep talk.

You'll be fine. Now that you're aware of the problem, you'll be on guard in the future. Just remain calm, cool, and aloof—and keep reminding yourself he's married and off-limits. This is just some weird chemistry thing.

Right.

She took a deep breath. Let it out. Took another.

Okay. Better. She had it under control.

Yet as she set the cup back on the desk, she noticed her hand was trembling.

Just like her heart.

And there didn't seem to be a thing she could do to stabilize either.

Juggling the ice pack in his hand, David paused outside the door to his office. Wishing he could avoid going back inside.

How was he supposed to deal with all the electricity zinging between him and Val—especially when he had no idea what had prompted it?

It wasn't her lovely face or great figure or the honey-blonde hair that called out to be touched, that much he knew. He'd run into plenty of attractive women in the past few years who'd sent clear signals about their interest, yet none of them had knocked him off balance like this.

And he didn't like this slightly out-of-control, unsettled feeling.

At all.

His fingers started to grow numb, and he switched the ice pack to his other hand. Even as a teen with raging hormones, he'd kept his emotions on a tight leash and stuck to the principles of his faith. Unlike a lot of his buddies, he'd never gotten carried away and done things he later regretted.

But he had the distinct feeling Val could easily carry him away and leave him with regrets.

The question was, why?

He transferred the ice pack again and raked his fingers through his hair.

This didn't make sense.

He hadn't even thought about her since their first encounter. Settling into life in Washington and worrying about whether Victoria was adjusting had required his total focus.

But today those deep blue eyes had sucked him in again, just as they had at their first meeting. And like that first day, he sensed that beneath the confident facade she presented to the world, Val was vulnerable. Searching. Scared. Unsure of her future. Alone.

As he was.

Could loneliness have prompted that buzz of attraction?

Maybe—on his end, anyway. Victoria's exuberant joy and boundless love might soothe his soul and give meaning to his days, but it couldn't take the place of love shared with a special woman. The kind he hoped to find again someday.

But not yet.

And not with Val.

She was only here for a few weeks, and he wasn't interested in a summer fling.

Bracing himself, he twisted the knob, reentered the office, and handed her the ice pack.

"Thanks." She gave him a polite but distant smile as she took it, careful not to let her fingers come into contact with his.

The tension in his gut relaxed. They seemed to be on the same page about how to deal with the unexpected high-voltage electricity between them. Good.

"No problem." He picked up his file and moved behind his desk.

She pressed the pack to her forehead while he explained the changes to her mother's program. Thanked him again when he finished. Politely shook his hand before she exited the office and disappeared down the hall.

But as he picked up the file for his next patient and stood, David realized she'd left something behind.

A faint, appealing fragrance that was a little exotic. A touch alluring. And hard to forget.

Just like the woman herself.

"Tell me how Mom liked the ratatouille." Karen dropped a box of low-fat, low-sodium, whole wheat crackers into her shopping cart as Val read the label on the package in her hand.

"She said it was edible. Trust me, that's high praise in light of some of the comments my culinary efforts have prompted."

"It smelled delicious. Is it hard to make?"

"Piece of cake. I jotted down the recipe for you, plus the ones for the stir-frys I mentioned on our first outing in case you want to try them too." Val withdrew several index cards from her purse and handed them over.

As Karen perused them, she pushed her cart past a cookie display. Val was right. The recipes were neither difficult nor time-consuming. "These sound very healthy."

"And they're good too. A winning combination."

"I wonder if Kristen would like them. She's developed some weird eating habits lately. For a while, she wouldn't eat meat. Next, she was off carbs. Desserts were on the restricted list for several weeks too. And it's not like she needs to lose weight. She's thin as a rail."

"Sometimes people focus on food because it's one of the few things they can regulate when other parts of their life are out of control."

"Like the divorce?" Karen tried to keep her voice nonchalant as she checked one of the stir-fry recipes and put a bag of brown rice in her cart. Even after a year and a half, it was hard to talk about the mess she'd made of her life without getting emotional.

"Could be. I deal with teenagers every day. They try to act cool, but most of them are insecure. They can behave in unacceptable ways for all kinds of reasons—to get attention, or to exert control over their lives when things at home are in an uproar, or it can just be a simple cry for help. That's why I enjoy teaching drama. If I can help them channel some of those energies through theater, act out some of those emotions on stage, maybe they won't feel the need to do things in real life they might later regret."

"I'm impressed."

The ghost of a smile flitted across Val's lips. "I do have a deep thought or two on occasion." She paused at the poultry section. "Did you want to get some chicken for that stir-fry?"

"Yeah. I think I will." Karen rummaged around in the bin and selected a package of chicken breasts. "How did you learn so much about teenagers?"

"Experience. Been there, done that."

"I did too, but I didn't come away with all those great insights."

"That's because you had your act together."

Karen gave an unladylike snort that would have drawn a disapproving look from her mother. "Not even close."

Val shook her head. "Sorry. Not buying. You always had your head on straight, and you never struggled with a lot of the conflicts kids deal with at that age."

"Are you kidding? I felt like conflict was my middle name. I just kept my feelings bottled up, toed the line, and did what was expected. More to try and win Mom's approval than anything."

"That was a lost cause." Val selected some yogurt, and Karen added a few containers to her cart too.

"Yeah, I know. It still is."

"Then why keep trying?" Val led the way to the checkout.

"I don't know." She shrugged at the question that had plagued her for years. "I wish I could be more like you and let her criticism roll off. But it bothers me."

"Can I tell you a secret?" Val leaned close and lowered her voice to a conspiratorial whisper as they got in line. "It bothers me too."

Karen didn't try to hide her skepticism. "Not that I ever saw."

"Cross my heart. But I learned long ago not to let her know that. It only motivates her to criticize more. Instead, I pretend like nothing she says ruffles me."

"Now I really am in awe of your acting talents." Aiming an admiring glance her sister's direction, Karen nudged her cart forward. "I had no idea Mom was able to get under your skin."

"Mom doesn't, either. Let's keep it our little secret, okay?"

"Sure."

As she began unloading her cart, Karen took a quick inventory. Fresh vegetables, yogurt, lean meat—what a change from two weeks ago. She picked up a bag of Fritos. Started to lay it on the conveyor. Hesitated when she realized Val was watching her.

"I know Fritos aren't all that healthy, but they'd be hard to give up."

"You don't have to give up everything you like. Almost anything is okay in moderation." Val dug a bag of M&M's from beneath a package of bean sprouts in her cart. "My weakness. But I limit myself to a couple dozen a day."

"You'd better hide those or Mom will clean you out."

"Don't worry. They're stashed in with the tofu. Trust me, she'll never look there."

Laughter bubbled up inside her. Had Val always had such a great sense of humor—or had she honed it in her theater work? Whatever, Karen was still smiling when they finished checking out and settled in for their weekly latte at the coffee shop next door.

"I forgot how hot and humid it can be in Washington this early in the summer." Val fanned herself with a paper napkin as they chose a table near the blower from the air conditioner. "I may have to switch to frappuccino."

"Yeah. And we might need to reverse our agenda and have our coffee first. I don't want to leave meat in the car for too long in this weather. Especially chicken."

"Good point. You'll have to tell me how Kristen likes those recipes I gave you, by the way."

Karen stirred her latte, watching the whipped cream dissolve in the dark liquid, diluting the blackness and tempering the strong taste with a touch of sweetness. "You know, I've been thinking about what you said in the store. How Kristen's odd eating habits might be a control issue. Her fixation on food did start a few weeks after Michael and I separated."

"Divorce is hard on kids."

Taking a sip of her drink, she debated how much she could share and still preserve some dignity. The whole notion of talking about the breakup of her marriage left a bad taste in her mouth—but Val was sharp and insightful; she might have some good thoughts.

Just do it, Karen. Take a chance. Don't overanalyze everything.

Heart hammering, she fiddled with her napkin. "Part of the problem is that she's never given up hope we'll get back together."

"I thought Michael was involved with some student."

Margaret must have told her that; she'd certainly never discussed Michael's love life with her sister.

"He is. Stephanie. But on her last outing with them, Kristen sensed there was trouble in paradise."

"Hmm. I'll bet the problem is he can't keep up with her. What is she, twenty, twenty-five years younger than him?"

"Something like that."

"He always did like younger women. You were almost a child when the two of you tied the knot."

"Twenty-one isn't a child."

"Seems like it now."

"True." Karen rested her elbow on the table and propped her chin in her hand. "You know, that was one of the few times I went against Mom's wishes. She told me I was too young to get married and that I should finish school first. She predicted it would never last."

"I bet she's never let you forget that, either."

"Bingo."

"I take it Kristen still misses her dad?"

"Yeah. A lot. But I think she misses the whole notion of 'family' more."

Val sipped her drink, her expression thoughtful. "A lot of kids from troubled homes are actually happier after their parents separate."

"I guess we did too good a job of keeping up appearances. I don't think Kristen suspected there were problems between us until Michael left."

Val squinted at her. "Why do I have a feeling you were the one who made the sacrifices to keep your home life as normal as possible?"

"Because you have great instincts?"

Val lifted her cup in mock salute. "All accolades graciously accepted."

"That wasn't an empty compliment. You nailed it." Karen stared down into her cup. Why not spill it all? Who knew what Margaret had passed on already, anyway—and what sort of spin she'd put on it? This way she could give Val her side of the sordid mess. "Things hadn't been good between us for quite a while. I knew Michael was restless and unhappy, but I couldn't understand why. I thought I was the model wife. I deferred to his opinions. I didn't take offense at his condescending manner or bad moods. I overlooked his patronizing attitude about my faith."

She sighed and shook her head. "I guess I thought acquiescence was the secret to winning his approval—and his love. I made that mistake with Mom too. In the end, though, people lose respect for doormats. Even Kristen noticed. She says I let them both walk all over me."

"You can change that."

"What's that cliché about an old dog?"

"You aren't old."

"I am next to Stephanie."

"No." Val touched Karen's hand as if to emphasize her point. "You're mature, not old. And don't ever forget that. Besides, it's not as if you want Michael back."

Karen dropped her gaze and busied herself wiping up the messy drips from her caramel latte. This was getting sticky—both the drink and the conversation.

Maybe Val would move on.

Narrowing her eyes, her sister leaned forward. "You don't, do you?"

So much for that hope.

Taking a deep breath, she wadded the napkin into a tight ball. "Not for myself. But Kristen misses him so much, and I want her to be happy. If he's breaking up with Stephanie, maybe . . ."

Val gripped Karen's hand. Hard. "You're doing it again."

"What?"

"Making decisions to please someone else."

"But I love Kristen, and she's been miserable since Michael and I split. It breaks my heart to see her this unhappy."

"And breaking yours will fix everything? Don't be a martyr, Karen. Not for this cause. Kristen is old enough to understand that sometimes it's better if two people don't stay together. Have you talked to her about the problems you and Michael had?"

"No. I thought she was too young at the time."

"She's not anymore."

"She'll think anything negative I say is sour grapes."

"That might be true at first, but she'll come to recognize the truth. Taking Michael back won't make you happy, and Kristen is older now. She'll see through the pretense. You won't be doing anyone any favors in the end."

Her sister's reasoning was sound—and on a rational level she accepted it. But when it came to Kristen's happiness, her heart usually trumped logic.

"Karen?"

At Val's prompt, she dropped the wadded-up napkin onto the table. "I guess you're right."

Once more, Val squeezed her fingers. "Promise me one thing. Before you make any rash decisions, call and we'll have coffee."

"I'm not going to do anything rash."

"Promise."

The passion in her sister's voice, and the concern etched in her features, tightened Karen's throat. Strange. After years of hardly speaking, years when Val had been more stranger than sister, they were finally beginning to connect—all because of a stroke.

The old adage was true—God often worked in mysterious ways.

"Okay." The word came out scratchy.

"Good." Val glanced at her watch. "Now we'd better rescue that chicken or it will cook in the car." She took the last swallow of her latte and started to rise.

On impulse, Karen reached out and laid her hand on her sister's arm. "For the record, Val—I'm glad you came home."

"Of course you are. I saved you from the dragon lady."

"That's not what I meant."

Val's wry smile softened. "I know. I feel the same way." She hesitated, but only for a moment. "And since we're in true-confessions mode today, I want you to know I appreciate how you've dealt with all the Mom-related issues through the years. I know it wasn't fair to dump all that on you, but I couldn't stay here—for a lot of reasons."

Such as?

The unspoken question hung between them—but instead of answering it, her sister rose, gathered up their cups and napkins, and crossed to the trash can near the door.

As she followed more slowly, Karen considered Val's comment. Had there been more to her reasons for abdicating family responsibilities than mere selfishness, after all? Was it possible Val's motives for leaving were less career-related than she'd always thought?

Val wasn't going to answer those questions today—but the whole summer stretched ahead . . . with a lot more trips to the coffee shop. A lot more one-on-one conversations. A lot more opportunities to exchange confidences.

And before her sister returned to her life in Chicago, maybe she'd open up enough to share the real reason she'd left Washington behind nearly two decades ago.

6

"Yoo-hoo! Anybody home?" Val peered into Karen's house through the screen in the open window.

Kristen looked up from the video she was watching. "Hi, Aunt Val." She rose awkwardly to her feet, tucked her crutches under her arms, and thumped across the room to open the door.

"Sorry to make you get up." Val stepped inside. "How come your air isn't on?"

"The repair guy's working on it now. And don't worry about making me get up. I need the exercise. I'm starting to feel like a slug. I'll be back to square one with my gymnastic training when this stupid thing comes off." She grimaced and banged her cast with the edge of the crutch.

"Can I cheer you up with some strawberry trifle?" Val held up a glass bowl.

Her niece's expression brightened at once. "Awesome! I bet it's healthy too."

"As healthy as possible for a dessert."

Kristen led the way to the kitchen. "How did you escape from Grandma?"

"She's napping."

"What do you guys do all day, anyway?"

"She reads a lot, and watches her soaps. I help her with her exercises twice a day, and once in a while we go for a drive. Sometimes she has company."

Kristen pulled two bowls out of the cabinet and set them on the counter. "I guess I ought to visit her more."

"She'd like that."

"Yeah. That's what Mom keeps telling me. But I see her every Sunday, when we pick her up for church. Besides, she's not a lot of fun to be around, you know? She criticizes everything. My hair, my clothes, my boyfriend, my fingernail polish. You name it."

While Val scooped generous servings of the trifle into two dishes, she found herself echoing what her father had always told her. "That's just how she is."

"How did you and Mom stand it all those years?" Kristen rummaged through the utensil drawer for spoons. "I mean, she drives me nuts after an hour. You guys had to live in the same house with her." She followed Val to the table, settled into a chair, and dug into her dessert.

"People can get used to almost anything."

Almost.

"Yeah?" Kristen sent her a skeptical look, then turned her attention back to her dessert. "You didn't hang around Washington once you were old enough to go to college, though. Mom should have left too."

"If she'd done that, you wouldn't have been born."

"So?" Kristen's face darkened as she jabbed at a strawberry. "Life stinks, anyway."

Val took a bite of her dessert. "Divorce is a nasty thing."

"Yeah."

"But in some situations it's better than the alternative."

The stubborn set of Kristen's jaw conveyed her reaction even before she spoke. "Not in ours. We were a family."

"Were you?"

"What do you mean?" Kristen sent her a wary look.

"How exactly were you a family?" Val kept her tone conversational. "Other than the fact you lived in the same house, I mean."

"We did stuff together."

"Oh, like picnics and vacations and going to church? Those kinds of things?"

Kristen chased a piece of angel food cake around her bowl. "No. Dad was always busy at work. He didn't have time for that kind of stuff."

"Hmm. I guess you guys watched movies together or barbecued in the backyard. That's nice too."

"We didn't do a lot of that, either." Kristen fidgeted in her seat, and twin creases appeared on her brow. "Dad said barbecuing made his clothes smelly. But Mom and I did all that stuff while Dad was working at night or on the weekends."

"It sounds like he missed a lot."

"Some. He tried to come to most of my school stuff, though."

"And I bet he did his best to spend time with your mom too. Took her out to dinner, or sat around and talked with her over a soda at the end of the day."

The creases on Kristen's forehead deepened. "He didn't talk to Mom a lot, and when he did, he always sounded kind of . . . annoyed. Like she was bothering him." She jabbed at a strawberry. "I think it made her sad."

"Is she happier now?"

"I guess. But . . . it's like with Grandma. Mom always lets herself be pushed around. She let Dad do that to her too. If she'd stood up for herself, maybe Dad wouldn't have left and maybe Grandma wouldn't be so bossy." Kristen sighed, settled her elbow on the table, and propped her chin in her palm. "I wish Mom had been more like you. You don't let Grandma bully you. And I bet you wouldn't let any man push you around, either."

Val forced down her last bite of trifle. "Sometimes it takes a long time for people to learn to stick up for themselves." She rose and picked up Kristen's empty bowl. "I think my dessert was a hit."

"Yeah. It was great. Would you give Mom the recipe?"

"Sure."

"She's been trying some of those other recipes you gave her too. We had that chicken stir-fry last night. It was awesome."

Silence fell as Val rinsed the dishes. A dog barked, the hall clock chimed, a faint train whistle sounded in the distance. The ordinary sounds of an ordinary day.

There was a certain comfort in that. Ordinary was very underrated.

When Kristen spoke again, her voice was more subdued. "Aunt Val, do you think Mom is happier without Dad?"

She picked up a dish towel and dried her hands. "What do you think?"

"Maybe." Kristen tapped a hot-pink nail on the table. "I guess he wasn't around much, anyway. And he wasn't always real nice to her. But I still miss him."

"That's understandable. Why don't you try to see him more often?"

"He's always busy."

"You know how you said your mom should have stood up for herself? Why don't you do the same thing? If you tell your dad you miss him, he might visit more often."

"I guess I could try."

"It couldn't hurt." Val hung up the dish towel. "I left some dessert for your mom in the fridge."

Kristen propped her chin back in her hand, her expression pensive. "Okay."

"I'll let myself out."

As Val dug through her purse for her keys, she felt Kristen watching her.

"I'll try and come see Grandma this week. And I'll think about calling Dad."

"Sounds like a plan. See you later."

"Yeah."

When she reached the threshold, Val glanced back. Kristen remained at the table, lost in thought.

With a satisfied nod, Val turned to go.

Mission accomplished.

So that was Dorothy Walker's son.

As the departing choir director introduced the midthirtyish man who was standing off to one side of the sanctuary, Karen leaned sideways in her seat to get a better view of him. He was nice looking in a brooding sort of way, with neatly trimmed dark brown hair and dark eyes. On the tall side at six, six-one, with a lean, muscular physique. Nicely dressed too, in pressed khaki slacks and a blue oxford shirt.

But he didn't exactly ooze warmth. As soon as possible after the introduction, he moved back to his seat in the shadows.

Karen gave him another discreet scan. Odd. Dorothy had said he'd had a traumatic accident, yet there was no evidence of physical injury.

Perhaps the invisible scars his mother had mentioned were the bigger problem.

During the remainder of the rehearsal she focused on her music, but afterwards she joined the group of choir members waiting their turn to welcome Scott. Interesting how the man was there, yet not there. He replied to their comments. Shook their hands. Smiled in the appropriate places.

But the smile never reached his eyes. They remained dark and distant and bleak.

After adding her own words of welcome, she headed for her car. Their exchange had been polite, nothing more. She'd gleaned no more insights about him, learned nothing new. Yet she felt reasonably certain about one thing.

He might have accepted the job. And he might have shown up at the rehearsal.

But he absolutely did not want to be there.

"Daddy, I have tangles."

David continued to stir the pot of oatmeal on the stove. "I'll help you in a minute, sweetie."

"Okay." Victoria set the brush and a barrette on the table and climbed onto a kitchen chair. "Do I have to go to day care today?"

It was the same question she asked every weekday morning. And he gave the same answer. "Yes, sweetheart. Daddy has to go to work. But I'll come get you at three-thirty, like I do every day, and we'll have the whole rest of the day together."

What would he do if he didn't have that kind of flexibility in his work? His career choice had served him well on that score—though who could have known shift work would be such a blessing?

Another example of Jeremiah 29:11 in action.

"I wish I didn't have to go." Victoria fiddled with the barrette, shoulders hunched.

A pang echoed in his heart. So did he. But there was no alternative.

He finished stirring the oatmeal, scooped it into a bowl, and added brown sugar and cinnamon. After pouring a glass of juice, he set both in front of her. "Eat up while I fix your hair."

She handed him the brush. "Don't make ouches."

"I'll try not to."

He eased the brush through her thick, wavy hair. Natalie's had been similar, until she'd had it cut into a short, chic, easy-care style better suited to her busy lifestyle. "You have beautiful hair, sweetie. Just like your mommy."

"Mommy was pretty, wasn't she?"

Her wistful tone tightened his throat. "Very."

"I wish I could remember her better."

"You were very little when she went to live in heaven."

"Did she love me?"

"Very much."

"I wish I had a mommy now."

"I do too." David set the brush aside and secured the barrette. "Okay. All done. Now finish your oatmeal."

After shaking some dry cereal into a bowl for himself, he joined Victoria at the table. "What do you say we go on a picnic this weekend?"

Her eyes lit up. "That would be fun!"

"Okay. We'll come home after church, change clothes, pack a lunch, and go exploring. We'll have an adventure."

"What's an adventure?"

"It's going somewhere new or doing something you've never done before."

She wrinkled her nose. "Like coming to Washington?"

"Sort of."

No response.

He tried again. "This will be fun. I promise."

Still no response.

Time to change the subject.

"When we get home today, why don't I put up that swing we bought for the backyard?" He added some more milk to his cereal, which seemed drier than usual today.

She gave a disinterested shrug.

Spoon poised over his bowl, David studied her. What had happened to her initial excitement about the project? "I thought you were looking forward to having your very own swing in our yard?"

"I was." She poked at her oatmeal. "But swinging all by yourself isn't very much fun."

Appetite fleeing, David pushed his cereal aside. Victoria was right.

About swinging.

And about life.

"I don't understand why Val has to run back to Chicago tomorrow. She's only been here for three weeks." Margaret dropped the piece of newspaper she'd been reading, letting it fall to the floor.

Karen tuned her out as she continued to try and balance her mother's checkbook. It had been challenging enough years ago. Now that Margaret had grown more lackadaisical about keeping up with her entries, it was downright difficult.

"Mom, there's a notation here for sixty dollars, but no check number and no indication who it was for."

Margaret gave a long-suffering sigh. "Let me see."

As she handed over the checkbook, Karen noted the improved dexterity in her mother's left hand. The physical therapy program—and Val's diligence in seeing that their mother did her exercises—were paying off.

Margaret lifted her chin and peered at the entry through her bifocals. "Oh. That was for trimming the tree out in front."

"Who was it made out to?"

"The man who came by and offered to trim the tree." Impatience nipped at her words. "He said if I didn't have it done, it might fall on the roof in a storm."

"What was his name?"

"I don't remember."

"Did you keep the carbon?"

"Is it in there?"

"No."

"It must have stuck to the back of the check. They don't make checks like they used to."

Karen reined in her own annoyance. “It would help if you either kept the stubs or filled out the register more completely.”

“I do the best I can. And this isn’t high finance. You have a business degree. I should think you could figure it out. Anyway, I don’t know why Val has to run off like this.”

“She told you she had a couple of modeling commitments to fulfill this summer. It’s only for one night.”

“I don’t care how long it is. It’s still an inconvenience for everyone.”

“She’s spending the summer here, Mom. That’s not exactly convenient for her.”

“She was due for a visit, anyway. Overdue.”

Resigned, Karen closed the checkbook. She’d have to straighten out the mess later, when she wasn’t distracted. Besides, there was another issue she needed to tackle before Val got back from running errands. One that would require her full attention.

As her pulse tripped into double time, Karen forced herself to speak the words she’d practiced. “Mom, while Val is gone I’d like you to come and stay in our guest room.”

Margaret stared at her as if she’d lost her mind. “What?”

“I’d like you to stay in our guest room. I don’t want you or Kristen to be alone at night, and it will be easier for you to come to our house than for Kristen and me to come here.”

“Easier for you, maybe.”

“And Kristen will be home all day.” Karen continued as if her mother hadn’t spoken. *Lord, give me the fortitude to stay the course.* “She can see to anything you need and get dinner started.”

“I want to stay here. I sleep better in my own bed.”

“We have a nice guest room. You’ll be very comfortable.”

“Not as comfortable as I would be in my own house.”

“Mom, be logical. It will be a lot less hassle for one person to spend the night elsewhere than for two people to haul all their stuff to another house. And I’ll be very busy tomorrow, working late in preparation for the second-quarter closing. Plus, Kristen is still having trouble getting around.”

Margaret glared at her. "I had a stroke. Doesn't that count for anything?"

Karen's stomach spasmed, the way it always did when Margaret was displeased with her. But she was tired of being manipulated. If Val could stand her ground with their mother, so could she.

"I'm not keeping score, Mom. This is just the best solution."

"I'm not going." Margaret's jaw settled into a stubborn line.

Her mother had called her bluff, just as she'd feared.

But it wasn't going to work. Not this time.

Struggling to maintain a placid expression, she slung her purse over her shoulder. "Okay. I guess you know what's best for yourself." The line of Margaret's jaw slackened—until Karen continued. "I'll call throughout the day to check on you."

The look of surprise on her mother's face was almost comical. "You mean you're going to leave me by myself? All night?"

"That was your choice, wasn't it?"

"Karen Marie, I've never seen you act this selfish."

That hurt.

Nevertheless, Karen managed to hold on to her neutral expression—by a hair. "I'm sorry you feel that way." She tucked her mother's checkbook into her purse. "Val should be back any minute. I'm going to head home and start dinner."

She got all the way to the door before her mother spoke.

"I suppose I could manage to come to your place for one night." Margaret said the words as if she had to pry each one loose like a stuck window.

Thank you, Lord! Karen closed her eyes and let out the breath she'd been holding.

When she turned, her mother was scowling. But for once, she didn't care. She'd stood her ground and done the logical thing instead of acquiescing to please someone else. It might be a small triumph, but it was a victory nonetheless.

"I'm glad you're being sensible."

"Do I have a choice? At least I'll get a decent meal instead of that weird food Val's been fixing."

Time to play her trump card. "As a matter of fact, I'm planning to try a new tofu recipe I clipped out of the paper. It sounds delicious."

"Tofu?" Shock flattened her mother's features.

"Yes. It's very healthy. Well, I have to be off. Kristen's heating up the leftover turkey lasagna we had for dinner last night, and I don't want to be late. Dorothy Walker gave me the recipe. Have a nice evening."

As Karen shut the door, she kept a firm grip on the handle, pausing to give her legs a chance to steady. That had been tough. And scary. And it had taken her way out of her comfort zone.

But she'd won.

Best of all, there was no lingering sense of guilt or remorse or shame.

In fact, there was only one word to describe how she felt.

Satisfied.

7

"So how did it go with Mom while I was in Chicago?"

Karen took a sip of her skim-milk frappuccino before she responded to Val. "I think she thinks we're conspiring against her."

"How so?"

"She grilled me about why we started shopping together, and commented that it was odd how we want to spend time together now when we never did as kids. Then she asked me what we talked about."

"What did you say?"

"This and that."

"I bet that drove her nuts."

"It frustrated her, anyway. When she couldn't get any info out of me, she started interrogating Kristen about her boyfriend. She knows I don't approve of him, and I guess she assumed that would get a rise out of me."

"Did it?"

"Nope. In fact, I came to his defense. Which surprised Mom—and Kristen. Mom's next strategy was to criticize the dinner."

"What did you have?"

"Tofu stew."

Val burst out laughing. "I wish I'd been there."

"She tried to enlist Kristen against me on the food front, but believe it or not, my daughter took my side. She said she thought it was not only delicious but healthy and good for the waistline. Mom never misses an opportunity to point out that I've gained a few pounds, so Kristen also told her I'd lost seven pounds—and that she could afford to do the same."

"I bet that didn't meet with a very favorable response."

"Give the lady a gold star." Karen took a sip of her drink. "She accused Kristen of being disrespectful and told me I should have raised her better."

"Sounds like a jolly meal. Did you, by the way?"

"Did I what?"

"Lose seven pounds?"

"Uh-huh." It wasn't much, but the accomplishment still gave her a small rush of pride. "Just eighteen more to go."

"Good for you. Listen, I'm sorry I had to bail for a day. I would have gotten out of the commitment if I could, but modeling is a nice supplement to my income and I don't want to turn down too many jobs or my agent will put me at the bottom of her call list."

"It wasn't a problem."

"I'm booked for one other assignment too, remember."

"I know. I have it jotted down." Karen tipped her head and pursed her lips. "Maybe I'll make turkey lasagna that night."

Val laughed again and shook her head. "You're bad."

"Aren't I, though?"

But she didn't feel in the least repentant.

"Martha!" Karen waved at the middle-aged woman across the church parking lot. At the summons, Martha Ramsey halted her trek toward the dumpster.

As she drew close, Karen's heart contracted at the weary slope of the woman's shoulders and her careworn face. Martha might only be in her midfifties, but she'd aged a decade since her son's debilitating accident. Yet she continued to find time to keep the sanctuary in the church decorated with fresh flowers supplied from the gardens of the congregation. Amazing—and inspiring.

Shifting her folder of music from one arm to the other, Karen stopped in front of the woman. "How's Steven?"

Martha set down a bucket filled with withered, dying blooms redolent with the pungent scent of decay. "About as well as can be expected, I guess. It's hard for a young man with such athletic promise to give up his dreams. Thank you for asking." She brushed a dead petal off her blouse and cleared her throat. "How is your mother? I'm still keeping her in my prayers."

"Improving every day."

"I'm glad to hear that." The woman stooped and picked up the bucket. "I need to get home and help settle Steven in for the night. Take care, and give your mother my best."

"You too. And I'll pass on your message."

Turning back toward her car, Karen rummaged in her purse for her keys. Considering how fast the lot had emptied, the other choir members had been as eager to leave as she was. And no wonder. Their second choir rehearsal with Scott Walker had been as unpleasant as the first one.

She continued to feel for her keys as she walked toward her car. If the man didn't want the job, why had he taken it? His flat tone, his cursory review of the music for Sunday, his early dismissal all reeked of indifference. If this continued, the already small group was certain to shrink. They'd all joined the choir in search of fellowship and spiritual enrichment, not friction and stress.

Rotating her taut shoulders, she tried to cut him some slack based on the little he'd told them about his accident. A partially paralyzed hand would wreak havoc with a musician's career. She could understand how that would turn a person's world upside down. So could the rest of the choir members. They were all kind, caring people.

But given the stoic expressions on their faces as the rehearsal ended, along with their silent exodus, the well of sympathy was fast running dry.

Karen stopped beside her car and frowned. No keys. Had she left them on the music cabinet? It was possible. She'd stopped there on her way in to retrieve a copy of a hymn the former director had passed out at a rehearsal she'd missed a couple of weeks ago.

Hand on hip, Karen surveyed the church. She hadn't seen Scott come out, but there was only one car left in the lot beside hers, and Martha was still here. If he'd slipped away while the two of them were talking, she'd have to ask Martha to reopen the door. But better to check first rather than delay the other woman, who was anxious to get home.

And if she was lucky, Scott would still be there and the door would be open.

Scott slowly lowered himself to the piano bench and expelled a long breath.

Tonight had been a disaster.

Even worse than last week.

He ought to just throw in the towel on this gig. His mother and the minister would be disappointed, but he didn't much care.

About anything.

Positioning his hand over the keyboard, he plunked out the melody line from one of the hymns they'd been practicing tonight. Something about eagle's wings and being freed from the terror of the night.

Too bad the nice words were a lie.

Nobody could save him from the kind of suffocating darkness, the vast, hollow emptiness that enveloped his soul.

Including God.

He knew that for a fact.

Because in his darkest, most desperate hours, when he'd pleaded for mercy, for release, for help—for anything that would lift the burden of darkness from his soul—the Almighty had been silent. Maybe he was there; maybe he wasn't. All Scott knew for sure was that he was on his own.

Rotating his injured hand left and right, he studied the fingers. Was it possible the doctor had been right when he'd said the disability could be partly psychological? That if he wanted to recover, he could? Was there some truth to the whole notion of mind over matter?

Closing his eyes, Scott gave himself a silent pep talk.

I want to play this piano. I will *play this piano. I will command my brain to send the correct impulses to my left hand, and it* will *respond.*

After repeating that mantra several times, he flipped through a book of hymns and selected a song that would have been a piece of cake to sight-read in the old days. Then, positioning his fingers on the keys, he attempted to play it.

His left hand refused to cooperate.

He repeated the mantra and tried again. And again. And again. Until whatever dim hope had flickered to life in his soul sputtered and died.

Tears pricking his eyelids, Scott banged the keys with all the force he could muster. As the jarring, discordant sound echoed in the empty church, he dropped his head into his hands and sucked in a harsh breath.

He might as well face it. His music career was toast. He needed to move on.

Except he didn't know where to go.

At the loud, dissonant crash from the piano, Karen jerked to a stop near the entrance to the sanctuary.

What was going on in there?

Edging closer to the door, she cracked it open and peeked in. Scott was sitting at a right angle to her, his elbows propped on the keys, his head buried in his hands.

Not an opportune moment to intrude.

But a quick glance confirmed that her keys were on top of the music cabinet two feet inside the door. Close, but just beyond her grasp—and she wasn't going anywhere without them.

Could she sidle in far enough to snag the ring and disappear without disturbing Scott?

Taking a cautious step forward, she reached for the keys—and watched in dismay as a loose piece of music slipped from her folder and fell to the floor with a clatter.

Her gaze flew to Scott. His head jerked up, and as his expression morphed from surprise to anger, her stomach twisted.

"Were you spying on me?"

Wrong word choice.

That was exactly what Michael had accused her of whenever she'd called his office on the nights he worked late during the months preceding their separation.

The accusation had been as misplaced then as it was now—and just as insulting.

"I forgot my keys." She lifted her chin, snatched them off the cabinet, and jangled them.

Some of the tautness in Scott's features dissipated, but his anger didn't abate. "Too bad you didn't come a little sooner. You would have heard my pathetic attempts to play this." Bitterness etched his words as he flung the music on the rack to the floor. "This job was a mistake. I knew it from the beginning."

Despite his hostility, her heart contracted at his almost palpable pain.

She took a tentative step closer and gentled her voice. "We're not the St. Louis Symphony Chorus, you know. We don't expect perfection."

He turned to her, his eyes raw. Bleak. "But I'm a trained musician, and I'm not satisfied with less than that."

"Perfection is a high standard to apply to anything—with or without an injury. It's a recipe for frustration."

"Yeah. I know all about frustration." He slammed the keyboard cover shut. "And I don't think there's much chance it's going to disappear anytime soon."

"Is your injury . . . permanent?"

The personal question was out before she could stop it, and Karen expected him to stiffen and tell her it was none of her business.

But to her surprise, he answered. "Who knows?"

"You mean there's a chance you might recover?"

"No one's ruled that out."

"Then that's good news, isn't it?"

He gave a mirthless laugh. "Depends on your definition of good." He stood abruptly. "I need to lock up."

Karen searched for other words of comfort but came up empty. Besides, she doubted anything she said would alleviate Scott's pain.

So she simply walked out in silence.

And said a silent prayer for the troubled man still inside.

8

Val pulled into a parking place, set the brake, and looked around the small park, deserted—as she'd expected—on this Sunday morning. The last thing she wanted was a bunch of strangers witnessing her journey into the past.

Leaning back in the seat, she scanned the cloudless late-June sky. The summer was flowing by as swiftly as the river below, and she hadn't made any progress toward her goal. Simply being back in Washington, back in her childhood home, hadn't proven to be the catalyst she'd expected.

Changing her environment—to one even less comfortable than the girlhood bedroom that held physical evidence of her dark secret—had seemed like a logical next step.

Now she wasn't so certain.

Stomach knotting, she surveyed the green expanse in front of her. It didn't seem possible that eighteen years had passed since her last visit here. Yet in some ways it also felt like a lifetime ago.

If only she'd known then what she knew now.

Swallowing past the bitter taste on her tongue, Val pushed open her door and stood. Below, the winding path of the glistening river led to the distant horizon, its serenity and peace a stark contrast to her turbulent emotions.

She shut the door and scanned the grassy knoll, where a few unoccupied picnic tables were scattered. Later, the park would be filled with family groups, but if all went according to plan, she'd be long gone by then.

Besides, the open area wasn't her destination. That lay in a small cove at the base of the bluff, down by the river. And on a Sunday morning, it would be populated only by memories.

Her pulse ratcheted up, and she tightened her grip on the door, fighting the temptation to get back in her car and drive away as fast as she could. But she'd been running away for too many years. It was time to face this and deal with it.

Or at least take the first step.

Without giving herself a chance to entertain any more second thoughts, she strode toward the edge of the woods on the far side of the knoll. At first glance, the perimeter appeared to be nothing more than dense brush. Where was the entrance? She did a second scan. Nothing . . . nothing . . . there! Some trampled undergrowth.

The path was still in use.

Pushing aside the brush, Val stepped into the shadows. Here, the path was clearer. Meaning it must still be a Saturday night gathering place for teens.

She picked her way down the sloping trail, trying to avoid the brambles that snagged at her legs. Good thing she'd worn jeans. But that didn't help her bare arms. She slowed her pace when thorny tentacles reached toward her, cautiously brushing them aside. Perhaps the path wasn't used quite as much as it had been in her day.

As she emerged from the woods onto a small, sandy beach at the river's edge, she came to an abrupt halt.

It was like passing through a time warp.

The spot was exactly the same as the day she and Corey had come down here with three other couples for an end-of-the-summer picnic. The blackened remains of a campfire were surrounded by sturdy logs deposited by the relentless motion of the river. Driftwood lay about, and beer cans littered the sand. Cigarette butts were strewn around the logs, and small stones rimmed the water's edge.

The only thing that had changed since her first—and only—visit was her.

Dread clogging her throat, she forced her gaze to move on to the first of the tiny crescent inlets that dotted the shore on either side of this main gathering place. The secluded nooks where the kids disappeared, two by two, after they'd consumed their fill of liquor.

She and Corey among them.

She choked back her revulsion as the events of that long-ago summer night played out in her memory like one of those jerky old-fashioned home movies her dad used to take.

"See? I told you everything would be okay." Corey scooted closer to her on the dead log and tipped back his third bottle of beer, chugging it down.

Was it? Val looked around. A lot of the kids were zoning out. Maybe, for once, Mom had been right to caution her about the rowdy parties that took place here. But Corey was leaving tomorrow to start his freshman year at Northwestern. She wouldn't see him again until Thanksgiving. After dating him all summer, how could she say no when he'd pleaded with her to attend his going-away party?

But this didn't feel right.

"Val." He nudged her with his elbow and passed her a plastic cup. "Try this. It'll put you in a party mood."

She squinted at the clear liquid in the dim light of the campfire. "What is it?"

"Happy juice. Trust me on this, okay?"

She took a sip. Coughed as it burned down her throat. Made a face.

He laughed. "It'll grow on you. Don't be a party pooper."

Somehow she managed to choke it down, sip by sip. No way did she want to embarrass him in front of his friends by being a wet blanket.

By the time she drained the cup, she was feeling relaxed and a little giddy. She even took a few drags on the joint someone passed her. Smoking had never appealed to her, but this wasn't too bad. She took a few more. The conversation around her grew distant, and an odd, floaty sensation overtook her.

That was when Corey pulled her to her feet and suggested a walk.

Not a bad idea. Maybe some fresh air, away from the acrid smoke, would help clear her head.

She let him lead her down the beach, but less than a dozen yards from the party crowd he guided her into a tiny alcove. From somewhere he produced a blanket. Spread it on the sand. Pulled her down beside him.

"I'm leaving tomorrow, Val."

"I know. I'll miss you."

"How much?"

"A lot."

"Show me."

It started as a kiss . . . and grew from there. The next thing she knew, they were lying down and Corey was tugging her T-shirt out of her shorts.

Alarm bells went off somewhere in the recesses of her mind.

"Corey . . . no. I . . . I don't do the heavy stuff."

"Even for me, babe? I love you. Don't you love me?"

"You know I do. But this is . . . it's wrong."

"How can it be wrong if we love each other and plan to get married?"

Val tried to think through the haze in her brain. "Married?"

"Do you think I'd ask you to do this if I wasn't planning to marry you? Not now, but after we finish school."

Val tried to sort out the sequence of intimacy and marriage. Something was out of whack here, but Corey's lips, and his urgency, were robbing her of rational thought.

"Are you sure about this?" Her words came out slightly garbled.

"Sure enough for both of us. Just go with the flow."

His hands were all over her. Her brain froze. She couldn't think.

And so she didn't.

She followed his advice and went with the flow.

A shudder rippled through Val as the images in her mind faded to black.

So many mistakes. And for what? She'd never even seen Corey again—and when she'd sought him out in desperation, he'd left her to deal with her darkest hours alone.

Sinking to her knees in the sand, Val dropped her face into her hands. If only she could turn back the clock, live that one night over again, how different her life might have been.

But it was too late for second chances.

A sob ripped through her. Then another. The memories crashing over her were too intense. Too disturbing. Too heart-shattering.

She had to leave.

Fast.

Pushing herself to her feet, she took off running for the trail, oblivious to the brambles snagging her hair and scraping her arms as she ascended. Up, up she climbed, until at last she emerged from the shadows into the sun on the knoll.

Bending forward, hands on knees, she sucked in deep, shuddering breaths, her heart thudding as if she'd just finished a five-hundred-yard dash.

So much for finding answers in the place where it had all begun.

And if she'd fallen apart here, how would she survive a visit to the place where it had ended?

"Daddy, can I go see that butterfly up close?"

Following the direction of Victoria's finger, David spotted a monarch hovering over a nearby patch of clover. "Sure. But be very slow and quiet or you'll scare it away. And don't touch it, okay?"

"Why?"

"Because butterflies are very fragile."

"What's fragile?"

"That means they break easily."

Tilting her head, Victoria studied him. "Like Mommy's vase?"

A vision of the piece of Venetian glass Natalie had brought back from a business trip to Italy flashed through his mind.

He'd never cared for the ornate vase, and he wasn't sorry it had slipped from his fingers while he was unpacking and shattered into a thousand pieces. But for whatever reason, the image of the brilliant crimson shards on the white tile floor in their new kitchen was etched in his mind.

They'd reminded him of blood.

He shut out the picture as best he could. "That's right. Like Mommy's vase."

"I'll be real careful."

"Okay." She took off, and David watched her approach the gossamer-winged creature. It flitted to the next flower as she drew close, and she stopped. After a brief hesitation, she started forward again. The same scenario was repeated again. And again. This game could keep Victoria amused for hours—and that was fine. Whatever made her happy.

He stretched out his legs on the blanket, leaned back on his hands, and lifted his face to the sun. It felt good to relax after all the upheaval of their move, and he intended to savor every minute of this gorgeous day.

A movement in his peripheral vision caught his eye, and he idly turned his head—then stiffened. A blonde woman had emerged from the woods, and she was bent over, holding on to a tree.

He straightened up and took a closer look. Was that a streak of blood running down her arm?

A second later she raised her head, and his heart stopped.

It was Val!

David catapulted to his feet, darting a quick glance toward Victoria. Her back was to him, and she'd bent down to examine the butterfly, oblivious to everything else. She'd be safe and occupied for a few moments.

As David sprinted toward Val, his alarm escalated. The closer he got, the worse she looked. Her hair was tangled, and he hadn't imagined the blood. A nasty scratch ran from her elbow halfway to her wrist. When he touched her arm and felt the tremors coursing through her, his gut clenched.

"Val?" His voice came out in a hoarse croak, and he tried again. "Val, what happened?"

No response.

He gave her a slight shake. "Val!"

Slowly she raised her head. Her eyes were glazed, and there was evidence of recent tears on her colorless face. She blinked once . . . twice . . . three times before she began to focus. "David?"

"What happened?"

She pushed her hair back from her face. "What . . . do you mean?"

"You stumbled out of the woods. Your arm is bleeding. You're shaking, and I can see you've been crying."

Val examined her arm. "It's just a scratch. From the brambles."

David narrowed his eyes. Was she avoiding his question on purpose, or was she in shock?

"Val, something happened in there. Should I call the police?"

"No. I'm fine. I . . . took a hike and I . . . I got lost in the woods. I was s-scared for a few minutes. That's all."

She was lying.

But if he pushed, she might shut him out completely.

"Okay." Far from it, but he'd play along. For now. "Your arm needs attention, though."

"I'll take care of it when I get home." She tried for a smile. Managed only a twist of her lips. "What are you doing here, anyway?"

"Getting ready to have a picnic." He gestured behind him.

As Val glanced over his shoulder toward Victoria, her features softened. Then she dipped her head again and fumbled in the pocket of her jeans. "Listen, I'm sorry I disturbed your day." She pulled out her car keys and clasped them in a tight fist.

"You're in no condition to drive."

"I'm fine. Really." She started to walk past him, but she stopped when he touched her arm.

"Look—why don't you join us?"

She glanced again toward his daughter. "No, thank you. I wouldn't want to barge in on a family outing."

"It's just Victoria and me."

She frowned. "Isn't your wife with you?"

"Natalie died two years ago."

"Oh." Her eyes widened. "I-I'm sorry."

"Thanks." He stepped aside and indicated the blanket where he'd been sitting. "Anyway, Victoria and I would welcome your company."

She edged back. "I-I don't think so." Her gaze was riveted on the blanket.

The blanket was freaking her out.

Why?

But he didn't have time to figure it out. She was still moving away, and in another moment or two she'd flee.

"I was just about to move to the picnic table. It looks like a more comfortable spot. Won't you reconsider? We have brownies for dessert." He gave her a teasing grin he hoped didn't look as forced as it felt.

Some of the tension in her features relaxed. "Brownies, hmm? That's hard to pass up."

"Then stay. I brought plenty."

Indecision flitted through her eyes, and he had a feeling she was going to decline. But much to his surprise, she relented.

"Okay. For a few minutes."

The tautness in his smile eased. "Good. Let me gather up our things."

As he shook out the blanket and folded it, Victoria looked his way. He waved at her and she bounded toward him, apparently more intrigued by their guest than by the elusive butterfly. Her step slowed as she approached, however, and she moved beside him to shyly regard the new arrival.

"Victoria, this is Val. She's a friend of mine. Can you say hello?"

"Hello." The little girl echoed his words in a soft voice.

"Hello, Victoria. I saw your picture in your daddy's office. You're even prettier in person."

"You're pretty too." She inspected Val's arm. "But you have an owie."

"A big thorn scratched me in the woods."

"We need to take care of that." David deposited their picnic supplies on the table and dug out his car keys.

"I can deal with it later."

He ignored her. "I'll get the first aid kit from the car."

"You carry a first aid kit in your car?" She shot him a surprised look.

"I have a five-year-old. That means I follow the Coast Guard motto: Always ready."

Val's lips curved. "Okay. Victoria and I will visit while you're gone."

David returned to the car, pausing at the trunk to glance back at the twosome. An exuberant Victoria was talking to Val, who was leaning forward as she listened, her mouth curved into a smile. He couldn't hear the conversation, but all at once his daughter's laugh floated through the air.

Man, he'd missed that sound. He'd almost begun to think she'd left it in St. Louis, along with her friends from day care and the familiarity of their old routine. Most days since the move, she'd been subdued. And how many nights had he awakened and found her at his bedside, complaining of having bad dreams and wanting to sleep with him?

Too many.

He fitted the key in the trunk, lifted the lid, and pulled out the first aid kit. So they'd had some transition problems. That was to be expected. But once they settled into small-town life, things would get better. They'd adjust to their new routine. Turn their new house into a home. Make new friends.

Like Val.

Already she was bringing laughter back into Victoria's life. Adding a spark to her eyes.

And to his.

Yet as he started back toward the picnic table, he frowned. Val was leaving Washington in a few weeks. Letting himself—or Victoria—get too involved with her would be a big mistake. He and his daughter had had enough loss and disappointment to last a lifetime. The key was to play this cool. Casual. Enjoy her company, but focus on making more permanent friends.

So they'd eat their lunch, have a few pleasant moments—and leave it at that. Even if Val seemed as much in need of a friend as Victoria did.

Because keeping things light and friendly would be a whole lot safer.

For everyone.

9

"I still don't know how you talked me into this." Karen shot Val a disgruntled glance.

Her sister grinned at her from the adjacent salon chair. "Trust me. You'll love it."

Karen cringed as another length of her hair fell to the floor. "I've always had long hair."

"Shoulder length is still long. Everything else is extra weight. This style will highlight your excellent bone structure. Am I right?" Val directed her question to the woman deftly wielding a pair of scissors behind Karen's chair.

"No question about it." The stylist continued to snip like there was no tomorrow. "And adding in layers will give your hair more body and fullness."

"See?" Val leaned back in her chair and linked her fingers over her nonexistent stomach.

Karen watched another long lock bite the dust. "It's not like I have much choice at this point."

"You could start a new trend. Half long, half shoulder length. Lots of kids do stuff like that."

"I'm not a kid." Karen scrutinized her reflection in the mirror. She had to admit the shorter length suited her face better. Softened it. But it didn't alter the mousy brown hue. "I do like the style. Too bad it doesn't help the color."

"Why not change that too?"

"No way. This is a big enough step for one day."

"How about sticking your toe in the water with some highlights? You have some natural auburn in your hair that we could bring out a little. Right?" Val pulled the stylist back into the conversation.

"Absolutely. That's a great idea."

"I don't think so."

"Why not? If you don't like it, it will grow out. Come on, Karen. Be daring."

"I'm not the daring type." Another length of hair dropped into her lap, and Karen picked it up. "You know, there is a little bit of red in here."

"Auburn," Val corrected. "A much richer color. The highlighting will enhance that. It won't change the basic color of your hair."

"I don't know . . ."

Val made the decision for her. "Do it," she told the stylist. Then she looked back at Karen, heading off her protest. "Consider it a birthday gift."

"My birthday's not until September."

"I'll be back in Chicago by then. This is an early present. And I bet you can be daring if you put your mind to it."

Could she?

Yes!

"Okay, I will." She waved a hand at the stylist, determined to rise to the challenge even if she was quaking on the inside—and already wondering if she was making a mistake. "You heard the lady. Do it."

An hour later, when they emerged from the salon into the sunlight, Val stepped back and inspected Karen. Shaking her head, she uttered one word. "Wow!"

"A vast overstatement, I suspect." Nevertheless, a heady rush of pleasure swept through her. "But I do feel pretty. Maybe for the first time in my life."

"You *are* pretty. And you'll be even prettier once we buy a little mascara and some blush and lipstick."

"Wait!" Karen grabbed Val's arm when her sister started forward. "What about our grocery shopping? We're already running late. Mom will wonder what happened to us, and Kristen will be livid that we left her with her grandmother for so long on a holiday weekend. As she reminded me this morning, she has places to go."

"They'll both live. We'll be quick. Besides, we're celebrating Independence Day, remember? What better way than this?"

Before Karen could reply, Val towed her down the strip mall toward the drugstore. "Nothing fancy or expensive, I promise. Just a few touches to enhance your coloring."

Those few touches turned into a major makeover—by her standard, if not her sister's.

And an hour later, as they pulled onto Margaret's street, her nerves kicked in big time. What in the world was her mother going to say?

As if sensing her trepidation, Val spoke. "Don't be intimidated. No matter what snide remarks Mom might make, you look great. Hold that thought."

Karen tried, but by the time they pushed through the back door she was as close as she'd ever been to a panic attack.

Kristen jumped to her feet the instant they stepped into the kitchen, clearly way past ready to end her extended visit with her grandmother. "I thought you guys got lost or . . ." Her voice faltered and her mouth dropped open as they walked into the room. "Wow!"

"See?" Val sent her a smug look.

Margaret's response, however, was far less affirmative. "What on earth did you do to yourself?"

"Mom! You look great!"

One yea, one nay. But Kristen's enthusiastic expression more than countered Margaret's dour demeanor.

"Don't you think that hairstyle is a little young for you?" Margaret gave Karen a critical once-over.

"She *is* young." Val dropped her purse on the counter.

Kristen limped over to inspect Karen up close, blessedly more mobile in her new, smaller walking cast. "I love how you brought out the red in your hair!"

"Auburn," Val corrected.

Margaret squinted at Karen. "Did you color your hair?"

"What shade of lipstick is that?" Kristen inspected her mouth.

"Desert rose." Val crossed her arms and leaned back against the counter.

"It's perfect! Why didn't you do this ages ago, Mom?"

"Because she was sensible before." Margaret sent a pointed glance toward her younger daughter.

"Before what?"

At Val's too-innocent question, Margaret glared at her. "You haven't been the best influence, you know. Karen used to be levelheaded. She respected her elders. She cooked decent food. She wasn't vain and didn't see any need to dye her hair or wear makeup."

"I could leave."

As mother and daughter faced off, Karen jumped back into the fray. No point letting this escalate. "No one wants you to leave, Val. And it was my choice to do this, Mom. It's no big deal. Kristen, did you and your grandmother have lunch?"

"If you could call it that." Margaret sniffed in disdain.

"Val left an awesome bean sprout salad." Kristen went to retrieve her backpack. "You have to get the recipe."

"I'll do that. Are you ready to go home?"

"Yes." She started toward the door, but at a raised brow from Karen she sighed and retraced her steps, planting a brief kiss on Margaret's forehead. "Bye, Grandma."

"Good-bye, Kristen. I'll see you at church Sunday, won't I? You don't want to disappoint God."

Kristen rolled her eyes. "Yeah, I'll be there."

"Good. You'll pick me up as usual, Karen?"

"Of course." Karen gave Margaret a brief peck on the cheek.

"I thought I'd better check. Things seem to be changing around here."

"Yeah. Isn't it great?" Val winked at Karen.

Ushering Kristen toward the door, Karen whispered to Val as she passed. "Good luck."

"No worries."

The breezy response didn't surprise her. Val had her act together. She knew how to cope with Margaret—and with everything else.

And one of these days, if she kept working at it, Karen might be as much in control of her life as Val was.

Her life was out of control.

Running her fingers through her damp hair, Val checked the clock on the nightstand as she paced. If she could hang on three more hours, it would be light again. Things never seemed as bad when the sun was shining.

When exhaustion at last turned her legs to rubber, she sank onto the window seat. She could blame her insomnia on the decrepit air-conditioning system struggling to cool the brick bungalow, but why kid herself when she knew the real cause—the familiar nightmares that had returned with a vengeance since her trip to the river last Sunday.

Val leaned back against the wall and massaged the bridge of her nose. If only there was someone she could talk to. Someone who could listen without judgment and offer guidance.

But she'd shared her secret once, long ago. With one person.

And that mistake had led to a far bigger one—and to rejection. She wasn't going to take that chance again.

Sweat beaded on her brow, and she swiped it off. Too bad she didn't have Karen's faith. Or her sister's relationship with God. Then she could ask the Almighty for assistance. But she didn't—and she couldn't. Why should he come to the aid of someone who'd rejected him long ago?

She pulled up her legs and rested her chin on her knees. At least her mother had stopped badgering her about going to church with them. They'd fought that battle years ago, and it was one of the few times she'd prevailed. Thankfully, Margaret's attempts since her return had been halfhearted at best. Poor Kristen, however, was getting the full guilt treatment, based on the exchange today.

Funny thing about that, though. She almost wished someone *would* nudge her back. Not that she expected to discover an answer to her dilemma written in the clouds afterward, or get some bolt-of-lightning revelation. But other people found comfort in their faith. Maybe she just hadn't tried hard enough.

Then again, maybe it was too late.

With a sigh, Val swung her legs to the floor and rose. She had to get some sleep, even if that meant facing the nightmares that were more vivid than ever, thanks to her visit to the river. Nightmares she suspected would get even worse if she visited the other places on her list.

No. Not if. When.

Because deep inside, she knew she'd never attain the peace she sought until she did.

And one day soon, she'd find a way to dig deep and summon up the courage to take the next step.

Karen grabbed her purse and music folder and stuck her head into the living room. Kristen was slouched on the couch, staring at the TV. As usual.

"I'll be home by nine. Sooner, if choir practice ends earlier."

"Okay."

At her daughter's dejected tone, she hesitated. "Everything okay?"

"Yeah. I guess."

Not convincing.

She moved closer. "You seem kind of down."

"I'm bored."

"Why don't you call Erin and get together with her?"

"The gang went to the water park."

"Oh." Water activities would be out until Kristen's walking cast came off in three weeks. "Couldn't you have gone along and visited?"

Kristen gave her a "get real" look. "They'll be in the water. Who would I visit with?"

"Maybe Gary would have kept you company." While she didn't much care for the long-haired kid Kristen had taken a fancy to, he'd be safe in a group setting. And it was better than the one-on-one dating Kristen kept pushing her to approve.

"I haven't talked to Gary for a while." Kristen's jaw quivered, and she averted her face.

Ah. A pothole on the rocky road of teenage romance.

Karen walked all the way in and perched on the edge of the sofa. "What happened?"

"How should I know? I've been sidelined with this stupid leg all summer. I guess he found someone else to do stuff with."

"Or he might be busy. He has a summer job, doesn't he?"

"Yeah, but he's got plenty of free time. Erin says she's seen him bumming around with Paula."

Another woman.

Even worse.

Karen thought about telling her daughter she'd get over her current heartthrob, that there were other fish in the sea, that someone better would come along who would be more loyal. But those platitudes wouldn't mitigate teen angst.

She leaned down and kissed the top of Kristen's head. "Always remember I love you."

"I'm glad someone does."

The tears in her daughter's voice tightened her throat. It might not be the most Christian thought, but she hoped Gary found out what it felt like to be dumped too. Soon.

"Would you like me to stay home with you tonight?"

"No. That's okay. I'm going to watch a movie."

"If I get back early enough, would you like to run down to Mr. Frank's?"

"I guess."

Not good. If a trip to the popular frozen custard stand didn't raise Kristen's spirits, she was in serious doldrums.

After giving her daughter's arm one more encouraging squeeze, Karen continued toward the front door. She wasn't going to renege on her choir obligation, but she'd make it a point to get back in time for an outing with her daughter, even if she had to leave early. No hardship there, considering Scott Walker's attitude problem.

She exited, pulling the door closed behind her, and walked toward her car. If things didn't improve with the choir soon, people were going to start dropping out and . . .

"Hello, Karen."

She pulled up short at the greeting, hand flying to her chest. "Michael! You startled me. What are you doing here?"

"Kristen called and said she'd like to see more of me. I decided to pay her a surprise visit. Is she home?" He stuck his hands in his pockets, the move calling attention to the weary droop of his shoulders. There were also faint shadows under his eyes, and fine lines had appeared on his forehead.

For the first time since she'd met him, he seemed old.

"She's inside watching a movie. And your timing is impeccable. She's in a funk and feeling neglected. The broken leg is keeping her from hanging out with her friends, and I think her boyfriend dumped her. Your visit will cheer her up."

He gave a distracted nod, but his focus remained on her. "Have you lost weight?"

"Some."

"And you did something different with your hair. I like it."

"Thanks." Much to her disgust, his compliment pleased her.

"Well . . . I guess I'll see what Kristen is up to."

"And I'm late for choir practice."

Karen started toward the car, sorry now she'd left it parked in front of the garage instead of pulling in after work. He followed, reaching down to open the door for her. She slid in, and after he shut it he leaned on the roof and gazed down at her with the intimate look that had turned her insides to jelly during their courting days.

"You really do look good, you know."

At his husky tone, she blushed—like in the old days.

Oh, for goodness' sake.

How sad was that?

This man had cheated on her. Dumped her for a newer model. How could she still be susceptible to his flattery?

She jammed the key in the ignition and looked away. "I'm late, Michael."

"Okay." He took his time removing his arm from the roof. "See you later."

She didn't respond. Instead, she put her sunglasses on and backed the car out of the driveway. She would *not* look back.

Yet much to her disgust, she found herself glancing in the rearview mirror as she pulled away. Michael was still standing there, hands in his pockets, the familiar stance bringing back a rush of memories. He'd always waited like that after she left his apartment during their dating days, watching until she was out of sight. And just before she turned the corner, she'd flick her lights. One. Two. Three. I. Love. You.

Her hand was actually moving toward the light control when she caught herself and snatched it back.

No way.

Those days were gone. Forever. She was over Michael. Whatever love they'd once shared had died long ago.

He'd moved on.

And so had she.

Ten minutes later, when she arrived a bit tardy at choir practice, Scott was in the midst of berating the basses for a missed note.

"No, no, no! I've played this twice already. It's not that hard. Try it again."

She slipped into her seat and sent a sympathetic glance toward the three members of the congregation who constituted the bass section. Only one of them read music. The other two learned by repetition, and Marilyn had always been happy to pound out their line over and over again. Scott, on the other hand, expected them to pick it up after a couple of run-throughs. It was obvious he wasn't used to dealing with amateurs.

The basses made one more dismal attempt.

Scott glared at them. "Okay. We don't have any more time to waste on this. Work on it on your own. I'm moving on to the alto line."

He played through it once. "Okay, let's try it." He started to play again. Several measures in, after Teresa Ramirez went up a note instead of down, Scott stopped and rubbed his temples.

"I hope I don't need to tell you that you weren't even close." Sarcasm dripped from his words. "Let's try it again."

They did. Several times, with Scott stopping often to correct missed notes—and leaving the altos as upset as the basses.

"All right, let's see if the sopranos can do any better. Since you have the melody line, this should be simple."

He played through it once, then they joined in. It was an unfamiliar piece, with an odd key change halfway through, and Karen did her best. But the other sopranos were struggling too, and their rendition was far from perfect. The arrangement was much too advanced and complicated for a small, amateur church choir.

As the rehearsal progressed, the skin tightened over Scott's cheekbones, and the tension in the room grew thick as the humidity of a Missouri August. The muscles in Karen's stomach tightened, just as they had whenever Michael had gotten angry at her or berated her for one of her many shortcomings.

"Okay, let's try and put this together." Shoulders stiff, Scott launched into the introduction.

The choir made a valiant effort, but the piece sounded terrible, even to Karen's untrained ears. The altos kept going flat, and the basses wandered all over the scale, totally lost. The tenors and sopranos managed to hit a fair number of the notes, but not enough to salvage the song.

Halfway through, Scott stopped playing and stood. "It would be a travesty to bestow the term 'music' on what you all are doing. I don't know how you can call yourselves a choir. Let's start with the basses."

As Scott ripped their performance apart, something inside of Karen snapped. She'd had her fill of disapproval and sarcasm from Michael, was tired of it from her mother, and up to her ears in it from Kristen. She'd suffered through that kind of abuse for years, and she wasn't going to take it anymore. She would not sit here passively and let an arrogant jerk rebuke her for doing the best she could, as a volunteer, in an activity that had once given her great pleasure.

Lifting her jaw, she gathered up her things, stood, and made her way to the end of the aisle. Scott stopped speaking midsentence, and silence fell over the room. She could feel fourteen pairs of eyes boring into her back as she walked toward the exit; apparently everyone was as surprised by her show of assertiveness as she was.

But even though her hand was shaking when she reached for the door handle, she didn't pause. She pulled it open, stepped through, and let it shut behind her.

And this time, she didn't look back.

10

"Scott? Is that you?"

As he shut the front door behind him, Scott lifted a trembling hand to his forehead and kneaded his temples. "Yeah."

Dorothy stepped into the living room, took one look at him, and closed the distance between them in three long strides. "What happened? You look terrible!"

"Choir practice was a disaster."

She took his arm and led him to the sofa, pressing him down. "Where's your medicine?"

"In the bathroom."

She disappeared down the hall, returning a minute later with two capsules and a glass of water. Scott downed them in one gulp, then closed his eyes and leaned his head back against the couch.

After taking the glass from his hand, Dorothy sat in a chair beside him. "It must be a bad one."

"Yeah. It came on right after rehearsal started."

"Crummy timing."

"No kidding. And listening to a bunch of off-key amateurs didn't help."

"They do their best."

"It's not good enough."

"They try hard, though. I know you're used to working with professionals, but most of the choir members are there because they like to sing, not because they're Metropolitan Opera caliber. If your standards are too high and you get too upset with them, people won't enjoy the experience anymore and they'll drop out."

"I'm finding that out. I think I lost one tonight."

"What happened?"

"I was trying to teach a new piece, and I got a little . . . upset. My head was pounding, and we were getting nowhere with the music. I guess I was too hard on them. Hard enough that one of the choir members got up and walked out."

"Which one?"

"I don't know. A woman. One of the sopranos."

"Older or younger?"

Although he tried to conjure up an image, details of her appearance eluded him. No surprise there. He'd never bothered to focus on any of the faces. "Younger, I guess. Shoulder-length reddish-brown hair."

"That had to be Karen. But walking out—that doesn't sound like her. She's usually not a wave maker."

"Like I said, I guess I came on a little too strong."

"You must have, if Karen walked out."

"I ought to quit. This isn't going to work."

A beat of silence passed before his mother responded. "We need a music director."

"I don't think I'm the right person for the job."

"Okay." She leaned back in her chair. "What will you do instead?"

"Maybe I'll just veg."

"You've been doing that for two months. You need to start thinking about your future."

"I don't have a future." His response came out flat. Hopeless. The way he felt.

"That's nonsense." For the first time since he'd come home, Dorothy's eyes flared with anger. "You do have a future. It may not be the future you planned, but you do have one. It's up to you to find it—and to stop feeling sorry for yourself."

She leaned forward, her posture intent. "Lots of people face tremendous challenges. Lots of people see their lives turned upside down. Remember that student I mentioned, Steven Ramsey? He was a promising football star until an accident at practice a few months ago left him a paraplegic. Now there's a young man who has to rethink his entire life. Not just his career, but his everyday life. Next to him, your injuries are minor. You can still get out of bed. You can still eat and drive and go to the bathroom by yourself. He has to relearn how to do all those things."

She moved even closer. In-your-face close. "You can still have a career in your field if you want it. That option isn't available to Steven. You need to think about that and get some perspective." She paused before she delivered her zinger. "Maybe you should follow your doctor's advice and see that psychologist."

The pounding in Scott's head intensified. He wanted to lash out, to tell her she was wrong and that he had every right to feel sorry for himself . . . but he couldn't argue with anything she'd said. He *had* been too hard on the choir. It *was* time to decide what he wanted to do with his life. He *did* need to regain some perspective.

And perhaps he also needed help.

Reaching out, Dorothy laid her hand on his arm and softened her tone. "I'm sorry if that sounded harsh, but it needed to be said."

"That still doesn't mean the choir job is a good fit."

"Why don't you talk to Reverend Richards about it? Maybe the two of you can come up with some ideas about how to deal with the service music until he finds a replacement for Marilyn. I know he'd be open to suggestions."

He sighed. "I guess that's the least I can do."

Dorothy gave his arm an encouraging squeeze and stood. "Will you join me on the screen porch? I made some lemonade."

"I'll be out in a minute."

He watched as she left the room. There was that lemonade analogy again. If life handed you lemons, you were supposed to make lemonade. He hadn't discovered how to do that yet, but his mother was right. It was time he learned.

And he also needed to make amends. To the choir as a whole—and to one member in particular.

The door to the physical therapy waiting room opened, and Karen glanced up from the magazine she was paging through. A sandy-haired man holding two cups of coffee stood on the threshold. He scanned the room, then spoke over his shoulder to the receptionist seated behind a frosted glass window. "Judy, have you seen Mrs. Montgomery's daughter?"

Laying her magazine aside, Karen stood. "Excuse me . . . I'm Mrs. Montgomery's daughter."

At the man's puzzled expression, Karen put two and two together. This had to be David, her mother's therapist.

Smiling, she amended her reply. "I'm her other daughter, Karen. Val's under the weather."

The flash of disappointment on David's face was brief but telling. "Nothing serious, I hope."

"Just a summer cold, I think. Is everything okay with Mom?"

"Yes." He glanced down at the two cups of coffee he was holding, and a flush crept up his neck. "Would you like some coffee?"

"No, thanks."

"Margaret will be out in a few minutes."

As he disappeared behind the door, Karen sank back into her seat. So that was David. The man Val had described as good-looking in a boy-next-door sort of way. But she had definitely underplayed the considerable assets of the tall, muscular, handsome man who had wowed Margaret—and perhaps Val. Based on the little tableau that had just played out, there was certainly interest on his end. Did Val feel the same way?

An intriguing question.

One she intended to get an answer to come Saturday morning.

As Scott glanced around Reverend Richards's organized, uncluttered office, he tapped the arm of his chair in a rapid, staccato rhythm. He didn't belong in a minister's office. And if his mother hadn't laid that guilt trip on him, he wouldn't be here. She was the one who'd gotten him this gig; she could have gotten him out of it.

On the other hand, he was thirty-eight years old. If he wanted to back out of a job, he supposed he should do the dirty work himself.

The door opened, and Reverend Richards hurried in. "Sorry to keep you waiting. A water pipe in the basement's about to blow, and while a fountain in the sanctuary might be pretty, there are better ways to accomplish such an architectural feature."

Smiling, he held out his hand. Scott returned the man's firm clasp, and as the minister settled into the seat beside him, a ray of sun from the window highlighted the faint brushes of silver in the brown hair at his temples as well as his kind eyes. The man radiated the same peace up close as he did from the pulpit on Sunday.

Lucky him. It must be nice to feel that secure of your place in the world.

"What can I do for you on this glorious day?" The minister wasted no time giving him the floor.

Scott cleared his throat. "I wanted to talk to you about the music director job."

"I've been meaning to speak to you too. You know, the choir has never sounded better. I like some of the new music you've introduced."

"I don't think the choir does."

The pastor smiled. "We all have a tendency to get set in our ways and not push ourselves too hard. There's always some resistance to change and challenge."

Considering the stony faces on the other side of the piano, "animosity" might be a better term than "resistance."

"The thing is, Reverend, I don't think this is working out."

He expected the minister to be upset. Instead, the man's expression remained placid, his posture open, his tone conversational. "Why not?"

"For a lot of reasons. Physical ones, first of all." He lifted his left hand. "My hand doesn't work right, and the keyboarding has been difficult. I also get blinding headaches that make me impatient and difficult to deal with. You can ask the choir about that. I guarantee you'll get an earful." He gripped the arm of his chair with his good hand. "On top of all that, I'm not religious. I haven't attended services for years, and it feels wrong to be involved in church music. I just can't muster any enthusiasm for the job." He sighed and lowered his voice. "Or anything else, for that matter."

Leaning forward, Scott clasped his hands between his knees and studied the subtle pattern in the carpet beneath his feet. "The truth is, since the accident I've been living under this dark cloud. All I want to do is stay in my room and shut the door. Going to choir practice is a real stretch. I'm not ready to deal with people. Or, frankly, with life. I only took this job because my mother pushed."

Scott felt the minister studying him, but he didn't look up.

"Why don't you tell me about the accident?"

At the man's quiet request, he eased back, putting a bit more distance between them. "I don't remember much."

"That's okay. Whatever you can recall."

His pulse edged up, and he stared out the window at the huge, sheltering oak tree on the lawn. "I don't talk about it much."

"Then let's go back a little further. Tell me about your career."

His stomach contracted. That subject was almost more painful. "I don't have a career."

"The one you had before."

The man wasn't giving up. Might as well throw him a few crumbs and hope he'd back off.

"I thought Mom had told you. I was a jazz musician."

"Yes, she mentioned that. What was it like?"

Scott closed his eyes, recalling the moments when everything had clicked, when every note had throbbed with passion and feeling and meaning. When he'd lost himself in the melody and been one with something bigger than himself. When he'd carried the audience along with him, given them a glimpse of the power and beauty of music. The connection, the emotion, had been so intense it often took his breath away.

"Amazing." That single word summed up the awe and wonder of it.

The room was quiet for a few seconds. "I can see how much you love it."

He opened his eyes and looked at the man next to him. "There's nothing like it. Nothing. Music can touch the heart and soul in ways beyond description. Those moments are rare but worth all the effort."

"I have to believe the effort part is significant."

"Yes. Years of lessons and practice. Night after night playing in smoky clubs. Constant travel. It's a hard life, but all the sacrifices were about to pay off. I played with a trio, and we'd just signed a recording contract with a major label. We were on the verge of national recognition, which would have moved us to a whole new level. We'd have gotten the more prestigious gigs. Maybe even made a little money. Not that that was our main goal, but it would have been a nice bonus."

"Your mother told me you were the sole survivor of the accident."

A shaft of pain seared through him, and Scott sucked in a harsh breath. "Yeah. Except for the truck driver who feel asleep at the wheel seconds before he hit us. He only had minor injuries. But Joe and Mark, the other musicians, as well as our publicist, didn't make it."

"I guess you'd known the other members of the trio for a long time."

"Ten years. We were like brothers." His voice choked on the final word.

"In other words, you not only lost your career but your family."

"I've never thought of it quite like that, but yeah, I guess I did. And the thing is, I don't understand why I was the one who survived. What did I have to offer that they didn't? I wasn't any more talented than they were, or a better person. Why me?"

"God had a reason."

"You think?" Scott gave a bitter, mirthless laugh. "It might be nice if he shared it with me."

"He will."

"I'm not in a patient mood."

"Patience can be a difficult virtue to master."

"Tell me about it." Scott hoped his sarcasm didn't offend this man, whose concern seemed genuine. But what could a minister know about starting over? About having your life turned upside down and being forced to change plans midstream? "I'm sorry. No one really understands my situation."

"Oh, I don't know. Maybe more people can appreciate what you're going through than you think. That's one of the dangers of focusing only on our own problems. We start to get myopic and believe we're the only one in the world who's ever been tested in a certain way. But a lot of people start over." He leaned back. "I happen to be one of them."

Scott frowned. "What do you mean?"

"I wasn't always a minister. In fact, this is my first congregation. I spent most of my life in the corporate world. Quite happily, I might add."

Scott took a moment to process that disconnect. "But . . . deep inside you must have always wanted to be a minister, right?"

"Hardly. I only had a passing acquaintance with the Lord. Ministry wasn't even on my radar. I had my life all mapped out. I'd worked out my ten-year plan and knew where I wanted to be every step of the way. God wasn't part of my equation."

"So what happened?"

"Nothing as dramatic as your experience, but day by day I began to realize the path I'd mapped out might not be the one God had in mind for me. Even though I fought him every step of the way, he persisted. Eventually I went back to church, hoping to find some answers there."

"Did you?"

"In time. After believing for years that my future lay in the corporate world, it took me a while to recognize there were other options. That maybe the skills I'd developed in human resources and planning and mediation and communication might have broader applications. I also began to realize that the life I'd planned had some serious downsides. My job kept me on the road three weeks out of four, and that lifestyle wasn't conducive to a wife or family. I suspect if I hadn't changed direction, I might never have married—and I'd have missed an experience that has added incredible richness and dimension to my life."

Scott regarded the minister. Though the man hadn't been forced by traumatic circumstances to give up his dream, he *had* grappled with a powerful, compelling call to change course, one that had required serious soul-searching and had wreaked havoc with his plans—the very things he himself was going through.

"I guess maybe you do have some inkling of what I'm experiencing."

"And so do many others who've faced life-changing challenges. But the other point of my story is to suggest you can still have a career in music, one that uses your considerable skills—though it may be a different kind of music career than the one you planned.

Right now, you're on the same journey I was, searching for direction. And it will come. In time, you'll find your new path."

The upbeat platitude sounded nice, but it didn't mitigate the darkness in Scott's soul. "I wish I shared your optimism. Right now I feel totally lost—and alone."

The man leaned forward and touched his arm, his expression intent—and caring. "You're never alone. Never. It may be trite, but the footprints story is very true."

Scott tipped his head. "The footprints story?"

"You've never heard it?"

"No."

"It's a simple story, about a man who railed at God after feeling deserted in his times of deepest need. In response, God showed him the path of his life, in the form of footprints on a beach. In many spots, there were two sets of prints. But in other places, during his darkest hours, there was only one set. The man pointed out to God that on those occasions, he'd walked alone. And God's response was simple but profound. He said, 'No, my son. In the places where you see only one set of prints, I was carrying you.'"

The breath jammed in Scott's lungs.

Could that be true? Had God been with him all through these terrible days, giving him the courage to get up and face each new morning, helping him get through the hours one minute, one second, at a time?

Maybe.

Because he didn't think he could have survived the blackness on his own. Some greater force must have been at work.

The minister broke the silence at last, his voice gentle. "I think we've wandered far afield from the purpose of your visit. You came to talk about the choir, and the truth is, we could use your help until we find a replacement for Marilyn."

Scott did his best to shift gears. "I hate to leave you in the lurch, but to be honest, I think I've burned some bridges. The choir may not want to work with me anymore."

"You'll find they're a very forgiving bunch. After all, they put up with my off-key singing. And the phrase 'I'm sorry' has far more power than you can imagine."

"What about my hand?"

"I haven't noticed any negative impact on our service music as a result of your injury. Would you consider giving it another try?"

Half an hour ago, Scott would have said no. Now he wavered. For some reason, he felt less alone. Less hopeless. And more willing to try and see this commitment through.

"I can't make any long-term promises."

"I'm not asking for any. We'll take it week by week."

If the man was that willing to work with him, how could he refuse?

"All right. You win."

"I hope it will be a win/win. Now, can I ask you one more favor? If the darkness starts to close in on you again, call me. Any time. And I mean any time." He withdrew a card from his pocket and held it out. "My office and cell numbers are on there."

Scott took the card. And as his fingers closed over it, the tangible symbol of caring and support felt like a lifeline. His throat clogged, and he gave a brief nod.

"I know you don't think of yourself as a religious man, but can you indulge me while I speak to God?" Before Scott could respond, the minister bowed his head and clasped his hands. Scott found himself doing the same, though the unfamiliar posture felt awkward.

"Heavenly Father, I ask your continued caring and support for Scott as he seeks a new path for his life. Please let him feel your abiding presence and know that even when he feels most lost, you are beside him, watchful and loving and ready to assist. I also pray that your healing touch will help Scott recover from his injuries so he may once again find joy in his music—and have the ability to share that joy with others. Amen."

The minister raised his head and placed a hand on Scott's shoulders. "Now go out and enjoy this beautiful day the Lord has made.

Try to leave your problems, if only for a little while, on his capable shoulders."

Scott didn't know if that was possible, but as he emerged from the building into the sunlight, his heart did feel lighter.

And for the first time since the accident, he began to believe that maybe, just maybe, he might have a future after all.

11

"Feeling better?"

At David's question, Val looked up from the book she was reading to find him smiling at her from the doorway of the rehab waiting room.

"Yes, thanks. It must have been a summer cold."

In truth, she didn't know what she'd had. Cold feet, perhaps, masquerading as the sniffles. Whatever, the brief illness had kept her from following through on her plan to revisit the other painful spots from her past. But she was determined to go this Sunday, sick or well.

"I didn't mean just that." He closed the distance between them.

Forcing herself to maintain eye contact, Val swallowed. She knew what he meant. Although he hadn't pressed her about the day two weeks ago when she'd almost collapsed in his arms after stumbling into the clearing at the park, it was clear the incident was still on his mind.

"I'm okay." She tried for a convincing tone, but the reassurance came off sounding weak even to her ears. To her relief, he didn't push.

"Glad to hear it. How about some coffee?" He held out a disposable cup. "Black, as I recall."

"Thanks."

She took the cup, and he dropped into the chair beside her. A whisper away.

Her pulse leapt, and she held the cup with both hands as she took a sip. "How's Mom doing?"

"She's making excellent progress. I expect full function will be restored to her left side by the end of the summer. A good thing, since she tells me you'll be heading back to Chicago in about a month."

So he knew the timing of her departure. What else had her mother relayed?

"What do you two talk about during therapy, anyway?"

"For the most part, she talks and I listen."

Val rolled her eyes. "I can imagine. It must be gossip central in there. As if you care about her whole cast of characters."

"I care about one of them."

At his quiet—and unexpected—response, Val shot him a startled glance. His perceptive eyes were fixed on her, and she forced up the corners of her stiff lips, determined to keep things light. "If she's talked about me, I suspect you've gotten more than a few soliloquies."

"I hear a lot about the meals you prepare."

"I'll bet."

"And the glamorous life you lead in Chicago."

"Trust me, Mom's exaggerating. I teach high school drama. I do a little modeling on the side. It's not glamorous."

"It is to her. Though not as glamorous as the life she thinks you could have had. On Broadway, no less."

She took another sip of her coffee and shook her head. "Mom always did have delusions of grandeur about my talent. I wasn't Broadway material."

"Did you ever think about giving it a shot?"

"Yes, and I did. For a year. But the realities of making it in New York didn't quite live up to my teenage fantasies. Being a big fish in a little pond is a lot different than being a minnow in the ocean. You have to have singular focus and a driving commitment to have even a minuscule chance of making it, and the whole thing was kind of overwhelming. Besides, my heart wasn't in it." Nor in much of anything else after that fateful summer of her seventeenth year.

"Do you like what you do now?"

"Very much." That was a question she could answer with absolute honesty. "Working with young people is interesting—and satisfying."

"Then that's all that counts." He crossed an ankle over his knee. "Margaret also told me about her church and invited me to visit. Victoria and I went last weekend. I thought you might be there, but I guess you were still sick."

Val ran a polished nail around the rim of her cup, where traces of lipstick clung precariously to the edge. "I was. Besides, I'm not much of a churchgoer anymore."

"Meaning you used to be?"

"Years ago."

"What changed?"

His tone was conversational, not accusatory, but he was getting way too personal. She sent him a pointed look that conveyed that message loud and clear.

"Sorry." He held up his free hand, palm forward, in a placating gesture. "I didn't mean to pry. My faith is such an important part of my life, I'm always curious why people fall away. I could never survive the dark times without God by my side." He checked his watch and rose. "Margaret should be finishing up on the equipment. I'd better get back inside."

"Smart plan. It's never wise to keep Mom waiting."

One side of his mouth quirked up, and he gestured toward her empty coffee cup. "Can I pitch that for you?"

"Thanks." As she handed it over, their fingers brushed. It was a fleeting touch, but even that slight contact sent a tingle down her spine—and made her wish she could share her secret with this man. That she could spill her heart to him, and that he would listen without judgment, pull her into his arms, and hold her until all her guilt melted away.

As he disappeared through the door, Val shook her head. Now there was a teenage fantasy if ever she'd heard one. Problems weren't that easily solved. Nor was forgiveness that easy to find.

Even from a man of faith.

"Aren't you going to be late for choir practice, Mom?"

Karen straightened from loading the dryer. Kristen stood in the doorway of the laundry room, a chocolate chip cookie in one hand and a glass of milk in the other. "I'm not going tonight."

"How come? You never skip."

"I had a busy day at work and I'm tired." She continued to transfer wet clothes from the washer to the dryer, hoping Kristen would let it go. She wasn't in the mood to discuss her decision tonight.

No such luck.

Her daughter clumped into the room and propped her hip against the counter. "That never stopped you before."

Karen shut the dryer and flipped it on. Might as well just spill it. "Actually, I'm thinking of dropping out."

"You're kidding." Kristen followed her into the kitchen. "I thought you loved singing in the choir."

"I used to love it. But the new choir director is . . . difficult."

"I think he's hot—for an older guy."

Her eyes widened. Scott Walker, hot?

No way.

Then again, his dark good looks might appeal to some people. Too bad his personality was equally dark.

"I won't debate that. Beauty is in the eye of the beholder and all that." She folded the dish towel she'd tossed on the table earlier and hung it on the door rack under the sink. "But he's hard to deal with. He talks down to people, and he raises his voice a lot."

Kristen stopped chewing. "Kind of like Dad used to?"

At the quiet question, Karen turned toward her and curled her fingers around the edge of the counter behind her. "Your dad never behaved that way with you."

"No, but he treated you like that. A lot."

As the comment hung in the air between them, Karen tightened her grip. Great. Despite all her efforts to shelter Kristen from the problems in their marriage, it seemed her perceptive daughter had picked up on them anyway.

"Your dad and I should never have married, Kristen." *Careful, Karen. Don't cast all the blame on the father she loves or let this come across as sour grapes*. "We weren't compatible."

"Then why did you?"

"I don't know. I was young. He was older and attractive and attentive. My self-esteem wasn't that high. Remember, I grew up in the same house as Val, and it was hard to compete with her. She was always gorgeous and self-confident. The boys didn't even notice me when she was around—except for your dad. I was flattered by his attention, and I guess that clouded my judgment."

"But you must have loved him back then. And he must have loved you."

Was her daughter ready for the truth? Val had suggested she was—and her sister could be right. Maybe it was time to test that theory.

She gestured to the kitchen table. "Let's sit for a few minutes, okay?"

Following her lead, Kristen slid into a chair at the polished oak dinette set where the three of them had shared too few meals as a family.

"To be honest, I'm not certain love ever played a role in our relationship. I was enamored and I mistook a lot of other emotions for love. As for your dad, I think he liked the fact that I always gave in to him and let him take charge. It fed his ego. But after a while that got old, and he lost respect for me, leading to problems later in our marriage. In the end, both of us regretted the mistake."

"But I thought marriage was supposed to be forever. Till death do us part and all that stuff, like Reverend Richards talks about."

"It is. But people do make mistakes."

Kristen chewed at her lower lip. "Do you think you'll ever get married again?"

"I don't know. Even though we're divorced, I still feel married in God's eyes."

"I don't think Dad would have any qualms about remarrying."

"He and I didn't have the same core beliefs about marriage, honey. Mine are based in faith. That's another thing we didn't share."

"Yeah. I know." Kristen traced one of the knotholes in the wood with an iridescent fingernail. Turquoise was the color of the week. "I remember that Christmas morning when I was about eight and he made fun of you for going to church. You tried to pretend it didn't bother you, but I heard you crying later in your room."

Another jolt ricocheted through her.

So that day was as etched in Kristen's memory as it was in her own.

"I'm sorry you heard that. I tried to shield you from the stuff that was going on, but that day was especially bad." Bad enough that the memory still left a bad taste in her mouth.

"I remember he wanted you to make breakfast for him before we went to church and was mad when you didn't."

"That's right." She could recall the sequence of events as if they'd happened yesterday. Most of the time, Michael had condescendingly tolerated her convictions despite his attitude of academic elitism that regarded religion as a simplistic panacea to life's problems. But not that day. He'd risen in a bad mood. Ranted that she was a fool for letting her faith run her life. Accused her of being selfish to put church attendance above family obligations. Sulked for the remainder of the day.

It had not been her best Christmas.

Nor Kristen's, it seemed.

When her daughter remained silent, she spoke again. "That was one of the few occasions I went against his wishes. In those days, I used to think being passive and giving in would smooth things out and help me get along with people—including your grandmother. But I'm learning that's not always the best way to be."

Kristen swirled the milk in her glass, closer and closer to the top. Playing the spill odds. "Do you think if you'd been different with Dad back then, you guys might have stayed together?"

"I used to wonder about that, but I don't think so. In fact, the marriage may not have lasted as long as it did. We'd probably have clashed sooner. Your dad and I are too different."

"Maybe he's changed."

Not that she'd noticed.

But instead of voicing that opinion, she reached over in silence and brushed a long strand of blonde hair back from Kristen's face.

"I wish we could have been a family forever." Kristen whispered the choked words as moisture beaded on her lashes.

"I do too. I'm so sorry your dad and I made such a mess of things."

Kristen gripped her glass. "You know, I used to think the breakup was all your fault." She sniffled and swiped at her eyes. "But inside I always knew it wasn't. Dad's a pretty good dad, when he's around, but I guess . . . I guess he wasn't the best husband. He wasn't very nice to you. And I don't want you to be unhappy."

Her little girl was growing up.

A lump formed in Karen's throat. For the past two years she'd been praying her relationship with her daughter would stabilize, that they would recapture the closeness they'd once shared. Tonight it felt as if they'd taken a giant leap forward.

Giving her yet another reason to be glad she'd skipped choir practice.

Scott stopped outside the church door and took a deep breath. He was a few minutes late for practice—by design. This way, everyone would be seated and he wouldn't have a chance to let second thoughts deter him from his mission once he stepped inside.

As he grasped the handle of the door, his heart began to thud the way it always did before an important performance. He'd read once that an adrenaline rush was a survival mechanism, designed to heighten the senses and increase alertness so a person was better equipped to deal with danger . . . or a hostile enemy.

And considering the expressions on the faces that swiveled toward him as he entered, the latter was an excellent description of the choir members.

The room fell silent as he approached the piano, and Scott did his best to rein in his pounding pulse. Stress could bring on one of his debilitating headaches, and he didn't need that complication tonight. At least not until after he got through his apology.

Once he set his folder of music on the piano, he faced the silent choir. For the first time, he looked—really looked—at the members as individuals. The emotions they were displaying were as varied as their appearance. Some were hostile. He hadn't misread that as he stepped into the room. But others appeared uncertain. Nervous. Cautious.

He scanned the group for the woman who had left the last rehearsal. Karen, according to his mother. What emotion would he see on her face? But her seat was empty—surprise, surprise.

Summoning up his courage, Scott rested one hand on the piano. "Before we work on music tonight, there are a few things I'd like to say. First, as you know, I'm only the interim music director while Reverend Richards searches for a permanent replacement for Marilyn. Frankly, I've never thought I was the best choice for the job. I have no experience directing a church choir. I'm used to dealing with professional, trained musicians who spend hours a day practicing and honing their craft. As a result, I have very high standards.

"However, in the past few days I've come to realize that while those expectations might be appropriate for my colleagues, they're far too strict for people who gather once a week on a volunteer basis because they love to sing. I apologize for being too hard on you last week.

"My patience is also being taxed by some health issues, including severe headaches that are a by-product of the concussion I suffered in the accident. I had one of those at the last rehearsal. I'm sorry to say, I took it out on all of you. I apologize for that as well.

"Finally, I realize that in spite of your busy lives, you give up several hours a week to enhance the worship service for the congregation. You don't need to add a difficult choir director to the stresses in your lives."

Scott cleared his throat. "For all those reasons, I spoke with Reverend Richards a couple of days ago, planning to resign. I didn't feel it was a good fit—but your minister can be quite persuasive, in a very gentle way." Scott saw a few tentative, knowing smiles. Empathy. That was a positive sign. "Anyway, he encouraged me to stay on for a while. I agreed to think about it, but I felt the decision should be up to you."

He jammed his left hand into his pocket. He'd have liked to ball it into a fist, but all he could manage was a slight flex of his stiff fingers.

"I want to tell you I'm sorry for causing too much anxiety at rehearsals, and to promise you that in the future I'll do my best to make the experience a pleasant one for you. I ask for your forgiveness for my behavior, and for your patience as I try to learn how to be a church music director. I know I've been difficult to work with, but I'd like a second chance. If things don't improve, I promise to step aside. Do you think we can give this another try?"

During his speech, the mood in the room had undergone a subtle shift. Scott wouldn't call it friendly. That would be too generous. But willing, perhaps. And more relaxed, as if a collective deep breath had been exhaled. He even saw a number of nods.

It appeared Reverend Richards had been right. The choir was a forgiving group. The members seemed willing to give him another chance.

Except maybe the woman who had walked out. Karen.

"Can I take the silence as a yes?" Scott searched their faces.

A murmur of assent supplied his answer.

As Scott thanked the group, then took his place at the piano, a burden seemed to lift from his shoulders. But his task wasn't finished yet. Nor would it be until that one empty seat was filled again.

And that meant he had one more apology to make.

As Karen deposited two frappuccinos on the table and took her seat, Val appraised her. "I'd say the weight-loss program is continuing to reap benefits."

"Yep." Karen lifted her drink in a mock toast. "Thirteen pounds down, twelve to go."

"That's terrific! And I love your new hairstyle."

"I do too. Even Michael noticed."

"Is he still hanging around?" Val wrinkled her nose.

"He comes to see Kristen. On his last visit he even said I was looking good." She rested her elbow on the table and twirled her straw in her drink. "He also looked at me the way he used to. Like I was attractive. I have to admit, that felt kind of good."

Val's eyes narrowed. "Uh-oh."

She stopped twirling. "What does that mean?"

"Are you still susceptible to that—excuse me for being blunt—jerk's compliments? After the way he treated you?"

Karen's face warmed. "It surprised me too. I mean, I don't have any feelings for him anymore."

"Hmm." Val tapped a polished nail on the surface of the small round table. "I think I know what the problem is. You need some romance in your life."

Karen coughed as her mouthful of frappuccino went down the wrong way. "You can't be serious!"

"One hundred percent. You need a new guy in your life."

"Sorry. Not in the market." With a resolute shake of her head, Karen took a cautious sip through her straw.

"Why not?"

"Believe it or not, Kristen and I just had a similar conversation. As I told her, we might be divorced but I did take vows before God. I can't discount those."

"Michael has."

"That's his issue, not mine. Besides, there aren't exactly a lot of guys tripping over themselves trying to date me. And I don't need male attention to make my life complete."

"If that's true, why did Michael's compliment turn your head?"

"I don't know."

"I do. Male attention is nice. Having a man in your life can be a positive thing."

"I've had a man in my life, thank you very much. I'll pass."

"I'm talking about a man who treats you right. Respects you. Cherishes you. You deserve that, Karen." Val studied her. "Look, I understand and respect your feelings about the sanctity of marriage. But even the Catholic church, which frowns on divorce and remarriage, grants annulments in cases where one of the partners never intended to abide by their vows. Do you really think Michael ever took his vow of fidelity seriously?"

Karen frowned. Val might have a point. Maybe he'd never intended to remain faithful. And if he hadn't, did that kind of deceit undermine their vows?

Possibly.

"I can see from your expression that I got you thinking."

As Karen poked at the whipped cream with her straw, it began to deflate. "I'll admit you've offered a perspective worth considering." Then she turned the tables. "But you're single too. What about romance in your life? And marriage?"

A mask dropped over Val's face. "That's different."

"Why?"

"I'm not wife material."

"Baloney." Karen sent her a teasing look. "And I suspect a certain physical therapist would agree with me."

The sides of the cardboard cup in Val's hand flexed under the sudden pressure of her fingers. "What are you talking about?"

"Your friend David was mighty disappointed the day I took Mom to physical therapy. He came out to talk to you and got me instead. I wonder what he did with that second cup of coffee he was holding?"

"You always did have an overactive imagination." A pink tint suffused Val's face.

"Uh-uh. *You* had the imagination. I was always the sensible, straightforward, analytical one. And I know what I saw. His disappointment went way beyond mere friendliness. He likes you—a lot. I think you've been holding out on me."

Val shook her head and spoke in a flat voice. "Trust me, Karen. There is nothing between David and me, and there never will be." She glanced at her watch. "Are you ready to tackle the grocery store?" She stood and turned toward the door.

Obviously, that subject was closed.

But why?

Despite her curiosity, Karen left the question unasked. Why jeopardize their developing relationship?

"All set. Listen . . . I'm sorry if I overstepped. I was just kidding around."

Her sister's smile seemed forced. "No problem. I have thick skin, remember? I'll pitch that for you." She took Karen's cup and walked away.

Although she tried to restore the prior easy give-and-take with small talk during the rest of their shopping trip, the strain between them didn't diminish much. Not until they were preparing to head home did Val start to relax.

And then her mood took another sudden turn.

As Val leaned forward to put the key in the ignition, she angled toward the passenger seat. "Let me know if you'd like that recipe for . . ."

All at once she froze, and the color drained from her face.

Alarm bells ringing in her mind, Karen checked out the activity beside her. A man stood on the other side of the car next to them, strapping a toddler into a car seat as an older child climbed into the backseat on their side. There was nothing unusual about the domestic scene.

She refocused on her sister. "What is it? What's wrong?"

Instead of responding, Val averted her face, put the car in gear, and backed out. "Nothing."

That was a lie.

For the second time that morning, something had disturbed Val. A lot, based on the tremors in her sister's hands. She looked so shaken that Karen almost offered to drive. But making a big deal out of the situation might do more harm than good.

Unwilling to take that risk, Karen remained silent as she tried to make sense of what had happened. Val wasn't easy to rattle, so whatever was going on was significant. Yet for the life of her, she couldn't figure out what the problem was.

As they pulled away, she studied the car next to the spot they'd vacated. It was just some guy with his two kids. What in the world about that scenario could freak out her always-in-control sister?

Karen had no answer.

And a quick glance at her sister told her Val had no intention of providing one.

In the darkness of the early morning hours, Val reached to the back of her bureau drawer and carefully withdrew the familiar cardboard tube. Cradling it in her hands, she sank onto the side of the bed.

Talk about weird coincidences. The odds of running into Corey in the parking lot at the grocery store had to be minuscule.

And not only him, but two children.

His children.

Val closed her eyes and tightened her grip on the tube.

Seeing him hadn't been part of her agenda for this trip. It hadn't seemed important to her healing process.

But perhaps she'd been wrong. Perhaps she'd needed to learn that he'd moved on. Married. Started a family. That he was living an ordinary, conventional life. That he hadn't been held a prisoner of the past, as she had been.

Yet how could he have gone on as if nothing had happened? How could he have felt he deserved a normal life? Had their tragic decision meant so little to him?

Val clutched the tube closer to her chest and closed her eyes. She had no answers to those questions. But if he could find a way to move on, perhaps she could too.

So tomorrow she'd drive to St. Louis. To the place where she'd received this. And if her courage held, she'd continue on to the final place, where she'd followed through on their fateful choice.

She'd do it alone too. Just as she had the first time.

Yet how much less painful it would be if someone was by her side!

An image of David flashed through her mind, and she squeezed her eyes shut. How ridiculous was that? She barely knew him—yet she'd learned enough to know he was a man of deep faith, with a solid moral character. The kind of man who would never be able to understand, or forgive, her mistake. A loving father who wouldn't want anything to do with her if he knew the truth.

And she couldn't blame him. She didn't deserve someone like him. Or anyone, for that matter. The guilt was too great. That may not have stopped Corey from leading a normal life, but for her, life had never been normal again.

Val rose and padded over to the window to stare out into the darkness. Could she share her story with Karen, ask her to go? In these past weeks they'd connected far better than she'd ever imagined.

But she, too, was a person of faith. And while she and David might both buy into the notion of forgiveness, it was one thing to believe it in theory and another to put it into practice. Val didn't want to risk their newfound friendship by putting the strength of Karen's faith to the test.

So who was left—except God?

She sank onto the window seat, shoulders drooping. Too bad she didn't have her sister's faith. Or David's. He'd told her once it had allowed him to survive the bad times. That even at his darkest moments, he'd felt God's presence. What a comfort that must be.

Val ran her fingers over the crude cardboard tube, suddenly toying with a radical notion.

Why not go back to church? Seek some of the comfort and strength David and Karen talked about? At worst, she'd waste a couple of hours. At best, the service might offer her some nugget of solace that would help get her through tomorrow.

And anything that could do that was worth a try.

12

As Scott finished arranging the service music on the piano, Karen slipped into her place. When their gazes brushed, she bent her head and opened her folder.

Not a positive sign, but at least she'd come, despite missing rehearsal. And he wasn't letting her get away without delivering the apology he owed her.

As the service began and the choir launched into the opening hymn, Scott took a closer look at the woman with the auburn highlights in her hair. In retrospect, he was surprised he hadn't noticed her. He certainly would have in his pre-accident life.

He repositioned himself slightly on the bench as he played to get a better view. Her head was bent over her music, and her hair fell forward, obscuring part of her face. But the soft strands couldn't hide her elegant bone structure or the full lips that moved with fluid grace as she sang. She struck him as the studious, serious type—in sharp contrast to the glamorous, flamboyant women he'd met in the music world who'd long ago lost their appeal. And while many of them had had flashy good looks, this woman possessed a timeless, classic beauty that wouldn't fade with age.

She could sing too. It was easy to pick out her pure, clear soprano as she hit the final note. Nice.

All at once she lifted her head and looked his way. Her lips parted in surprise when she found him watching her, and a flush crept across her cheeks—as if she was worried she'd made a mistake. He sent her a small smile of reassurance, but her color deepened and she dipped her head again.

Now he'd embarrassed her.

Seemed he'd have two things to apologize for after the service.

Angling toward the sanctuary, he tuned in to Reverend Richards. As long as he was here, he might as well listen to what the man had to say.

"The story we heard today in John's Gospel is one of my favorites because it's so rich in meaning and symbolism. Here we have a man born blind. A man who lives in darkness, groping through life, stumbling and falling, often losing his way because he can't see the road ahead. He feels apart from the world, an outcast, alone and abandoned.

"Then Jesus enters his life and cures him. When asked later by the Pharisees to explain what happened, the once-blind man utters those wonderful words that continue to resonate with meaning in their simplicity and power: 'I was blind and now I see.'"

The minister surveyed the congregation. "My friends, the Bible is filled with stories of people whose lives were transformed after encountering Jesus. There are dozens of examples of physical cures. The ten lepers. The man with the withered hand. Peter's mother-in-law. But many spiritual cures are recorded too. The tale of the adulteress is one of the most famous—a beautiful, inspiring story of forgiveness for a woman caught in sin, whom Jesus refused to condemn.

"God sends that same message to us today. Just as he did two thousand years ago, he stands ready to forgive us. To light our path. To guide us if we lose our way. To give us strength and hope. And God offers these things without our asking. The blind man didn't seek God. God found him and opened his eyes, dispelling the darkness. For as Jesus said earlier in that same Gospel, 'I am the light of the world.'

"I think it would be safe to assume that most of us experience dark times. It's part of being human. But during those trials, I ask you to remember that God stands ready to guide you. To forgive you. To offer you new hope and a new beginning. Pray to him for those things. It doesn't have to be a formal prayer. Just talk to him, in the quiet of your heart. And, like the man in today's reading, once we open ourselves to his abiding grace and loving presence, we too will be able to say, 'I was blind and now I see.'

"Now, let us pray . . ."

As the pastor continued, Scott drew a long, slow breath. It was almost as if the man had written that sermon for him. He too was living in darkness, groping, stumbling, and falling like the blind man. Not only had he lost his way, he didn't even know his destination. All he'd been able to think about was the life that had vanished in a few terrible seconds. It was no wonder he'd stumbled; he'd been looking behind instead of ahead.

Yet looking ahead was terrifying. The future loomed as an endless black void, empty and meaningless. While there might be other possibilities for his life, he was blind to them.

If Reverend Richards was right, however, help was there for the asking.

Scott wasn't convinced a simple conversation with God would put his life back on track—but if the pastor and his mother and all the other people who gathered in this church each week believed prayer had such power, it was worth a try.

Val stared at the minister as he finished his sermon. It was as if he'd written the words for her. Could they be true? Did God grant forgiveness that easily to a repentant heart? Was it possible to leave the past behind and start anew?

As for prayer . . . she didn't remember any formal ones. But talking? No problem. Finding the words to ask for forgiveness would be a piece of cake.

Except—wasn't that too simple? How could a mere "I'm sorry," no matter how sincere, rid her of her guilt?

On the other hand, this prayer thing was important to a lot of people. Like David, despite his absence today. And Karen. Even Margaret prayed. It may not have helped her disposition, but apparently God listened to her. When Val had announced this morning that she planned to attend services with the family, Margaret had recovered from her shock with surprising alacrity and said, "Well, I guess the Lord heard my prayers after all."

Still, asking for absolution struck Val as way too presumptuous.

Maybe she could ask for strength, though, on her journey to the past—and for guidance. Like the blind man, she was groping her way down this rocky road, unsure of her steps, stumbling and falling and fearful of what lay around the next corner. If nothing else, God might take pity on her, as he had on that poor blind man, and light her path.

Not that she expected the light to penetrate into the deep, dark crevices of her soul, of course. That would be too much to expect. But even a few beams to dispel some of the shadows that had darkened her days for more than seventeen long years would be a welcome gift.

"Sorry to interrupt." Scott joined Karen and another choir member as they chatted after the service. "Karen, do you have a minute?"

Surprised by the call out, Karen switched her focus from Ellen Sullivan to the dark-haired man. She hadn't realized he even knew her name. "Yes. Would you excuse me, Ellen?"

"Sure. I'm just glad you came to services today. The soprano section would have been in dire straits without you. See you soon."

As Ellen walked away, Scott gave her a smile that seemed a tad . . . nervous? “We missed you at choir practice.”

Heat crept up her neck. She hoped it wouldn’t spill onto her cheeks. “I had a long day at work. I couldn’t handle any more . . .”

Her voice faltered, and he finished the sentence. “Stress?”

The flush moved higher. “I should have come. I heard it was better.”

“I hope so. I apologized to the choir for my bad temper and asked them to give me another chance.”

“Ellen called to tell me that.”

“I’m glad. But a secondhand apology isn’t sufficient. I know you were very upset at rehearsal two weeks ago, and I wanted to tell you in person I was sorry for my behavior. I hope you aren’t thinking about dropping out.”

“No. I’ve been in the choir too long for that. I’ll be back next Wednesday.”

He smiled. A real smile this time, bigger than that tiny lip tip he’d given her earlier after the opening hymn.

The transformation took her breath away.

His dark eyes, usually brooding and distant, grew warm and vibrant. The angular planes of his face softened, and the tiny crinkle lines beside his eyes told her he had once smiled far more than he did now. As for those lips . . . Karen’s glance lingered there. No longer taut, they were supple and appealing and . . .

She swallowed, resisting the urge to fan herself.

No wonder Kristen had said he was hot.

“I’m glad you’re sticking with us. Now I’ll be able to report to Reverend Richards that I didn’t drive away any choir members after all.”

“Karen, are you ready to go?”

Yanking her gaze away from him, Karen turned toward her mother. Margaret was bearing down on her, Kristen and Val on her heels. “Yes. I was just gathering up my music.” The words came out in a breathless rush.

"Good. Val needs to get home. She has someplace to go today. Don't ask where. She isn't saying."

Instead of the saucy reply Karen expected from her sister, Val fiddled with her purse. Her cheeks were a bit pinched, and Karen wondered if she was feeling ill again.

"Young man, since Karen hasn't introduced us, I'll do it myself. I'm her mother, Margaret Montgomery. This is my other daughter, Val, and my granddaughter, Kristen." Without giving Scott a chance to respond, Margaret continued. "We're very pleased you were willing to fill in after Marilyn left. Why she couldn't give poor Reverend Richards more notice, I'll never know, but you're a godsend."

One corner of Scott's mouth quivered, and Karen caught the amused glint in his eyes. "I must admit, no one's ever called me a godsend before."

"I'd say the term fits in this case. I understand from Dorothy that you have extensive training. But I expect you'll be disappointed in our little choir. They'll never live up to your standards."

His gaze swung to Karen . . . and stayed there. Once again her cheeks warmed.

"I've learned that setting standards too high can be discouraging instead of motivating. All the choir members do their best, and that's really all you can ask of people, isn't it?"

Instead of responding to his comment, Margaret gestured toward Val. "You ought to try and convince Val to join while she's here for the summer. She has the real vocal talent in the family. Such a beautiful voice. And professional training too. She'd be a good addition to the choir."

"Talent must run in the family, then. Karen also has an exceptional voice. I was admiring it today during the opening hymn. I believe she has perfect pitch."

Karen stared at him. Surely he was just being kind. Val *did* have the real talent.

Still, she couldn't quite contain the sudden glow in her heart.

"Hmm." Margaret peered at him over the top of her glasses. "I see you're quite the diplomat."

"Tact and sensitivity are great assets. Ones we all need to work on, don't you think?" Without waiting for her to answer, he continued. "But in this case, I wasn't being diplomatic. Just truthful. Perhaps your daughters inherited your talent?"

Stifling a smile, Karen glanced at Val. Though her face was still a bit tense, her sister gave a subtle thumbs-up. Margaret had been insulted so charmingly she didn't even recognize the slight.

"I did do a little singing in my younger days." Margaret seemed pleased—if a bit flustered—by his question. "But my husband had a wonderful tenor voice. I suspect they got their talent from him."

Now that was a switch. Margaret had gone from disparaging her oldest offspring's talent to acknowledging both daughters' singing ability. Karen shook her head. Amazing.

"Ready?" Val moved closer and nudged her.

"Yes." She ventured a look at Scott. For a brief second, she had the absurd notion he was going to wink at her. Instead, he smiled. But she didn't imagine the twinkle in his eye.

"Then I can count on you to be at practice Wednesday?"

"Yes."

"I'll look forward to seeing you."

He moved back toward the piano, and Karen found Kristen regarding the musician with a speculative expression as Val and Margaret began to weave through the crowd, leading the way toward the exit.

"He likes you." Kristen gave her a smug smirk.

Karen frowned. "What in the world are you talking about?"

"The new music director. He likes you."

"You, my dear, are imagining things." She tried for a dismissive tone. "He's never said a word to me until today."

"So? There are lots of other ways to communicate besides words. Didn't you see that look in his eyes?"

"That look was not aimed just at me. He's trying to make amends with all the choir members. Trust me. He wasn't singling me out for special attention. Now let's go. Your grandmother won't be happy if we keep her waiting in the car." She started to turn away.

"I bet he *was* singling you out. Let's get Aunt Val's opinion."

Kristen started after the departing duo, but Karen grabbed her arm. "No!" The last thing she needed was a discussion about romance—or even the suggestion of it—in front of her mother. "I told you the other day—I'm not looking for that kind of . . . involvement."

Planting her hands on her hips, Kristen faced her mother. "I bet God wouldn't want you to spend the rest of your life all alone just because you and Dad made a mistake."

After her conversation with Val on that very topic, she was beginning to think the same thing. But she wasn't ready to talk about it with her daughter.

"The subject's closed, Kristen." She adopted her this-isn't-open-for-discussion tone. "Let's go."

Although Kristen acquiesced, Karen had a feeling her daughter would follow up on the topic in the not-too-distant future.

As for Scott—if Kristen happened to be right about his interest, she had a feeling he'd follow up too. He couldn't have risen to the brink of success in the cutthroat music business without being single-minded about going after what he wanted.

Meaning she'd better get her feelings about the status of her marriage resolved.

Pronto.

Val edged into a parking spot across the street from the small brick building in St. Louis that had once housed the Women's Health Clinic. It had a new, more descriptive name now, but it was in the same business, providing services like fertility testing, birth control assistance, and ultrasounds.

Summoning up her courage, Val picked up the cardboard tube on the seat beside her and slid the paper out. With shaking fingers, she unrolled it across the steering wheel. To the untrained eye, the old technology was hard to interpret. If the technician hadn't pointed out the head, the feet, and the hands, Val doubted she could have deciphered it.

But even if she couldn't quite discern the outlines of her baby, the ultrasound had made it tangible. And once the nurse had let her listen to the heartbeat, the baby growing within her had become all too real. That thump of life had been seared into her memory, haunting her dreams for close to two decades.

Maybe the whole thing would have been less traumatic if she hadn't gotten the ultrasound and seen such compelling evidence of the life growing within her. Corey had tried to dissuade her from doing so, and he'd refused to pay for it. But she'd done it anyway, even though it had taken most of her summer savings from her waitress job at Harry's Bar and Grill.

She stroked her finger over the crinkly paper. She hadn't analyzed her motivations at the time, but they were clear to her in hindsight. She'd hoped some medical issue would be discovered that would justify the solution Corey had proposed to their "problem."

Her baby, however, had been fine. Healthy and normal and expected to arrive at the end of May. He or she would have been seventeen this year. Poised on the brink of adulthood, with a future filled with endless possibilities.

Except Val's tragic mistake had robbed her baby of that future, stilling the heart that now beat only in her memory.

With shaking hands, she lay the ultrasound on the seat beside her and pulled into traffic. One more stop to make. And for that, she needed all the courage she could muster.

Replaying the minister's words from this morning, she sent a desperate plea to God.

Lord, I know I don't deserve anything from you. Certainly not forgiveness. But I could use some strength and courage. Could you be with me for the next few minutes? Help me feel I'm not quite so alone? Please!

As she approached her destination, Val looked around. The neighborhood had deteriorated over the years. Dramatically. Under normal circumstances, she'd have worried about her safety, but today she didn't care. The danger within loomed far larger than any external threat she might encounter.

Once she arrived, Val pulled to the curb, set the brake, and lifted her head toward the third floor. To the window of the shuttered room where the procedure had taken place. She could have gone to a legit clinic, but she'd been afraid they'd ask too many questions and then notify her family. She'd wanted a place where she could walk in the door anonymously and leave the same way, with her shame the only evidence of her visit.

Corey had found this place. She'd been afraid it would be seedy, but while the outside of the brick tenement had been a bit rundown, the small facility had been clean and businesslike inside. She'd filled out minimal paperwork using a fake name, and then she'd been ushered into the "treatment" room. The whole process hadn't taken more than an hour. She'd paid in cash and driven back to Washington in a friend's borrowed car. Feeling dirty. Tainted. And the hour she'd spent in the shower after arriving home hadn't made her feel any cleaner.

In the end, she'd given up, crawled into bed, and curled up into a knot until her mother had called her for dinner. Although she'd picked at her food, for once Margaret hadn't commented on her eating habits. She'd been too busy talking about the problems her friend, Alice Martin, had been having with her son, who'd been cited by the police for underage drinking.

Val hadn't been able to get too excited about that transgression. It had paled in comparison to her own.

No one ever found out about her trip to St. Louis. The secret remained known only to her and Corey and God. Nor had she suffered any physical trauma because of it. Only later, after reading plenty of horror stories about back-alley practitioners and patients who ended up with massive infections or who hemorrhaged or were left barren . . . or died . . . had she realized how lucky she'd been to breeze through the procedure and emerge unscathed.

Except for the emotional scars.

A silent tear slid down her cheek, and Val closed her eyes. *Dear God, I'm so sorry! If I could do it all over again, I'd live with the consequences. I'd see the baby to term and either keep it or put it up for adoption. I wouldn't care about the shame or humiliation or my mother's wrath. I'd do the right thing, Lord! I would!*

She rested her forehead on the steering wheel. A sob caught in her throat. Then another. And another. Until the tears were coursing down her cheeks.

Only a persistent tapping on her window pulled her out of her funk.

Wiping the back of her hand across her eyes, Val raised her face to find a vacant-eyed man peering at her from the other side of the glass. He was dressed in a torn T-shirt and a filthy baseball cap, and based on the coarse stubble on his gritty face, he hadn't shaved in quite a while. Or had a bath.

For a moment, she panicked. But all at once, the man backed off. Perhaps her mascara-streaked face had scared him as much as his disheveled state had frightened her. For whatever reason, after one more glazed look in her direction, he wove down the street as fast as he could.

Swiping at her cheeks, Val twisted the key in the ignition. She needed to get out of this place. She didn't belong here, and it wasn't safe.

Hands shaking, she put the car in gear and aimed for the highway. It was time to go back to Washington. To do what she'd done that day almost eighteen years ago.

Pretend everything was normal.

13

"Okay. Great job. We'll try the new hymn on Sunday. Thanks, everybody."

A rustle of papers, accompanied by conversation and laughter, followed Scott's dismissal as Karen and the other choir members put away their music. What a change from previous rehearsals. True to his word, he'd been far more pleasant and patient with the group, and she'd enjoyed the session.

As she stood, Reverend Richards waved at her from the back door and walked over. "Hi, Karen. How are things going?"

"Can't complain, thanks."

"Margaret seems to be doing well."

"She is. Val's been keeping a close eye on her."

"I got to meet your sister last Sunday after services. I'm sure her presence this summer has been a great blessing."

"Absolutely. I was in desperate need of the help."

"Speaking of needing help . . ." He gave her a rueful smile. "I wondered if I could borrow your great organizational ability for a special project our church has been asked to take on."

"I'll be glad to help if I can. What is it?"

"You're familiar with Hope House, I believe—the counseling center for unwed pregnant teens?"

"Yes. They do important work. I'm glad we take up an annual collection for them."

"So am I. But that won't be enough this year. They've had some unexpected expenses in recent weeks, and it doesn't appear they'll have sufficient funds to get them through the end of their fiscal year in September. To help shore up their coffers we've been approached about doing a benefit dinner that would include musical entertainment. A number of area choirs have agreed to participate—including our own, I hope—but I need a chairperson who can organize this and pull it off by the third week in August."

"Wow." Her eyes widened. "That's only a month away."

"I know it's ambitious timing. I think we can get a lot of volunteers from the congregation to chair committees, but I need someone with strong managerial skills to oversee the whole process. You were the first person I thought of."

She gave him a teasing look. "Resorting to flattery, are we?"

"Is it working?"

At the twinkle in his eyes, she smiled. "Maybe."

"Good. You're the perfect person to spearhead this. I always know when I ask you to take on a project that it will be done right, and on schedule."

As he waited for her response, she took a quick inventory of the demands on her time. Kristen was doing much better. Val had things under control with their mother. Work was slacking off a bit too. Yes, she could manage a project like this. "Okay. I'll be happy to help."

"Thank you." He motioned toward Scott, who was closing the piano. "Now I want to talk to our music director and see if he'll agree to tackle a couple of new pieces with the choir for the event."

"Why don't I stop by your office Saturday morning about nine and you can go over the details with me?"

"Perfect. I'll see you then."

Even before he turned away, Karen was already formulating a list of things to do. Give her a problem, and her brain immediately transitioned to analytical mode. Must be a DNA thing.

But as Scott turned in response to the pastor's greeting and his gaze connected with hers, the left side of her brain disengaged. His warm smile seeped into her heart, tripping her pulse into double time despite her best efforts to rein it in.

And Karen suspected that no matter how hard she tried to analyze that particular problem, the solution would defy logic.

Stifling a yawn, Scott inserted his key in the church door. Must be all the carbs from the Thursday night fried chicken special at home, a childhood tradition his mother had revived since his return. Not the best thing for his waistline—or cholesterol—but he had to admit the comfort food was soothing.

As it turned out, the door was unlocked, and when it swung open, soft piano music spilled out.

Huh.

Who else would be playing at this hour?

After a brief hesitation, he stepped inside. Maybe he could find some pieces in the music file for the choir to work on for the benefit without disturbing whoever was inside.

Taking care to be as quiet as possible, he moved into the cool interior, a welcome respite from the oppressive July heat. For a moment he stood in silence, letting his eyes adjust to the dimness. The music was more audible now. Except . . . it wasn't exactly music. It sounded more like someone was just fooling around on the piano.

As he edged toward the choir area to check out who was playing, a wheelchair came into view. A young man with broad shoulders was picking out a melody with one hand and using the other to experiment with chords. The piano bench had been moved aside to accommodate him.

Scott's step faltered. Was this the young man who'd been injured in a football accident? Steven something. And if so, why was he here?

As Scott moved into the young man's field of vision, the teenager stopped playing and started to push back from the piano. "Sorry. I didn't know anyone was here."

"No. Stay there. I just stopped by to look through some music." Scott held out his hand. "Scott Walker."

The boy took his fingers in a firm grip. "I know. I listen to you play every Sunday. I'm Steven Ramsey."

"Nice to meet you. And make it Scott. Do you play?"

"No." The single word was tinged with regret.

"It sounded like you were putting some notes and chords together."

Steven skimmed his fingers over the keys. "I like music. But I . . . I used to play football. You have to take lessons, and practice a lot, to be good at music. I didn't have the time. Besides, lessons are expensive." He looked back at Scott. "I bet you took a lot of lessons."

Scott moved to the piano bench and sat on the edge. "I majored in music theory and composition in college, and I do have a fair amount of classical training. But the keyboard isn't my main instrument."

"You could've fooled me. What do you play?"

"Clarinet in the beginning, but for the past ten years I've focused on saxophone."

"Cool. What kind of music do you like?"

"I used to play jazz."

"What do you play now?"

The bottom dropped out of his stomach. "I don't play anything." Lifting his left hand, he demonstrated the unresponsiveness of his fingers. "I injured this in an accident a few months ago."

"Will it get better?"

Karen had asked him that once. And he gave Steven the same answer he'd given her. "No one knows."

"But there's hope, right?"

Hope.

It wasn't a word he used much anymore. But it was clear he had more of it than this young man whose own dreams had been shattered forever. Steven would never walk again, let alone play pro football. Scott, on the other hand, had some chance of recovery—however slim. "Yeah. I guess."

"And you can still play the piano."

"Not very well."

The boy's expression grew bleak, and he stared down at the keys. "Better than I can play football."

The boy's soft comment was like a punch in the gut.

His mother had told him not long ago that he needed to get some perspective. Well, he'd just had a whole boatload of it dumped in his lap.

And Steven was right—as his mother had been right. He could still do many things. Maybe not with the skill he once had. Yet. But he had hope . . . and a future of some kind in his field, if he wanted it, as Reverend Richards had pointed out.

Steven had none of those things.

"I'm sorry." He didn't know what else to say.

The teenager gave a stiff shrug. "I'll survive, I guess."

As Steven began to idly plunk the keys, an idea began to percolate in Scott's mind. "Now that you have the time, why don't you pursue your interest in music?"

The young man stopped playing. "I'd need lessons."

"So?"

"I have three brothers and sisters. And we've had a lot of medical bills in the past few months. Mom and Dad both work, but . . ."

He didn't have to finish the sentence for Scott to understand the problem. Money was tight.

But the solution seemed obvious.

Nevertheless, Scott hesitated. He'd avoided making commitments of any kind since the accident, except for the part-time choir gig. And if his mother hadn't pushed him, he wouldn't have pursued even that.

This, however, was different. This was a task he wanted to take on. The first one that had interested him since his life had been turned upside down.

"I'll tell you what . . . I don't have much teaching experience, but I do have a lot of time on my hands. I'd be happy to spend some of it showing you the basics on the keyboard."

"For real?" A glimmer of interest sprang to life in the boy's eyes.

"For real."

The glimmer flickered. "The thing is, we don't have a piano. I don't have anywhere to practice."

"How about here?"

The spark rekindled. "Do you think Reverend Richards would let me?"

"I can talk to him about it. Do you have a way to get here every day?"

"I have a lot of friends. One of them would give me a ride."

A middle-aged woman appeared from behind the tabernacle carrying a huge vase of flowers. Spotting him, she hurried forward, her expression apologetic. "We'll be out of here in a few minutes. I didn't realize you'd be working."

"No problem."

"This is my mom," Steven offered.

Rising, Scott held out his hand. "Nice to meet you, Mrs. Ramsey."

"Mom, Scott says he'll give me piano lessons."

The young man's eagerness tugged at Scott's heart.

"That's real kind of you, Mr. Walker . . ."

"Scott."

"Scott. And I'm Martha. But the thing is, we've got a lot of other expenses now, and . . ." She gave him a what-can-you-do look, regret pooling in her eyes.

"There wouldn't be any charge. You'd be doing *me* a favor. The doctors want me to exercise my injured hand as much as possible to increase flexibility, and working on the keyboard with Steven will give me more of a chance to do that."

When she hesitated, Steven spoke again. "Please, Mom."

At his quiet, intent plea, she searched his face. Swallowed. Gave Scott a tremulous smile. "I know Steven would enjoy it. He's always had an interest in music but never had an opportunity to develop it. Thank you."

"It's my pleasure." Scott directed his next comment to Steven. "I'll talk to Reverend Richards about using this piano for practice. What do you say we start tomorrow?"

"Cool. Thank you."

They shook hands, and at the new spark in Steven's eyes . . . of optimism . . . anticipation . . . hope . . . a shaft of sunlight pierced the darkness in his soul.

And suddenly Scott realized that Steven had it all wrong.

He should be thanking him.

"Okay, what's the total now?" Val smiled as Karen deposited her fat-free frappuccino on the table and settled into a chair across from her at the small café table.

"Eighteen and dropping."

"Way to go! At this rate, you'll be back to your old svelte self before I leave."

"Don't talk about leaving yet." Karen wrinkled her nose. "I'm getting kind of used to having you around. It'll be lonely after you're gone."

"For me too." She gave Karen's hand a quick squeeze. There were definitely things she would miss when she returned to Chicago. Becoming friends with her sister had been an unexpected bonus of this visit.

"I wish it hadn't taken so long for us to connect." Karen took a sip of her drink. "Why do you think it did?"

"Lots of reasons, I suspect. You went away to college when I was fifteen. I left for school at eighteen, a month after you got married. Before that, there was too much rivalry, thanks to Mom—and too many hormones as well, I imagine."

"I suppose." Karen sighed. "I'll miss you."

"We can keep in touch by phone."

"It's not the same."

"True. But we have almost four more weeks. It's much too soon to haul out the Kleenex. Let's talk about something more cheerful. Like the way your choir director zinged Mom without her knowing it last Sunday. I like that guy!"

"He saw right through her, didn't he?"

"I'll say. It was great! What's he like to work with?"

"Why? Are you thinking about joining the choir?"

At the alarm in her sister's voice, Val hastened to reassure her. "No. I have no intention of encroaching on your turf."

Karen's brow furrowed, and she caught her lower lip between her teeth. "Sorry. I didn't mean to overreact. Of course you can join if you want to. It's just that . . . well, music is one more thing you can best me at. I have a niche in the choir, but if you're there I'll fade into the background. Mom was right. I don't have any great singing talent."

"Your choir director doesn't agree—and neither do I."

"You're both just being nice." Karen dismissed the compliment with a flip of her hand. "Anyway, I'm working on the jealousy thing, but I guess it's going to rear its ugly head now and then."

"Welcome to the human race. As for the choir . . . since I'll be heading back to Chicago next month, it wouldn't make any sense to get involved even if I was so inclined, which I'm not. I promise to leave all church-related matters in your very capable hands."

"Oh! That reminds me." Karen set her drink aside and leaned forward. "I met with Reverend Richards this morning about a fund-raising event we're going to have in mid-August. He asked me to coordinate it."

"Don't you have enough on your plate without taking on another project?"

"This is for a good cause, though. Hope House. Was that around when we were kids?"

Searching her memory, Val came up blank. "Doesn't ring any bells. What is it?"

"A counseling center for pregnant teens. They offer medical referrals, adoption assistance, and emotional support as an alternative to abortion. The problem is, they're running close to the red and they asked Reverend Richards if our church would sponsor a fund-raising dinner, with entertainment. It's a few days before you have to go back, and I wondered if I could persuade you to be the emcee. You'd be perfect, Val. Your background and training would add some professional polish to the evening."

As Karen lobbed the ball into her court, it took every ounce of her acting skill to maintain a placid demeanor. Her sister wanted her to help raise money for an organization that offered help—and hope—to girls who found themselves in the same situation she'd been in at seventeen? Talk about irony—and strange timing.

Or . . . maybe not.

Could this be a chance to make amends? By supporting an organization that helped other young girls make a better decision than she had, could she take a step toward atoning for her mistakes?

It might be worth considering.

"What would I need to do?"

"Welcome the attendees, introduce the different groups that are going to entertain, thank people at the end of the evening." Karen ticked the items off on her fingers. "It's very simple. The kind of thing you could do in your sleep."

From a technical standpoint, Val didn't have any doubt she could handle the job. Emotionally . . . that might be a different story.

When she hesitated, Karen spoke again. "I know I dumped this on you, and I know you didn't come down here to perform. Why don't you think about it and let me know in the next few days?"

Val gave a slow nod. "That sounds fair enough."

Smiling, Karen laid her hand on Val's arm. "Thanks. I know it would be a piece of cake for you, and your flair would add some pizzazz to the evening."

Although Val tried to return the smile, she couldn't quite pull it off. No matter what Karen thought, emceeing this event wouldn't be a piece of cake. Not even close.

In fact, if she agreed to do this, it might end up being the most difficult performance of her life.

14

"Hello, Val."

At David's greeting, Val turned. She'd noticed him sitting up front with Victoria as she'd arrived for the service, but when had he spotted her?

She gave him a tentative smile. "Hi." Then she bent down to the little blonde-haired girl clutching his hand. "Hello, Victoria. I like your dress. And your hair is very pretty today."

"Daddy brushed it for me. He didn't make any ouches, either."

"I'm glad to hear that."

"We're going to the zoo today. Do you want to come?"

The suggestion seemed to surprise David as much as it did her. But before she could respond, he jumped in. "That's a great idea. How about it, Val?"

For an instant, she was tempted to accept his invitation. Then logic kicked in. Why start down a path that led nowhere?

Forcing up the corners of her lips, she stiffened her resolve. "This sounds like a father-daughter outing to me. I wouldn't want to intrude."

At his speculative expression, she braced. Was he going to press her to accept, as he had the day at the park?

"I was surprised to see you here today." He rested a hand on Victoria's shoulder. "I thought you said you weren't a churchgoer."

He'd let the invitation drop. Good.

So what was with that little niggle of disappointment in the pit of her stomach?

"I'm not." She forced herself to switch gears. "This is an aberration, trust me."

"Your mother told me you came last week too."

It figured. Her return to church was big news for Margaret, and David was a captive audience during the therapy sessions. But she owed God one for helping her through her journey to the past last weekend.

Besides, she had to admit that being in church made her feel less alone.

Instead of giving him a direct response, however, she turned the tables. "I didn't see you last Sunday, though."

"Victoria had a cold. She must have picked up the same bug you had. Anyway, I promised her we'd go to the zoo as soon as she got better, and we'd love to have you join us. As for father-daughter time, we have lots of that. We don't have many friends here yet, and I think we're both ready for some company."

So the subject wasn't closed, after all. In fact, based on that last comment, while the idea might have been Victoria's, he was all for it.

And wouldn't it be lovely to spend a carefree day with a handsome man and a little girl who could steal your heart with one sunny smile?

But she had to resist the alluring temptation. Dating could lead to romance. Romance could lead to love. Love could lead to marriage. Marriage could lead to children. None of which she deserved. Not after what she'd done.

Just say no, Val.

She tried, but the words dried up in her mouth.

As if sensing her indecision, David offered the one argument that was almost impossible to resist. "Come on, Val. It will be fun. And you'll brighten a little girl's day."

She glanced down at Victoria, who wore the expression of hopeful innocence reserved for the very young. There was no pretense there, no secrets, no hidden agendas or doubts or regrets. No worries about tomorrow, no consequences to deal with. She was just a little girl without a mom, excited about spending a day at the zoo with her dad—and maybe with the lady who'd shared a brownie with her in the park.

Val's shaky resolve disintegrated. How was she supposed to resist those big green eyes? Besides, attachments weren't formed in one day. It would be nothing more than a pleasant afternoon they could all tuck away in their memories.

With a sigh of capitulation, Val gave up the fight. "You win."

The smile David gave her warmed his eyes—and melted her heart.

"Is she coming, Daddy?"

"I think she is."

"Oh, goody!" The little girl jumped up and down and clapped her hands. "Can we get an ice-cream cone too?"

"I think that could be arranged." David gave the little girl a squeeze and looked back at her. "Why don't I swing by and pick you up around one?"

"That works." She rummaged in her purse for a slip of paper. "I'll write down Mom's address for you."

"Six-forty-seven West Madison." Her hand stilled, and he grinned. "It's on her records, and I have a good memory for numbers. Being new in town, however, I could use some directions."

It took less than two minutes to explain how to find the house, and as David left her with a wave and a "See you about one," she turned to find Karen watching her with a smug expression.

"It's not what you think." Despite her best effort, Val wasn't able to stop the blush that negated her words.

"Isn't it?"

"No. We're just going to the zoo. Victoria asked me."

"Looked to me like her father endorsed the idea."

"They're new in town. They don't know a lot of people yet."

"In other words, your decision to go with them was an act of charity?"

"Something like that."

"Nice try." Winking, Karen nudged her. "But I was watching your face—and his. Call it whatever you like, but I know a date when I see it."

"Karen! Val! I'm ready to leave."

Their mother's voice shattered the Sunday morning stillness outside the church, and Karen chuckled. "Lucky you. Saved by the bell. Or should I say bellow? Come on. We can chat about this later."

Not if she could help it. She didn't want to talk about her feelings for David.

And she was already beginning to think that accepting his invitation had been a huge mistake.

At the peal of the doorbell, Karen huffed out a breath. Great. Yesterday she'd spent two hours of her already packed Saturday meeting with Reverend Richards about the Hope House benefit. Now a visitor was interrupting her Sunday afternoon—and she still had another load of laundry to do before she hotfooted it back to her mother's to be on hand when Margaret woke up from her nap.

She dumped the armload of clothes from the dryer on the kitchen table and marched down the hall. Whoever it was, she'd make this fast. Listening to Mom complain if she wasn't back at the house on schedule was not on her agenda for the day.

At the door, she smoothed her hand over her hair, checked the peephole—and frowned.

What on earth was Michael doing here?

She shook her head and unlocked the dead bolt. If he was looking for Kristen, he was out of luck. Now that she was more mobile, her social life had picked up.

She pulled the door open and gave him the bad news at once. "Sorry, Michael. Kristen went to a sleepover last night, and they're having a barbecue this afternoon. She won't be home until this evening."

To her surprise, he seemed unfazed. "I knew it was a gamble. I was in the mood to go for a drive and thought if she was home, I'd take her to Mr. Frank's."

"I'll let her know you came by." Karen began to close the door.

He put a hand out to stop her. "I don't suppose I could get a cup of coffee, could I?"

She narrowed her eyes. Since when did they socialize during his visits? "Coffee?"

He gave her a weak grin and slid his hands in the pockets of his knife-creased slacks. "Yeah. You know. That black stuff full of caffeine. We used to drink some together in the morning."

Okay, this was weird. Michael never joked with her. And why would he bring up an intimate morning ritual they had shared only in the early days of their marriage?

When she didn't respond, he withdrew one hand from his pocket and ran his fingers through his hair. Fingers that weren't quite steady. She refocused on his face. The faint hollow in his cheeks and his slight pallor were also new. "Is everything okay?"

"As a matter of fact, no. I was hoping to tell you about it over a cup of coffee."

Karen hesitated. She didn't have time for this—but he *had* made a long drive.

Don't be a patsy.

Right.

She opened her mouth—but he spoke first.

"Please."

She closed her mouth. Wow. She could count on her fingers the number of times he'd used that word while they'd been married.

Fine. She'd listen—within reason.

She pulled the door wide and made a point of looking at her watch. "I only have a few minutes."

"I appreciate whatever time you can spare." He moved past her and headed toward the kitchen.

Karen followed, sweeping aside the clothes on the table to carve out enough space for two cups. Surprising her again, Michael went to work making the coffee—a task he'd always left to her when they'd lived together as man and wife.

As she folded her arms and watched him, he gave her a sheepish look. "I've learned a lot in the past few months."

You mean your new lady love doesn't wait on you like a slave, the way I did?

Clamping her lips together, she kept that thought to herself. Instead, she retrieved the cream and two mugs, then sat at the table. He joined her once the coffee began to brew.

As the seconds ticked by in silence, impatience began to thrum through her. How hard could it be to tell her that things had turned sour between him and Stephanie? And that had to be what he wanted to talk about. Though why he thought she cared was beyond her.

In the interest of expediting the conversation, she gave him the opening he couldn't seem to find for himself. "How are things with Stephanie?"

He played with his empty mug. "Not good."

If he expected her to offer condolences, he was out of luck. Her sense of charity only went so far.

When the silence lengthened again, he cleared his throat. "As much as I hate to admit it, I think it was a mistake from the beginning. We were too different." He wiped a hand down his face. "Long story short, we split up about three weeks ago. She met someone else. Someone younger."

Thrown aside for someone younger. Ha. Perhaps there was justice after all— even if that wasn't a very charitable attitude.

"The thing is, I should never have left." He played with his mug. "I guess it's that whole greener pastures thing. Or maybe a midlife crisis. Who knows? Whatever the motivation, it was a mistake."

Karen stared at him, suspicion niggling at the edges of her mind. Surely, after all that happened, he couldn't be implying that he might want to come back.

Could he?

Tipping her head, she gave him a cautious look. "I have some chores I need to finish, Michael. Is there a point to this?"

He leaned forward, his expression intent. "Yeah, there is. We had a good thing going once. Maybe we could again."

Unbelievable.

In his usual arrogant way, he wanted to waltz back into her life and pick up the dance without missing a beat.

But the music had changed.

"It wouldn't work, Michael."

"Look, I know I made a lot of mistakes. But you're the one who always preached forgiveness and repentance and turning the other cheek. Isn't this a perfect opportunity to put that into action? I truly am sorry, Karen. And we could make this work if we both committed to it. Why not give it another try?"

She tightened her grip on the mug. "I'm glad you're sorry, but our relationship was only good for you. I cooked your meals. Did your laundry. Took your clothes to the cleaner. Made your coffee. It was never a partnership of equals. You ran the show, made all the decisions, and I let you. That was my mistake, and I paid for it after you walked out and I had to create a new life, to survive on my own. But guess what? I did it. And believe it or not, I like my life now. I've learned to stand on my own feet, and to stand up for myself. I don't need you to make my life complete."

His incredulous expression suggested he thought some alien had commandeered her body. "That doesn't sound like the Karen I know."

"I told you. I've changed."

"Don't you believe in that till-death-do-us-part vow anymore?"

"When it's entered into with the right intent. But that doesn't mean I need to stay in an unhealthy relationship. Or put up with infidelity."

His complexion reddened. "I said I was sorry about that."

"And I said I was glad. But suppose I could forgive one fling. How could I be sure there wouldn't be more? Or that there weren't others before?"

She threw in the last comment as an afterthought, but when his ruddy hue deepened to crimson, a wave of shock crashed over her. "There *were* others, weren't there?"

"Look, I'm human, okay?" Irritation sharpened his voice. "I've slipped a couple of times. It happens. That's how men are."

So Stephanie hadn't been the first, after all. Michael had strayed more than once.

And Val had been right. Michael's "that's how men are" comment said it all. He'd entered into their marriage never planning to honor his vow of fidelity.

Their marriage had been a sham from the beginning.

As for his implication that his behavior was a normal male trait—she didn't buy that. Not for one minute. Not all men were unfaithful. There were plenty who had honor and integrity. Who were honest and true. Who might make mistakes but didn't break promises. Or vows.

For some reason, an image of Scott flashed through her mind. She didn't even know him, yet she had a feeling he could be counted on to keep his word. Perhaps because of the way he'd handled the choir situation. He'd made a mistake, yes, but he'd also made amends—and made a change. She didn't think he'd fall back to his old ways.

"You've met someone else, haven't you?"

Michael's comment jerked her back to the conversation. The man actually had the gall to sound aggrieved, as if he was the injured party.

"A counterpart to your Stephanie? And who knows who else? No, Michael, I haven't. But that doesn't mean I'm willing to go back to what we had before."

"It could be different this time."

"It wouldn't work."

"Would you be willing to try, for Kristen's sake? She'd like us to get back together."

Leave it to Michael to find her weak spot and try to exploit it.

But she knew something he didn't. Kristen was on to him. Their daughter had understood far more about the problems in their marriage than either had suspected. And based on the conversation they'd had recently at this very table—including Kristen's comment that Michael was a better dad than a husband—Karen knew that as much as Kristen had hoped for a reconciliation, she preferred her mother to be happy.

Michael's ploy wouldn't work. Not anymore.

She shook her head. "No. It's over."

For a few seconds, he appraised her. Then his shoulders slumped. Placing his hands on the table, he pushed himself to his feet. "I guess there isn't much else to say."

"I guess not."

"Tell Kristen I was here, okay?"

"I will."

"I'll let myself out."

As he left the room, Karen remained seated. She heard the front door open, then click shut. A few minutes later, a car engine kicked in. She listened as it faded into the distance, then slowly unwrapped her hands from around the unused mug. They'd never poured their coffee. Her cup was still empty.

But her life wasn't. Not anymore. She was finally taking control of her destiny. Trusting her own judgment. Standing up for what she believed. Cracking open the door to the possibility of love.

And it felt great.

15

"I think you've made a new friend."

At David's comment, Val took a lick of her ice-cream cone and shifted around on the bench to watch as Victoria enjoyed the antics of the zoo's prairie dogs.

"She's a sweetheart. And she's lucky to have a father who plans outings like this. A lot of men put their families in second place, behind their careers. It's a shame, don't you think?"

When David didn't respond, Val glanced toward him. A slight frown marred his brow. "We had sort of the opposite situation in our family. Natalie was very career-oriented."

The perfect opening to ask a few questions about his wife. "What did she do?"

"She handled marketing for her company's global brands. Since my hours were more flexible and I didn't have to travel or work overtime, I took on most of the child-care duties, which was fine with me. I've always believed that raising a child is the most important job in the world."

An opinion not shared by his wife, apparently. Though David hadn't said anything negative about Natalie, she sensed their different philosophies on child rearing had been a source of disappointment to him . . . and perhaps a point of contention.

"It sounds like she was very busy—and gone a lot." She kept her tone casual and conversational. No way did she want to come across as nosey.

"She was. We delayed starting a family, hoping that once her career was established things would slow down, but the opposite happened. As she took on greater responsibilities, her life got more hectic. It became obvious there was never going to be a 'good' time to have children. Finally we just decided to go ahead. As it was, she went back to work four weeks after giving birth."

He examined the remnants of his ice cream. The cone had collapsed, and the mess that remained wasn't salvageable. He wrapped it in his napkin and balled it in his fist. "Natalie always pushed herself too hard. I used to tell her to slow down and smell the flowers, that life was too short and should be enjoyed. But neither of us realized how short hers would be."

Val crumpled the napkin that had been wrapped around her own ice-cream cone. "Was it an accident?"

"No. Not in the way you mean. She was a borderline diabetic when we married, and after she had Victoria, her condition worsened. It got to the point where she needed to check her blood sugar level several times a day and give herself injections as needed. Two years ago, on an overseas flight, her blood sugar went haywire. Maybe, with the time change, she got out of sync, forgot to check . . . we'll never know. Halfway over the Pacific she fell into diabetic shock. There was a doctor onboard, and he did the best he could under the circumstances, but after she went into cardiac arrest . . ." His voice rasped, and he swallowed.

"I'm so sorry." Following her heart, she laid her hand over his as her gaze flickered to Victoria. "I can't even imagine how difficult that must have been for both of you."

"Yeah." His voice roughened again, and he cleared his throat. "At least I had my faith to sustain me. But Victoria was too young to find any comfort there, or even grasp what was happening. Children can sense when something's wrong, though, and for days after Natalie's death I couldn't get Victoria to eat more than a few bites at a time. For weeks, she'd wake up at night crying. She was only three, though, and kids that age rebound fast. The trauma fades—along with everything else, unfortunately. She has no memory of her mother. I show her pictures, and I try to tell her about Natalie, but to her they're just stories, with no more basis in reality than her fairy tales. All she knows is she doesn't have a mommy like all of her friends do."

David looked down to where her hand rested on his, and she removed it on the pretense of adjusting her purse.

"You know, I think I owe you an apology." He angled toward her.

"Why?"

"I promised you a fun day, but all I've done is depress you."

"I'm not depressed. Just sorry for all you've gone through."

"Close enough. Let's change the subject. Tell me about you."

If he thought that was going to cheer her up, he was dead wrong. "Now there's a boring subject." The comment came out light despite the heaviness in her heart—just as she'd hoped.

"Not according to your mother. She's always bragging about you."

"Bragging? Mom?" She gave him a skeptical look. "You're kidding, right?"

He held up his hand. "Scout's honor. I hear lots of flattering things about you and your sister."

"Are you certain we're talking about the same Margaret Montgomery? All Karen and I ever heard growing up was criticism. About ourselves, not about each other, mind you. We each felt that nothing we ever did was good enough, and that the other sister was the favored one."

"Interesting." He dabbed at a sticky spot on his lips with his napkin.

He had nice lips.

"Margaret *is* opinionated." He settled an arm along the back of the bench. Inches from her shoulder. "And I can see how she could be manipulative. But I don't hear too many complaints—except about food. Even those have tapered off since I started complimenting her on her weight loss, though. Was your dad critical too?"

"No." She pulled her gaze away from his mouth. "He was supportive and affectionate, and he always made us feel special. His unconditional love helped compensate for Mom's shortcomings in the parenting-skills department, and I vowed someday, when I had children, to emulate his example as best I could."

"So what happened?"

She tipped her head. "What do you mean?"

"As far as I know, you've never been married. Or had kids."

She'd walked right into that one.

Focusing on her fingers, she wiped off some sticky ice cream residue. "Too busy for either."

"That's a shame. I've seen how you interact with Victoria, and how she relates to you. You'd be a good mother."

Calling on every ounce of her theatrical training, Val managed to keep her expression placid. "Motherhood isn't for me."

"Why not?"

"I happen to agree with what you said earlier, about the importance of raising children. It's a full-time job, and I love my career too much to give that up."

"I didn't mean to imply a woman has to give up her career to have a family. I think there's a way to integrate the two. The key is to maintain perspective and priorities."

"Finding that balance is a challenge. It's better not to take the chance." Val tossed her wadded-up napkin into the trash bin beside the bench and gave David a too-bright smile. "So, tell me what you've been doing in whatever free time you have, now that you're settling into Washington."

If the abrupt change of subject disconcerted him, he didn't let on.

"I haven't had a chance yet to do much more than straighten out the house and help Victoria acclimate, but I think I might volunteer for a program at church."

"What kind of program?" That should be a safe subject, since she had no serious affiliation with the church.

"We're going to be sponsoring a benefit for an organization called Hope House. I think your sister is coordinating the whole thing. Maybe you know about it?"

So much for safe subjects.

"Karen mentioned it."

"It sounds like a good cause. I can't think of anything more worthwhile than saving the lives of innocent babies. The pro-life movement has always been near to my heart."

The bottom fell out of her stomach.

"But I'm afraid I can't contribute much to the effort. All of my theatrical talent could fit in my little finger." David gave her a self-deprecating grin. "I used to run lights and sound for shows in college, though, and I enjoyed that behind-the-scenes stuff. I thought I might volunteer in a capacity like that."

"I'm sure they'd welcome your expertise." Val played with the edge of her purse strap. "Actually, Karen asked me to be the emcee."

"No kidding! Are you going to?"

"I don't know. I told her I'd consider it."

"I think it's a great idea. With your background, you could bring something special to the event."

She averted her head on the pretense of watching Victoria. Yeah, she could bring something special, all right. But not in the way he meant.

Not even close.

And as the little girl's giggle infiltrated her defenses—and reminded her of all she could never have—she was sorrier than ever that she'd succumbed to temptation and accepted David's invitation to spend the day in their company.

"I had fun at the zoo today, Daddy."

David finished tucking in Victoria, then leaned down to kiss her forehead. "I'm glad, sweetheart."

"Did you have fun too?"

Not as much as he'd hoped. But he managed to paste on a smile. "It's hard not to have fun at the zoo."

"Yeah." She cuddled up next to her Raggedy Ann doll. "Do you think Val had fun too?"

Not much. Especially not after their little chat on the bench. Things had headed south for both of them at about the same point, near as he could tell. For him, talking of Natalie had reminded him of all he'd lost . . . and how much Victoria needed a mother. He hadn't been able to work up much enthusiasm for that task until Val had walked into his life. But her admission today that her career came first . . . bad news. Been there, done that.

As for why Val's mood had changed so abruptly—he had no idea.

"Daddy?" Victoria tugged on his shirt.

"I think Val enjoyed laughing with you about that goofy monkey that kept making faces at us."

Victoria giggled. "That was funny. And I liked how she rode the carousel with me too." Her expression grew more serious. "Do you think we could go somewhere else with her sometime?"

That question was tougher.

"I don't know. She's only going to be in town for a few more weeks. Val lives in Chicago, remember?"

"Is that far away?"

"Far enough. It takes a whole afternoon to drive there."

Victoria's face fell. "That's too bad. She's really nice."

Yeah, she was. Nice enough that he'd considered doing the very thing Victoria had suggested. One or two more excursions wouldn't be enough for his daughter to get too attached, and he enjoyed Val's company.

And until their chat on the bench, he'd felt certain Val would accept another invitation. She might be an actress, but her smiles had been genuine, and she'd been captivated by Victoria, reaching out every now and then to brush her hair back with a gentle hand when the wind tossed the soft strands.

But after their exchange, she'd grown quiet, and their parting had been polite, nothing more.

David bent down and gave Victoria another kiss. "There are a lot of nice people in the world. We'll meet some more of them."

"Not as nice as Val, I bet."

No argument there.

He crossed to the door and paused by the light. "Good night."

"'Night, Daddy." She snuggled under the blanket and closed her eyes.

He flipped off the switch and wandered into the kitchen. Maybe he'd unpack a few more boxes. Or fix that pantry drawer that kept sticking. Or put together the ceiling fan that had been delivered yesterday. The endless list of chores never seemed to shrink.

But in the end, he grabbed a soda out of the fridge and went out to the screen porch instead to think some more about Val.

Because the pieces weren't adding up.

He settled into a patio chair and ticked off what he knew. She was an actress. She had a less-than-perfect relationship with her mother. She'd left town for college and never come home. She was single, and maintained she intended to stay that way. She also claimed she didn't want children.

Yet he'd seen a different message in her eyes as she'd watched Victoria. They'd held longing. Tenderness. And an emotion he was tempted to classify as regret. As if the thing she wanted most was beyond her reach.

David took a swig of his soda and crossed an ankle over his knee. That didn't make sense. Val was a young woman. She was attractive, intelligent, and compassionate. She could have her pick of men. And she was smart enough to find a way to juggle a job with marriage and motherhood.

So why had she written off a family? Was there something in her past that was holding her back?

Maybe.

Because as she'd said good-bye today, he'd heard more in her words than a mere parting for the day. While their paths would cross again at the rehab center, he'd had the distinct feeling she was closing a door between them—and posting a No Trespassing sign.

He tipped the can against his lips again. Perhaps he should be grateful if she backed off. He didn't need another complicated relationship, and Val was complicated. Whatever secrets she harbored, whatever issues she was grappling with, could create problems for all of them. If he was smart, he'd do the safe thing. He'd write off her summertime visit as a chance encounter and move on.

With a sigh, he rose and crushed the empty can in his hand. That plan was sound. Logical. Smart.

But his heart and his mind were duking it out when it came to Val.

And he had no idea which one would win.

16

"Okay, I think that should do it for tonight. Those two pieces will be in great shape for the benefit, thanks to your hard work. I'll see you all on Sunday."

As Scott dismissed the choir and gathered up his music, he glanced at Karen. She was talking to Teresa Ramirez, but he didn't intend to let her leave without broaching the idea he'd been mulling over since he'd taken note of her lyrical soprano voice.

It wasn't going to be an easy sell, though. He'd been watching her, and she worked hard to blend in with the rest of the choir, trying her best not to stand out. After meeting her critical mother and beautiful, successful sister, he could understand why she might lack confidence in her singing ability—and perhaps in other things as well.

But her inferiority complex was undeserved.

As Teresa moved away, Karen began stuffing her music into her tote bag.

His cue.

Crossing the room to join her, he summoned up his most winning smile. "Do you have a few minutes to talk about the benefit?"

Her head jerked up, and she gave him a startled look. "Sure."

Man, she had beautiful brown eyes. Soft. Warm. Inviting. And as for those supple, expressive lips . . .

Focus, Walker. This isn't about your feelings. It's about helping this woman gain some confidence.

He swallowed and took the seat beside her. "I'm starting to work with Steven Ramsey on the keyboard. He happened to be here one night when I stopped in, and he has a strong interest in music. After only a couple of sessions it's clear to me he has real talent. Do you think it might be possible to include him in the program? It would build his self-esteem and give him a goal to work toward. I think he'd be ready to do one or two simple pieces."

Her eyebrows rose. "You're giving Steven piano lessons?"

"It's no big deal. I have a lot of time on my hands."

"Of course we'll include him! If you've discovered a way to give him a new sense of purpose and direction, you'll have done a great service to him and his family. That's a very thoughtful gesture."

His neck warmed. "There are benefits on both sides. But that's not the only thing I wanted to talk with you about. Did you notice that one of the selections we practiced tonight for the benefit has a solo soprano section?"

"Yes. This one." She picked up a piece of sheet music from her lap. "We skipped over that part."

"I'd like you to do it."

She stared at him as several beats of silence ticked by. "I beg your pardon?"

"I'd like you to do it."

"You mean . . . sing by myself?"

"Yes."

"You can't be serious."

"Yes, I am. I've been listening to you. You have a lovely voice, with a tonal quality that's perfect for that piece. Clear and pure and ethereal."

More silence as she regarded him with an expression of disbelief and alarm. "I couldn't sing in front of five people, let alone the five hundred we expect for the benefit."

"Why not?"

"I'm not . . . I've never had . . ." She fingered the piece of music and took a deep breath. "Look, I can carry a tune, and singing with the group is fine, but singing alone . . . I couldn't."

"I'll work with you on it. In private, if you like, until you feel ready to do it in front of other people."

Her mouth twisted. "That could take far longer than we have. Years, maybe."

"We could give it a try, at least. If you want to back out later, we'll eliminate that section, like we did tonight." When she hesitated, he rose. "I'll tell you what. Why don't we run through it, just you and me? See if the range is comfortable."

"Now?"

"To paraphrase a line from *The King and I*, now is always a good time. Unless you have another commitment?"

Again, she hesitated. "I do have some work to finish that I brought home from the office, but . . ."

He could see she was tempted, and he pressed that advantage. "Take the leap, Karen. Sometimes our biggest successes come when we take a chance."

Her grip on the music tightened, crinkling the edges. "There's also a risk you can fall on your face."

"That's not going to happen in this case. I've spent my life in the music business. I know how to evaluate talent."

Her cheeks pinked. "I appreciate that assessment, but talent is one thing. Confidence is another."

"I have enough of that for both of us. Come on. Give it a try. Trust me on this." He extended a hand—hoping she'd take him up on his offer.

For both their sakes.

As Karen looked at Scott's outstretched fingers, she bit her lower lip. Hugged her music folder to her chest. Tried to quell the butterflies in her stomach.

He was right, of course. Risk and reward went hand in hand. You couldn't succeed if you didn't try. Didn't stretch yourself. And he'd given her an exit strategy. She could back out if things didn't go well.

What did she have to lose?

Lifting her chin, she took his hand. His long, lean fingers gave hers an encouraging squeeze, and then he dazzled her with that killer smile. The one that transformed his face and never failed to make her heart stumble. Nor did her legs feel any too steady as he led her to the piano.

But that was nerves, pure and simple. What else could it be?

She dismissed the other possibility that came to mind.

"I'm still not comfortable with this, Scott."

"We'll take it slow and easy." He slid onto the bench and opened the music. "Don't push. Let the sound flow."

She lifted her music. It shook in her hands. As he began to play, her breathing went haywire. When he approached her cue, her throat tightened and she couldn't produce a sound.

Flushing in embarrassment, she laid the music on the piano. "I can't do it." Somehow she managed to choke out the words.

Scott spoke in a quiet but firm voice. "Yes, you can."

"I wish I could." She shook her head in regret. "But I can't."

"All right. We'll do it together until you're comfortable."

Before she could respond, he launched into the intro again, refusing to take no for an answer. Karen sucked in a deep breath and tried to pull herself together. Okay, maybe if he sang along she could manage to get through it. But she'd never be able to do it alone. And she could imagine what her mother would say if she knew her oldest daughter was even *thinking* about singing a solo!

Scott played the final chord of the intro, gave her an encouraging smile, and began to sing the melody in his pleasant baritone.

Karen did her best, but her voice was shaky and she wavered on the high notes. Still, she made it to the end.

Finishing the final measure with a one-handed flourish, he turned to her. “See. You did it.”

“True. But it was awful.”

One side of his mouth quirked up. “That’s a little extreme. The first attempt is always rough, whether singing or playing an instrument. Let’s try it again.”

Once more he played the intro, and once more he sang along with her. This time, her voice was a little steadier and she didn’t have quite as much trouble with the high notes.

“Better.” He gave her a pleased nod. “Let’s try it again.”

They ran through the song half a dozen times. The last time he dropped out halfway through. She glanced at him in panic and her voice wavered, but he gave her a steady look.

“Keep going.”

And she did.

As the last note died away, he angled toward her, resting an arm on the music stand. There was warmth in his eyes—almost as much as was in her heart. “I’d say we made great progress tonight. And the next rehearsal will be even better. We’ll try it with the choir next week.”

Karen’s brief spurt of elation evaporated. “I’m still not sure I can sing in front of anyone else.”

He studied her for a moment. “I’ll tell you what. Would you feel more comfortable if the two of us got together again first to rehearse?”

“I don’t want to impose.”

“I’ll be here Saturday morning with Steven. If you came around ten, we could spend a few minutes working on the piece after I’m finished with him.”

“Are you sure you don’t mind?”

“I’m sure.”

At his definitive tone—and the intensity in his eyes—her pulse tripped into a staccato beat again. "Okay. Thank you. I think that would help." Then she tacked on a caveat. "But I'm not ready to commit to anything. Singing with you, or with the choir, is a lot different than singing in front of an audience."

"Yes, it is. But in my experience, if you practice a lot, it's not as big a leap to a real performance as you think it is."

"Since Val is the only one with performance experience in our family, I'll have to take your word on that."

"It's true. Trust me."

Trust me.

His words echoed in her mind as she collected her music, said good night, and walked toward her car.

And even though she'd met Scott just a few weeks ago, even though she'd been betrayed by a man she thought she'd known well enough to marry, she did, indeed, trust Scott.

"How did practice go?"

Scott stopped rummaging in the refrigerator and turned toward his mother, who stood in the doorway. "Good. We worked on some pieces for the benefit. Is there any leftover pot roast from yesterday?"

"Yes. Are you hungry?" There was surprise—and hope—in her voice.

"Starved."

Some of the tension in her features dissipated. "I think there are some potatoes too." She crossed the kitchen and nudged him away from the refrigerator. "Do you want me to heat them up?"

"That would be great." He retrieved a glass from a cabinet and headed toward the sink. "Is there a YMCA anywhere around here?"

"Yes. Not too far from church. Why?"

"I think I might join. I need to get back into my exercise routine. I was always good about it on the road, but after the accident, I . . . anyway, it's time."

After punching a few numbers on the microwave, Dorothy leaned back against the counter. "How are things going with Steven?"

"Better than I expected. He's got great potential."

"His mother tells me your offer of music lessons was the answer to her prayers."

"She was praying Steven could have piano lessons?" Scott twisted the tap off.

"No. She was praying something would come along to make him want to live. To give him hope." She paused for a second, her expression troubled. "Did you know he tried to commit suicide right after the accident?"

Shock hurtled through him. "No. I didn't."

"According to Martha, he thought his life was over. Everything but his physical life, anyway. That kind of black despair can cause people to do uncharacteristic things."

That was true.

Scott examined the glass of water in his hand. It was half full. Or half empty, depending on your perspective. And he understood Steven's perspective. He'd been there himself. But bit by bit, the darkness was receding. While he still didn't know what lay ahead, the black void that had once dominated his vision of the future was beginning to brighten.

"In any case, the music lessons have been a turning point for Steven." Dorothy moved to the refrigerator and pulled out a bowl of coleslaw. "So, in a way, some good came out of your accident. Maybe not yet for you, but for others. If you hadn't come to Washington, who knows what might have happened to Steven?"

"Kind of like that old movie with Jimmy Stewart." Scott took a drink of water. "The one where he's shown what his town would be like if he'd never been born. About how one person can make a difference, and how lives are connected."

"*It's a Wonderful Life*."

"That's the one. Except in that case, I think an angel was the catalyst."

"Yes. Clarence. But humans can also be the source of great good. God often works through people to bring about miracles."

The microwave beeped, and as she crossed the room to remove the plate of food, Scott mulled over her words. He'd never given much credence to miracles. The word conjured up notions of amazing cures or tragedies averted, and he'd seen little evidence of those.

But maybe all miracles didn't have to be flashy. Maybe a miracle could also be a young man finding hope again. Or an insecure woman finding confidence. Or an injured musician finding his way out of blackness.

He took his place at the table as she slid the plate of food in front of him. Funny. His mother had credited him with offering Steven hope, but it had worked both ways. In helping the young boy find meaning, he was finding meaning himself. And in helping Karen build confidence, he was better able to face his own future with assurance and optimism.

As he dug into the food, a new lightness spread through him, lifting his heart and filling it with hope.

Maybe miracles were all around him, every day. But like the man Reverend Richards had spoken about in his sermon, he'd simply been too blind to see them.

17

Karen tucked her music folder into her oversize shoulder bag, squeezed her keys, and turned to Kristen. "Are you sure you don't want to come with me? I'll only be there twenty minutes, and we could stop at Mr. Frank's afterward."

Her daughter drained her glass of milk and made a face. "I told you, Mom. I don't want to go to church on a Saturday."

She was out of ammunition. Cajoling, guilt, a bribe—nothing had worked.

She'd have to lay her cards on the table.

Hugging her music folder to her chest, she took the plunge. "Look . . . I'd really appreciate it if you'd come. I need some honest feedback."

Kristen stopped rinsing her glass and cocked her head. "On what?"

"Scott . . . Mr. Walker . . . asked me to sing a solo at the benefit."

As her daughter's eyes widened, Karen's stomach clenched. "I knew it was a mistake. I'll call and tell him I—"

"No!" Kristen set the glass on the counter, now fully engaged. "I think it's a great idea! I'm just surprised you agreed."

"I haven't. Yet. I'll probably back out. I'm not solo material."

"Yes, you are! I hear you singing around the house sometimes when you think I'm not listening. You should go for it."

"I don't know . . ." She blew out a shaky breath. "Can you imagine what your grandmother will say?"

Kristen rolled her eyes. "She doesn't like anything anybody does. You might as well not try to please her. Did you tell Aunt Val about this?"

"No. Only you. And I haven't sung in front of anyone except Scott. That's why I wanted you to come today. I thought it would give me a chance to see how I do with someone else there."

"Okay. I don't have to meet my friends until after lunch, and besides—I think it's very cool you're going to do this."

"We'll see."

Kristen peppered her with questions as they made the short drive to church, but once they parked and started toward the entrance, she broke off the inquisition. "Listen."

They both stopped. Muted sounds of a simple, classical piano piece floated through the air.

"Isn't that pretty?" The piece was vaguely familiar, but Karen couldn't think of the title.

"Yeah." Kristen picked up the pace again. "Imagine how great Mr. Walker must have played before the accident."

But as they paused inside the door, Karen saw at once that Scott wasn't the pianist. He was standing behind Steven, who was giving the piece in front of him his rapt attention.

She and Kristen held back until he finished, then clapped with enthusiasm.

The young man twisted toward them, his complexion reddening.

"Wow! I heard Scott was giving you lessons, but I had no idea you'd progressed this much." Karen smiled at him as they joined the duo.

"That was great," Kristen echoed.

Steven looked away and straightened the music. "It's just a beginner's piece."

Scott laid a hand on the young man's shoulder. "Pretty soon you'll be passing me up. I never had the natural flair you do for the keyboard."

As Steven's flush went another shade darker, Karen rescued him by changing the subject. "I brought Kristen along as a sample audience."

"Great idea. I hope you can convince your mom to do the solo." Scott flashed her daughter a grin. "I'm afraid my powers of persuasion aren't working very well."

"I already told her to go for it."

"Keep pushing from your end." He gave Kristen a conspiratorial wink. "Steven, I'll see you Tuesday. Do you have a ride home?"

"My mom's going to stop by on her way back from the grocery store. She should be here soon."

"Okay. Then if you two will excuse us, Karen and I have work to do."

Steven pushed away from the keyboard, and as he and Kristen moved off to one corner, Scott focused on her. "I was afraid you'd get cold feet and not show."

His tone was teasing, but his eyes were serious. She lifted her chin a fraction, trying not to be distracted by the way his jeans hugged his lean hips or the impressive biceps beneath the sleeves of his black golf shirt. "I said I'd come, and I always keep my promises."

"I believe that." He gave her a long look, then reached for the music and set it on the stand. After sliding the bench back into position, he took his seat. "Ready?"

"No. But I'm here, so I guess I'll try it. Could you . . . would you sing through it with me once?"

"Sure. Let's do some scales first, to warm up."

They ran through a few vocal exercises, and despite the presence of Kristen and Steven, by the time they moved on to the piece, Karen wasn't nearly as nervous as she'd been the first time she'd sung it.

As the last note died away, Scott gave an approving nod. "Nice. Now try it on your own."

Her nerves spiked, but when she checked out Kristen and Steven, they were involved in an animated conversation, oblivious to the rehearsal.

So much for her audience.

For the next few minutes, Scott played through the piece several times, and with each rendition, her voice grew stronger and more confident. He began to offer suggestions on interpretation and dynamics, and she forgot to be nervous as she concentrated on his instructions.

"Okay. Let's do it once more, and try to focus on all the things we've talked about." Scott flipped back to the first page.

As he began to play, Karen closed her eyes, letting the music filter into her soul as her mind processed and implemented all of his suggestions.

The last notes died away and the church went silent—until the sound of clapping filled it. Karen opened her eyes to find Kristen, Steven, and Scott beaming at her.

"Wow, Mom! I had no idea you could sing like that!" Kristen bounded over.

"Me neither, Mrs. Butler." Steven wheeled up behind her daughter. "You should sing solo stuff more often."

The accolades of the young people were gratifying, but she valued Scott's opinion more. Summoning up her courage, she looked at him. His approving smile told her all she needed to know, but his words were the icing on the cake.

"I second that."

Karen was saved from having to respond by the arrival of Martha Ramsey, but as they all exchanged a few pleasantries, her heart continued to glow.

Only after Martha and Steven disappeared out the door and Kristen spoke to her did she come back to earth. "Are we still going to Mr. Frank's?"

"What's Mr. Frank's?" Scott closed the cover over the piano keys.

"You've been in Washington all summer and you haven't been to Mr. Frank's?" Kristen's eyes widened.

"No. What is it?"

"Just the best frozen custard in the world! Mom, he should come with us."

Her heart skipped a beat. "I've already taken up far too much of his time. We've been here forty minutes."

"Actually, I don't have any solid plans for the rest of the day." Scott leaned against the piano and slid his hands in his pockets.

"Awesome! Come on." Kristen took her mother's hand and hauled her toward the door.

"Give me a minute to lock up and I'll follow you. Is this okay with you, Karen?"

Before she could answer, Kristen chimed in.

"Of course it's okay." Her daughter gave another tug on her arm. "Everybody goes to Mr. Frank's. It's not like it's a date or anything."

Karen shot Kristen a narrow-eyed look. Leave it to her daughter to throw that word in.

Kristen ignored her.

Doing her best not to appear flustered, she answered Scott's question herself. "You're welcome to join us. Mr. Frank's is definitely worth a trip."

"Great. I'll meet you in the lot in just a minute."

She waited until they were outside to confront Kristen. "What was with the date reference?"

Her daughter gave her a look of feigned innocence. "I'm sorry. Did I embarrass you?"

"This has nothing to do with being embarrassed." Not much, anyway. "You know I don't date, and I don't want Scott to think I do."

"Why do you care what he thinks?"

She hit the automatic car lock on her key chain. "Because."

"Because you like him?"

"I'm not discussing this, Kristen." She slid into the car.

Kristen joined her a moment later. "You need to chill, Mom."

She watched as Scott exited and started for his car. "Man, he is one hot dude, even if he's old."

Old?

Karen eyed Scott's lean, muscular physique as he strode toward his car.

Hardly.

Rather than respond, however, she put the car in gear and changed the subject. "You and Steven seemed to hit it off."

"Yeah." Kristen settled back in her seat. "I never talked to him much at school. He was older, and the big football hero and all. Out of my league, you know? But he's cool. He thinks about stuff most kids don't. Heavy stuff. Like, about life and what's important."

She paused, and Karen took a quick peek at her. Kristen's expression was pensive.

"Being stuck in that chair has to be really hard. But he says he figures God must have something better than football in store for him. That's a pretty awesome attitude." Kristen hesitated, playing with the buckle on her seat belt. "He asked me to go to a movie with him."

"How do you feel about that?"

"I told him you don't let me date."

"I'd let you go with Steven. He's a good kid."

Kristen scowled at her. "And Gary isn't?"

Uh-oh. Careful, careful.

"It's just that I've known the Ramseys my whole life, and all of them have solid values. I don't know Gary very well." But enough to suspect he had questionable morals, at best. "Do you want to go with him?"

Thankfully, her daughter let the subject of Gary drop.

"Part of me does, but . . . I mean, I don't know how to relate to a guy who . . . who's in a wheelchair."

"He's the same guy he was before the accident in every way that counts, and I'm sure he'd like to be treated the same."

"But, like, who's supposed to get the popcorn? Usually guys

do that. And how would we get there? He can't drive. And what if he has to, you know, go to the bathroom? I mean, it's kind of awkward."

"That's true—especially for him. He's had to learn to do everything in a new way. But you know what? People cope. They figure it out. They adjust—often through trial and error. The important thing is to keep trying and not to treat every challenge as if it's life or death. If an awkward situation comes up, talk it through. You'll be amazed how a simple conversation can smooth things out."

"Does that mean you think I should go?"

"It's up to you, honey. Go if you enjoy being with Steven—but don't go out of pity. That won't do anyone any good."

"I guess I'll think about it."

Kristen lapsed into silence for the remainder of the drive, but she perked up when they pulled into the parking lot at Mr. Frank's a few minutes later. Hopping out of the car, she waved Scott into a spot farther down. The place was already crowded at eleven in the morning.

"I can vouch for the chocolate chip concrete, but they're all good," Kristen told Scott as he joined them.

"I'll go with your recommendation. Karen, what will you have?"

He started to retrieve his wallet, but she held out a hand to restrain him. "Uh-uh. Your first visit is our treat. Maybe you can find us a seat—although the prospects don't look too good." She scanned the scene. The few scattered benches were already occupied.

"I'll do my best."

By the time Karen and Kristen inched their way through the order line, Kristen had greeted several friends who'd also paid an early visit to the popular spot.

"Can I go talk to Erin while we eat, Mom?"

"Yes, but we're not going to stay long. I have to do some weeding before I go grocery shopping with Val."

"Okay. Wave at me when you're ready to leave."

As Kristen headed for her friends, Karen stepped away from the counter and searched the throng for Scott. To her surprise, he'd found a vacant bench.

Striking off in his direction, she surveyed the crowd as she grew close. "I can't believe you found a seat. This place is always packed."

"I could attribute it to good karma, but you'd discover the truth soon enough." He gestured to the wood plank beside him. A good third of it was covered with tree sap.

Lifting her head, Karen found the source. A large branch had broken off the pine tree above.

"I tried to clean it off, but all I got for my trouble was sticky fingers. We'll have to share this end."

Karen gave the bench a dubious scan. Two months and twenty-two pounds ago, there was no way she'd have fit in the spot reserved for her. Now, she would—but not unless she got cozy with Scott.

Tilting his head, he held out his hand and gave her a quizzical look. "So do I get to sample that before it melts?"

"Sorry." Karen thrust the cup of custard toward him.

He took it from her, hesitated, then moved over as much as he could without falling off the edge. "Join me?"

Wonderful. He'd picked up on her nervousness.

Telling herself to stop acting like an adolescent, Karen perched on the bench, keeping as much distance between them as possible. But unless she wanted to go home with tree sap all over her slacks, she had to sit too close for comfort. Close enough to smell the distinctive musky scent of his aftershave. To see the speck of chocolate that clung to his lips after he took a bite of his custard. To notice the tiny flecks of gold in his dark brown eyes.

"This is great." He took another bite, but his attention was on her, not the custard. "I'll endorse Kristen's recommendation any day."

Was he talking about the custard flavor—or her daughter's suggestion that he join them? Hard to tell from his expression, but for safety's sake, she'd assume it was the former.

"She likes Mr. Frank's a lot. Her dad and I used to bring her here, and they still come here once in a while when they get together."

Frowning, she poked at her custard. That was stretching the truth. Michael had rarely accompanied them on their trips to Mr. Frank's. Was mentioning her ex some sort of a subliminal defensive measure? A way to keep Scott at arm's length while she figured out what role romance might play in her future?

"My mom told me you were divorced. I'm sorry."

She spooned up a bite of custard, hoping the creamy treat would work its usual soothing, comfort-food magic. But when the sweet confection melted on her tongue, it left a bitter aftertaste instead.

The silence lengthened, and Scott spoke again. "I guess I shouldn't have brought that up. I'm sorry."

"It's okay. Separation and divorce are very sad—and very hard, even after a year and a half. I appreciate your empathy." She watched the custard dissolving in her cup.

"Is there any chance you two might get back together?"

"No."

"I guess there are some hurts that can't be overcome."

His gentle, empathetic tone soothed her—and encouraged confidences. Somehow she sensed that this man could be trusted with secrets, that he would respond with understanding and kindness.

Dare she open up a bit about her divorce? About Michael's infidelity?

Brow furrowed, she swirled the tip of her spoon through her custard. Strange. Those subjects had always been too painful—and demeaning—to discuss in depth with anyone. Yet for whatever reason, she wanted to tell this man more. To explain how devastated she had been by her husband's betrayal. To be affirmed in her refusal to agree to a reconciliation.

Maybe he wouldn't want to hear all that garbage, though. Maybe he'd back off if she opened up.

Still . . . she'd taken other risks lately—and been rewarded.

Why stop now?

As Karen stared at the dissolving custard in her cup, Scott debated his next move. She struck him as a very private person who might resent personal questions. Yet he wanted to know what had happened. Wanted to know what kind of idiot would dump such a strong, caring woman for a fling with a coed.

And Karen *was* strong, whether she realized it or not. According to his mother, she'd shouldered the burden of Margaret's demands for years, gone back to work when her husband walked out on her, and was now raising her teenage daughter alone. That took guts. And grit. And determination.

This was another woman who took the lemons life dealt her and made lemonade.

He was still struggling to come up with a diplomatic way to ferret out some information when she surprised him with a tentative, quiet overture.

"My husband and I weren't a good match from the beginning."

He latched on to the opening. "How so?"

She ran her plastic spoon round and round the custard, watching as it left soft trails in its wake. "He was a lot older than me, and I was flattered by his attention. You've met Val. Imagine what it was like growing up in her shadow. She was the popular and pretty sister. The boys never noticed me. So Michael's attention was great for my ego, and my acquiescence was great for his. But that wasn't enough to sustain a marriage. Especially after he . . . strayed. More than once, as I learned not long ago."

Her plastic spoon snapped in two with a loud crack, and she set the almost untouched custard on the bench beside her, folding her hands in her lap.

Scott studied her profile. The sun highlighted the soft auburn strands of her hair as they curved over her high cheekbones. Yet the harsh noonday light was also merciless, drawing attention to the shadows beneath her eyes and the creases at their corners—evidence of long-term stress and fatigue and tension more than age, he suspected.

Out of the blue, an overpowering urge to punch out the man who'd hurt her swept over him.

He frowned. How weird was that, considering he was usually repulsed by violence?

She slanted him a look, reminding him he owed her a response.

"It's hard to forgive a betrayal like that."

The faint parallel grooves on her forehead deepened. "I have to admit I'm still working on that. He's told me he's sorry. Even suggested we give it another try." She lifted her chin. "I'll get to forgiveness eventually, but that doesn't mean I have to put myself back into a bad situation. I'd rather live alone than return to a relationship where I'm not an equal partner."

"Maybe you'll marry again." Scott toyed with his own spoon, watching her.

"I don't know. I've always believed the vows we took before God were for life, no matter what Michael did. But I've been doing some praying about it lately . . . I guess I'll see where that leads."

"I doubt God wants you to spend the rest of your life alone."

"Some people stay single." She studied him. "You've never married, have you? If you don't mind me asking."

"I don't mind." Oddly enough, he didn't, even though he'd never talked much about his personal life with anyone but family. "No, I've never married. I was on the road too much, and I didn't have time for anything but my music. Now that I've been away from it, though, I don't think I could ever go back to that nomadic existence."

"What will you do instead?"

"Good question. I wish I had the answer." Lifting his left hand, he tried to flex the fingers. "A lot depends on this."

"Have you seen any improvement?"

"A little, maybe. Not enough to be noticeable to anyone else."

"Well, despite that liability, you're doing a great job as music director. And you've already demonstrated you can teach music."

"But the saxophone was my main instrument, and performance was my passion."

"Those things may still be in your future. You just have to be patient."

"Reverend Richards gave me the same advice—but patience isn't my strong suit."

"I don't know. You're pretty patient these days with a very mediocre choir. One member in particular."

He looked straight into her eyes. "In that particular area, I don't find it at all difficult to be patient."

"Hey, Mom, I need to get home and change."

As Kristen drew up beside them, Karen moistened her lips and checked her watch. "Wow! I had no idea we'd been here so long. We need to get going."

Kristen examined Scott's empty cup. "Did you like the custard?"

"It was amazing. I think I'll be visiting Mr. Frank's on a regular basis."

"So you're glad you came with us?"

"Absolutely." His gaze flickered to Karen, and an endearing blush crept across her cheeks.

"Cool. Come on, Mom." Without waiting for a response, Kristen started toward the car.

"I guess duty calls." Karen rose and took a step back.

"Yeah. For me too. I need to check out the gym at the Y. I'll see you tomorrow at the service." He reached over and plucked the custard cup from her fingers. "I'll get rid of these."

"Thanks. Well . . . until tomorrow."

Scott remained where he was as she set off for her car. Waited as she backed out. Waved as she disappeared from sight down the road.

But as he slid into his own car and buckled his seat belt, he had a feeling that a certain auburn-haired soprano wasn't going to disappear as quickly from his thoughts.

And that could be dangerous.

Because a woman with unresolved issues about her marital status—and who was also fast making inroads on his heart—could be a recipe for disaster.

18

"I have some good news to report."

Karen glanced at Val as they waited in line at the coffee shop to place their weekly orders. "Tell me. I could use some."

"Mom is doing so well that David has reduced her therapy sessions to once a week. By the time I leave, she should be finished."

"That *is* good news." Karen stepped to the counter and ordered an iced tea.

"What happened to the frappuccino?" Val gave her a quizzical look.

"Can't afford it. I indulged at Mr. Frank's this morning." Not quite true. She'd eaten no more than a few bites of the custard—but her stomach hadn't yet settled down from that cozy huddle on the sappy bench with Scott.

"Mr. Frank's before lunch? That *was* an indulgence."

"To be honest, it was a bribe. For Kristen." Karen tried to tamp down the sudden hammering of her heart. "I needed an audience, and I hoped if I offered her a trip to Mr. Frank's she might give me twenty minutes."

"Okay—now I'm intrigued. Why did you need an audience?"

Karen tried for a nonchalant tone. “Scott—the music director—asked me to sing the solo part in one of the songs the choir is doing at the benefit. He thinks I can do it, but I wanted to get Kristen’s opinion.”

Her sister’s mouth dropped open. “How in the world did he convince you to do that?”

“I haven’t committed yet. I’m reserving the right to change my mind up until the last minute.”

“I think you should go for it.”

The tension in Karen’s shoulders dissolved. “That’s what Kristen said you’d say.”

“I knew my niece was smart.”

As they took their drinks and settled at a small table, Karen played with her straw and sighed. “The thing is, Mom will think I’m nuts.”

“Forget Mom.”

“Also Kristen’s advice—but easier said than done. If I embarrass myself, I’ll have to listen to her ‘I told you so’ routine for months. Or years.”

“Somehow, I don’t think Scott would put you in a position to fail. Do you?”

“Not on purpose. I think he believes I can do it. The problem is me. My confidence level is so low it’s in the negative range.”

“You want my advice? Trust his judgment and stop worrying about what anyone else thinks. Oh, that reminds me . . . have you noticed Mom’s been kind of quiet the past couple of days?”

“I haven’t talked to her much since Wednesday, but *Mom* and *quiet* don’t belong in the same sentence. What’s up?”

“I don’t know. She did tell me she wants to go to the cemetery tomorrow, though. In fact, she wants the three of us to go. Is this some kind of annual ritual for Dad’s birthday or something?”

“No. We often go on the anniversary of his death, but she’s never asked me to take her on his birthday.”

“Interesting.” Val tapped the table, her expression pensive. “She had me stop at Walmart on the way home from therapy Thursday too. I offered to get whatever she wanted, but she told me she had to do this herself. For Dad. Any idea what that was all about?"

Curiouser and curiouser.

"I haven't a clue."

"Hmm. I told her I'd go tomorrow night, after dinner. Can you come?"

"Yeah. I guess." Karen propped her chin in her hand. "I wonder what she's up to?"

Val rolled her eyes. "With Mom, who knows?"

As she pulled to a stop in the deserted cemetery, Karen surveyed the parched grass. Even at seven o'clock in the evening, the mercury hovered near ninety and the humidity was close to 100 percent. Not a leaf was moving, and the limited shade in the small cemetery provided little relief from the relentless sun.

"Mom, it's stifling today. You shouldn't be out in this heat."

"I've seen worse." Margaret grasped the handle and opened the door.

Karen looked over her shoulder at Val, who lifted her hands in a "what can you do?" gesture. "Hold on a minute and we'll help you out."

Margaret waited until Val and Karen were both on her side of the car. With their assistance, she stood on the concrete drive and stepped onto the dried-out turf. Val leaned in for her cane, but Margaret shook her head.

"I don't need that anymore. David said it's all right to walk without it."

"Maybe you could use it on the uneven ground." Karen started to reach for it. With her mother making solid progress toward independence, the last thing they all needed was a sprained or broken ankle.

"I'll hold onto you girls. I'll be fine." She grabbed Karen's arm, but when she reached for Val, the bag from Walmart got in her way.

"I'll hold that for you." Val extended her hand.

After a brief hesitation, Margaret relinquished it and took Val's arm. She nodded to her right. "It's over there."

"I know, Mom." Karen kept a firm grip on her arm as they inched toward the familiar plot. How many solitary trips had she made here in the early years after Dad's death—and continued to make until her life had grown too hectic?

Too many to count.

As they reached the simple stone that bore only their father's name, the date of his death, and a brief paraphrase from Psalms—"My lines have fallen on pleasant places"—Karen's throat tightened. How she still missed him, even after all these years! But he *had* moved on to a more pleasant place. She believed that with her whole heart and soul. And he deserved it, for his life on earth with their mother couldn't have been all that pleasant.

As if reading her mind, Margaret spoke in what, for her, was a subdued tone. "Your father didn't have an easy life, but he loved you girls. And me, far more than I deserved."

Karen's eyes widened, and she exchanged a look with Val. Since when had their mother ever acknowledged her faults?

"Give me the bag, Val." Margaret held out her hand.

In silence, Val handed it over. Despite the significant improvement in her left hand, Margaret struggled to open the top, which she'd clutched into mangled crinkles.

"Can I help?" Karen stepped closer.

"No. I can get it." After working at the crimped plastic a bit more, the top gapped open and Margaret reached in. She withdrew a package of licorice and a safari hat, clutched them to her chest, and moved toward the headstone. Resting one hand on the top for support, she bent down and laid the items on the grave. Then she straightened up and stood in silence.

What in the world . . . ?

A tingle of apprehension raced along Karen's spine, and she glanced at Val. Her sister's shocked expression mirrored her own reaction to their mother's bizarre behavior.

When Margaret turned to them, however, her eyes were alert and lucid. "No, I haven't lost my mind. Though it probably seems so to you." She withdrew a handkerchief from the pocket of her dress and proceeded to pat her face. "It's a hot one, no question about it. Always was on your father's birthday."

She tucked the handkerchief back, steadied herself by resting a hand on top of the headstone, and gestured to the items on the grave. "I guess you're wondering what that's all about—and why I wanted to come here today."

Karen didn't respond. Neither did Val.

"Of course you are." Margaret continued as if she hadn't expected a reply. "And I'm going to tell you. It's a long story, so I'll start with those." She pointed again to the candy and hat on the grave. "Every year, I used to ask your father what he wanted for his birthday, and he always said the same thing. 'How about some licorice, Maggie? Or a safari hat. I always fancied one of those.'" The angular lines of her face softened. "He used to call me that sometimes, you know. Maggie. He was the only one who ever did."

After a few seconds, she coughed and cleared her throat. "Anyway, my answer was always the same. I'd say, 'Licorice will ruin your teeth, Bill. And what in creation would you do with a safari hat?' Then he'd say, 'Maggie, honey, these teeth will last far longer than I will. And if I had a safari hat, I could pretend I was hunting elephants in the wilds of Africa while I cut the grass.'"

She shook her head, but her eyes were filled with a rare warmth and affection. "Your father always did have a fanciful streak, you know." A few beats of silence passed, and when she continued, a hint of regret clung to her words. "I never did get him the licorice or the hat. I didn't think the candy was good for him, and I dismissed the hat as frivolous."

Her expression grew pensive as she examined the items on the grave. "I had a peculiar dream the other night, though. I've never been one to put much stock in dreams, but this one has been on my mind. I saw your father sitting on that old, rusty riding mower he loved. He was eating licorice and wearing a safari hat, and he looked happy. Then he spoke to me. 'It's important to give people the things they need, Maggie. And you still have time to do that.'"

She pulled out her handkerchief again and dabbed at her brow. "I pondered over that for a long while. At first I thought Bill was talking about the candy and that silly hat. But finally, I understood what he meant. He wanted me to tell you girls a story so you would understand why I am the way I am. Why I tend to push people away. Especially the people closest to me."

She tucked the handkerchief back in her pocket. "I know I haven't been the best mother. Or the best wife. I thank God every day that Bill saw the love in my heart, even though I don't always show it in the right way, and that he was willing to take me as I was. His devotion was the greatest blessing I ever received. Followed very closely by you girls."

Her voice caught, and she rested her hand on the headstone again. "I don't really know if that dream was a message from your father, or my conscience having its say at last, but after I prayed about it I decided to share my story with you girls. It's not an easy one to tell, even after all these years, and I'm not going to dress it up or belabor it. The fact is, when I was eleven years old, I was molested by my favorite uncle. My father's brother. A man I loved and trusted and admired. It happened three times. I never told anyone about it. I was too embarrassed and ashamed. Somehow I felt it was my fault."

She swallowed and tightened her grip on the headstone. "Until that happened, I was an outgoing, happy child. But afterward, I shut down. I didn't trust anyone, and I pushed away the people I should have loved the most. It was the only way I knew to protect myself. I was terrified of having my trust violated, of getting hurt again."

Loosening her grip, she stroked the top of the headstone. "The truth is, I'll never know why your father fell in love with me. Why he persevered. I'm just thankful he did. With him, I learned to let my guard down. And after I told him my story, he understood. He was able to see the woman I might have become—and did become, now and then, with him. But habits die hard, and once I had you girls, I reverted to my old ways. Not by choice, mind you; I couldn't help myself. I started doing things to push you away. I still do. The same with other people. It's just how I am."

Margaret refocused on the items resting on the grave. "As I spoke with God about it these past few days, I realized that if the stroke had killed me, I'd have left unfinished business here. I know it's foolish, but I wanted to bring these things to Bill and tell you girls what happened to me so maybe you'll understand why I was never the kind of mother I should have been—and never will be, at this stage of my life, I suspect."

She looked over at her daughters. "I know understanding doesn't change anything, but it might help you make some sense of it. Especially if you know I always loved you, no matter what my actions might have said. As for forgiveness, I leave that to God."

In the silence that followed her story, Margaret's lower lip began to tremble. "I'm ready to go now. And I don't ever want to discuss this again."

As Karen tried to digest her mother's startling story, Margaret sniffed and gave Val a bemused look. "Well, I can't say I've ever seen you speechless." Then she turned to her. "Are we going to stand around here all evening in this heat? The mosquitoes are out already and I'm being eaten alive."

Karen jerked forward and held out her arm. Her sister joined her on the other side.

No one spoke during the slow walk back to the car.

Once behind the wheel, Karen's shaky fingers fumbled with the key as she tried to insert it in the ignition.

What a strange few minutes.

Yet as she put the car in gear and drove away, her throat tightened. Today she'd seen a side of her mother she'd never seen before—and might never see again. She also now understood the events that had shaped her. That might not take away the sting of the hurtful things her mother had said and done through the years or improve their relationship much, but it helped to know Margaret's criticism had nothing to do with Karen herself and everything to do with a little girl who had been hurt and betrayed by someone she'd loved and trusted. A little girl who had been afraid, after that, to ever again let anyone get too close.

Karen checked on Val in the rearview mirror. As if sensing her sister's scrutiny, Val met her gaze. And in her eyes, Karen saw what was in her own heart.

Understanding that mitigated the pain of their rocky mother/daughter relationship.

And gratitude for a final gift from the father they had cherished.

"Karen, could you come in here, please?"

At her boss's summons, Karen surveyed her piled-high desk. Just what she needed—another assignment in the middle of reconciling the monthly department budget.

Stifling a sigh, she spoke into the receiver. "I'll be right there." After dropping the phone back into its cradle, she typed several more numbers into the computer, then grabbed a notebook and pen.

Harold Simmons was seated at his desk. As usual, the sun from the large window behind him bounced off his shiny bald head, reminding her of the silver reflecting ball in her father's rose garden.

But under his intent, no-nonsense scrutiny, those capricious thoughts disappeared as fast as the startled deer she'd seen by the side of the road a few days ago.

He began spitting out rapid-fire instructions almost before she cleared the threshold. "We got approval for a new position. An entry-level financial analyst. I need you to put together a job description based on comparable positions in the industry, along with a list of internal candidates for me to consider. As soon as possible."

Translation: by the end of the day. Two hours from now. Meaning she'd have to work late to finish the budget.

Her hopes for a quiet evening at home evaporated.

"Okay. I'll get on it right away."

Back at her desk, she put aside the budget work and focused on Harold's project. On the positive side, she'd been around long enough to establish contacts in human resources, compensation, and staffing who could provide the information she needed.

By ten minutes to five, she was putting the finishing touches on the report.

After proofing the job description, Karen gave the list of candidates a final scan. With a satisfied nod, she gathered up the material, started to stand—and froze.

Wait a minute.

She could do this job . . . couldn't she?

Yes.

She knew the company and the industry. Plus, since her promotion to administrative assistant eight months ago, she'd taken on responsibility for a significant amount of budget work and analysis.

It was a perfect fit—and this job would move her into the professional ranks, offer more perks, and pay a higher salary.

But did she have the nerve to apply for it?

She sat back down.

A few weeks ago, she'd have said no—but she wasn't the same person she'd been a few weeks ago. Thanks to Val and Scott's pushing and prodding, she was learning to take control of her own life. To stop worrying about pleasing other people or seeking anyone's approval. To reach higher than she'd ever dreamed.

Because as Scott had pointed out a few days ago, sometimes the biggest successes come when we take a chance.

Squaring her shoulders, Karen reopened the document of

candidates and added her name to the bottom of the list. Hesitated. Moved it to the top.

Five minutes later she marched into Harold's office and handed him the material. She might not get the job, but at least she'd put herself in the running.

And that, in itself, was a huge step forward.

Tapping a finger against the steering wheel, Karen checked her watch as she waited at yet another red light. Kristen would be starving by the time she fixed dinner, but what could she do? Her boss didn't care if his special project had thrown off her schedule; the budget work still had to get done. And she couldn't renege on her promise to Reverend Richards that she'd pick up the proof for the flier about the benefit on her way home.

Praying no cops were lying in wait to fulfill their ticket quotas on this Monday night, she pressed harder on the accelerator and zipped through several yellow lights.

Once in the church lot, she grabbed her purse and half jogged toward the door, scanning the portico for the envelope the minister had promised to leave if she was late.

Nothing.

Had he tucked it against the wall, behind one of the overflowing pots of petunias, to protect it from the gathering storm clouds?

As she ran up the stairs, the muffled but plaintive wail of a saxophone seeped through the thick, wooden front door, and she came to an abrupt halt.

It had to be Scott.

Errand forgotten, she moved closer and cracked the door. He was playing some sort of bluesy number she'd never heard, so raw with emotion a shiver snaked down her spine. Though she heard a few fumbled notes, the rendition was powerful, imbued with such anguish and loss and pain she felt as if she was reading a diary.

As the last notes died away, she drew an unsteady breath and pushed the door open. A shaft of light from the descending sun darted inside, illuminating the man standing in the sanctuary and bathing the interior in a golden glow.

She could manage only one word. "Wow."

Slowly Scott lowered the saxophone. "I didn't know I had an audience." Unlike the first time she'd appeared without warning, however, he sounded shaky rather than angry or accusatory.

"I didn't think you played the sax anymore."

"This is the first time since . . . since before the accident. It wasn't very good."

"I heard a few wrong notes, if that's what you mean, but the power of the music . . . the way you play . . . the emotion . . ." She shook her head as words failed her. "You have an incredible gift."

His color was high as he stroked the polished brass instrument with an almost reverent touch. "I never thought I'd pick this up again."

"Why did you?"

"Because of what happened yesterday after services. I stayed around to go through some music, and Steven came over to ask if I'd help him with a problem spot in one of the pieces he's practicing for the benefit. It's a tricky area, and instead of explaining the correct fingering, I decided to show him. As I played, I realized . . ." His voice rasped, and he cleared his throat. "My fingers were responding. Not perfectly, but there was enough improvement that I decided to pull the sax out of the mothballs."

"That's wonderful!" She moved closer and touched his arm.

He looked down at her fingers, and his Adam's apple bobbed. Seconds ticked by, the quiet broken only by a distant rumble of thunder. She told herself to pull back. Step away. Play it safe.

But before she could follow through, he laid his hand over hers and lifted his gaze.

She stopped breathing.

Something as compelling and powerful as the music he'd just played began to pulsate between them.

He lifted his free hand toward her, and her knees began to wobble. "Karen, I . . ."

"Scott? Is that you in here?"

At Reverend Richards's question, she gasped and jerked back. Scott dropped his hand at once, but she caught a glimpse of regret as he turned toward the door the minister had cracked open.

"Yeah. It's me." His words came out husky and ragged.

The man pushed through and crossed toward them. "I saw the lights. I didn't know you'd be here today. Karen, I have the proofs for you. I hope I didn't keep you waiting."

"No." Her assurance was little more than a croak. She swallowed and tried again. "I just got here."

"Great. I meant to walk these over here sooner, but things got hectic in the office." He spoke to Scott as he handed her the envelope. "What brings you here on a Monday evening?"

"I was, uh, working on some music."

The minister smiled. "Don't overdo it, okay? We don't pay you *that* much." He consulted his watch and shook his head. "Late for dinner again. Thank goodness I have a patient wife. I'll see you two Sunday."

As he started toward the door, Karen jerked forward and fell in behind him. "I-I need to go too. Kristen is waiting for dinner, and she isn't quite as patient as your wife."

At the door, the man spoke over his shoulder to Scott. "Will you lock up on your way out?"

"Sure."

Karen didn't want to look back—but she couldn't stop herself.

Scott was standing where she'd left him, watching her.

The sharp zing of electricity that zipped through her had nothing to do with the supercharged air of the approaching storm.

He took a step toward her.

Heart pounding, she stumbled toward the door and almost ran to her car.

And as she slid behind the wheel, one thing became clear to her.

In a perfect world, she might be able to put off decisions about romance until life slowed down and she had more time to think.

But her world wasn't perfect.

And she'd just run out of time.

19

Tuning out the conversation around her in the therapy center waiting room, Val tried to focus on the new suspense novel that had been garnering accolades. The praise was well deserved. The book had an excellent plot. Strong characterizations. Fast-paced action.

But it wasn't holding her interest—thanks to the drama in her own life.

With a resigned sigh, she closed the book and leaned her head back against the wall. In less than three weeks she'd be returning to Chicago, her quest for resolution and redemption a bust.

Still, there were some positive outcomes from her trip. She and Karen had become the sisters—and friends—they'd never been in their younger days. And Margaret's startling revelation had explained—if not justified—a lot about her behavior through the years.

As for David . . .

She closed her eyes.

How did you deal with a man who was tempting you to break every rule about relationships you'd followed for eighteen years?

But somehow she had to find the strength to do the right thing.

And she was trying. Hard. Maybe her evasion tactics were spineless, but they were working—more or less. Too bad Margaret had asked her to wait around today in case she was done early. Otherwise, she'd have dropped her off and ducked back just in time to pick her up, as she'd done the last couple of times.

The door to the treatment rooms opened, and she glanced up to find David on the threshold, holding two disposable cups.

He lifted one. "Can I tempt you?"

What a question.

Without waiting for a response, he crossed the room and dropped into the chair beside her. Other than an elderly man engrossed in a fishing magazine, they had the place to themselves.

"I haven't seen much of you lately." David handed her one of the cups.

"I've been at church."

"But you disappear before I can say hello. And you stopped staying for therapy sessions."

"I've been busy." She took a gulp of coffee. It burned her mouth.

"Victoria asks about you."

Val forced herself to meet his gaze. "I'll be leaving in three weeks. It's best if I don't see her. She might get attached, and she's had too much loss in her life already."

"I had a feeling that might be your reasoning—and I agree that it's very tough for people of any age to lose someone they care about." He took a slow sip of his coffee. "I heard there's an opening at the high school here for a drama and speech teacher. Someone with your qualifications would be a shoo-in."

It took a second for his implication to sink in.

When it did, her heart stuttered.

Oh. My. Word.

He wanted her to stay. To start a new life in Washington and become part of his and Victoria's.

Reminding herself to keep breathing, she gripped her cup with both hands. Not once since the day she'd left for college had she considered coming back to Washington to live. The very notion had been anathema.

It wasn't anymore, thanks to a sister she'd befriended and a man who was offering a tantalizing glimpse of a future she'd thought she could never have.

Except there wasn't any future with David. As kind and good as he was, he'd never be able to accept what she'd done. Not with his special interest in the pro-life cause. Not when he was working even now, through the church benefit, to help save the lives of unborn babies.

She might as well face the hard truth.

Staying in Washington wasn't any more of an option now than it had been the day she left for college.

When the silence lengthened, David spoke again. "Victoria would be happy if you stayed. I would be too."

She shook her head, blinking back the sting of tears. "It wouldn't work."

"How do you know if you don't give it a chance?"

"Trust me. I know."

The interior door opened, and the older man laid his fishing magazine aside in response to a summons from his therapist. Once he disappeared inside, David set down his coffee cup, took hers from her fingers—and before she realized his intent—enfolded her cold hands in his warm, comforting clasp.

Her lungs short-circuited.

Pull away! Now, before it's too late!

But she didn't.

"You must have realized by now that I think you're a very special woman, Val." His voice and expression were as serious as she'd ever seen them. "And I know you've felt the connection between us. I've seen it in your face. I also know there are some issues we'd need to work through if things got serious. Trust me, I've wrestled mightily with the ones on my side during many a sleepless night and some lengthy conversations with God. But I've come to believe we ought to explore this."

"David, I . . ."

He held up a hand. "Let me finish, okay? I'm not a speech-making kind of guy, so this isn't real easy for me."

She closed her mouth.

"I know you didn't come home this summer to find romance. I didn't move to Washington for that reason, either, but that's how things work sometimes. When we least expect it, someone walks into our life who may be destined to change it—or become part of it. I don't know if that's what will happen with us, but I'd like to find out. Will you do me a favor and consider the job for a few days before you make a decision?"

Don't build up his hopes—or yours. Just say no. End it now.

When she opened her mouth, however, different words came out. "I guess I can . . . think about it." At least she had the presence of mind to tack on a warning. "But I'm not making any promises."

"That's good enough for now." He smiled and squeezed her hands. "Margaret should be finishing up. I need to get back."

He stood, surprising her again by leaning down to brush his lips across her forehead in a whisper-soft kiss. "See you soon."

And then he was gone.

Yet he left behind the faint whisper of something she hadn't felt in a long while—and yearned to embrace.

Hope.

But did she dare?

Harold Simmons steepled his fingers as Karen stepped into his office. "Tell me why you think you can do this job better than the other candidates on the list."

She blinked, trying to regroup. She'd only given him the description for the new job and the list of candidates two days ago. When had he ever responded this fast to *anything*?

"You seem surprised by the question." He pinned her with one of the intimidating looks he usually reserved for his managers.

Okay. She'd watched him play this game numerous times. He called in a manager. Threw an unexpected question at him or her. Watched their response. Those who buckled under the pressure, who hemmed and hawed or got flustered, were toast career-wise.

She didn't intend to be one of them.

Settling into one of the chairs across from his desk, she rested her hands loosely on the arms, keeping her posture open rather than defensive. "I'm surprised by the timing, not the question. I just gave you the report Monday night and you were out of town yesterday."

"Things move fast in the business world—and they'll move faster in the new position we're creating. I need someone who has strong technical skills and can juggle multiple responsibilities."

"In that case, I'm a perfect fit. I have a business degree, with an emphasis in finance. In my present job, I handle all the budget duties for this department. As you know, that includes not only reconciliation but analysis and planning, not to mention my work on the month-end closings. I do all that as well as a multitude of other tasks. I've never missed a deadline, and my work is always accurate.

"As for juggling multiple responsibilities . . . my personal life is also a good example of that. In addition to my career here, with its often extended hours, I'm raising a teenage daughter alone. I'm active in my church, and I've been the primary caregiver for my elderly mother for many years. I'm an expert at multitasking."

There was silence while Harold digested her speech, and Karen held her breath. She'd recited her qualifications and accomplishments in a confident, concise manner, highlighting her strengths without exaggeration or bragging. Truth be told, she'd impressed even herself with her assertiveness and her credentials.

As Harold studied her, she caught a speculative gleam in his eyes—and a glint of admiration. Then he leaned forward and drew a stack of reports toward him, signaling the end of their meeting. "Give me a copy of your resume. We'll talk again later."

Not until she was back at her desk did she realize her legs were trembling.

But on the inside she felt rock solid.

Too bad Val wasn't around. It was definitely high-five time.

"Okay. Let's work on the second benefit piece. I've asked Karen to try the solo section. Karen, I'll sing through it with you the first time."

A wave of panic crashed over her as the other choir members sent curious glances her way. Her last rehearsal with Scott had gone well, and she'd thought she was ready for her solo debut in front of the choir.

Not anymore. Fear clogged her throat, and she doubted she'd be able to get out more than a croak.

"Ready, Karen?"

She refocused on Scott. His eyes were encouraging, his message clear.

You can do this. And I'll be there with you until you feel ready to sing it alone.

Taking a deep breath, she gave a slight nod.

The first run-through was rough. The second was better. When he dropped out on the third, she faltered but kept going. And with each successive repetition, her voice grew stronger.

At last Scott closed his music and stood. "That was great." His gaze swept the group . . . but lingered on her. "I think the audience will be impressed by this piece. I'll see you all on Sunday, and be careful going home. If this rain keeps up, we'll need to start building an ark."

His comment was met with chuckles, followed by the rustle of paper as the choir members tucked away their music. A number of them stopped to compliment Karen as she gathered up her own music, and by the time the place emptied, she was floating on a buoyant sea of praise.

"See? I told you that you're good."

At Scott's comment, she turned. He was leaning against the piano, ankles crossed, arms folded across his chest.

"I guess I'm not bad, anyway."

Instead of responding, he pushed away and strolled toward her, sliding his hands into his pockets. "It doesn't take much to make you happy, does it? A few compliments, and you're glowing."

"Actually, it's more than that. I got a promotion today at work too." She'd been bursting to tell someone ever since Harold had called her into his office at five o'clock, but Kristen was in St. Louis spending the night with her dad and Val wasn't answering her cell phone.

"No wonder you look so happy. It seems to me a celebration is in order. I'd suggest Mr. Frank's, but the weather isn't exactly conducive to sap-covered benches. How about dessert at that restaurant down by the river near the train station?"

She knew the one he meant. It was a special-occasion kind of place—meaning she hadn't gone there often. But if a new job and successful solo debut didn't merit a trip there, nothing did.

"That would be nice. Thank you."

His smile broadened. "Great. We can take my car."

Alone with Scott in his car. In a rainstorm. Insulated from the world, with lots of electricity flying.

Not the best idea.

She needed to get her act together on the romance front before she took that kind of risk.

"Actually, it will be closer for me to go home from there than to come all the way back here to get my car." She kept her tone matter-of-fact. "Why don't I meet you?"

He acceded with a nod. "Okay. I'll see you there."

Fifteen minutes later, as she dashed in from the rain, he was waiting inside the door.

"What a downpour!" She closed her umbrella and shook it out.

"But we won't let it dampen our party." He took her arm and guided her between the tables as they followed the hostess.

His touch was polite, nothing more—but still, a little tingle ran up her spine.

Once they were seated at a candlelit table, a server arrived to take their order.

Scott perused the menu. "What would you like?"

"They have a fantastic green apple cobbler here, with a wonderful sauce. It's totally decadent—but I'm not inclined to worry too much about calories tonight."

"You don't look as if you need to worry about them, period."

"That's because I do—and some days it's a struggle." Yet all at once, the forfeited Fritos and denied desserts didn't seem such a big sacrifice.

"Two green apple cobblers." Scott handed their menus to the waitress.

"Good choice. That's our house specialty." The waitress noted the order on her pad. "But I have to warn you, they're baked fresh. It's about a thirty-minute wait."

Scott looked at Karen. "I don't mind if you don't."

"I'm game."

As the waitress headed back to the kitchen, Karen shook her head. "I'll pay for this late night tomorrow—but rules were made to be broken, right?"

"Throwing caution to the wind, are we?"

"I'm too practical for that. But every now and then I go a little wild."

His lips twitched. "Staying up late and eating a fattening dessert hardly qualify as wild."

"They do for me."

He tilted his head, studying her. "Are you saying you've led a sheltered life?"

"Quiet might be a better word."

"Is that bad?"

"It is when you let people walk all over you."

"You don't strike me as that kind of woman."

Nice to hear.

She rested her elbows on the table and linked her fingers. "I'm not anymore. But for most of my life, my decisions were designed to please other people. My mother. My husband. My daughter. My friends. I'm learning, though, that there's a fine line between selfishness and self-esteem. It took me a lot of years to recognize that my value isn't based on my ability to meet the expectations of other people."

"Sounds like a healthy attitude to me. Now tell me how the new job came about."

She gave him the details, answering his occasional questions, and finished with a shake of her head. "To be honest, I'm still in shock at how things worked out."

"Why?"

"I didn't know I had it in me to be that assertive. But I've learned a lot from Val this summer. She's always been confident and self-assured, and she never lets other people dictate how she behaves. I wish I'd followed her example years ago."

"Personally, I like a woman who knows what she wants and goes after it."

At his slow, intimate smile, she changed the subject. "All we've done is talk about me. What about you? Tell me how it's been going with Steven."

He took her cue, and they were still chatting about his pupil when the waitress delivered their desserts.

"That looks great." Scott eyed the cobbler and wasted no time picking up his fork.

"It is." She dug into her own dessert. "So have you given any more thought to where you'll go from here? Especially now that you're playing the sax again."

"Believe it or not, I'm toying with the idea of staying in Washington."

Her spoon froze halfway to her mouth. "Are you serious?"

"Why not? It's a nice town, and St. Louis is a manageable commute for occasional performance gigs. I've also discovered I like teaching. There might be enough work here to keep me busy. What do you think?"

She lowered her spoon to the ramekin and made a pretense of scraping out some of the crust.

This was more than a discussion about locales.

Scott was asking her if she wanted him to stay, telling her he was interested.

And she was.

She knew that in her heart even if her mind hadn't yet come to grips with it.

Pulse accelerating, she gave him a steady look. "That sounds like a reasonable plan."

He searched her eyes, then sent her a smile so warm it curled her toes. "I'll have to give it serious consideration, then."

After that, their conversation moved on to less personal topics, and their parting when he walked her to her car was friendly, nothing more.

But as they said their good-byes in the fresh, rain-washed air; as he took her hand in his firm clasp and gave it a gentle squeeze; as a star peeked through the dispersing clouds to twinkle down on them; she knew much had changed this night.

And what had started out as an ordinary day was ending with extraordinary possibilities she'd never even dreamed of a few short weeks ago.

20

"Hi, Mom! I'm home."

At the upbeat greeting, Karen wiped her hands on a dish towel and headed for the foyer. Kristen must have had fun with her father on her two-day visit to St. Louis. A visit enhanced, no doubt, by Stephanie's absence.

To her surprise, Michael had followed Kristen in.

"I can take that, Dad. I'm fully mobile again." She shook her cast-free leg as she reached for her overnight bag. "Thanks again." Standing on tiptoe, she kissed his cheek.

"I'll call you soon, sweetie, and we'll schedule another visit before school starts." He gave her a longer-than-usual hug.

"Cool." She bounced over to Karen and planted a quick kiss on her cheek too. "Anything new?"

"Erin and Steven called this morning when they couldn't get you on your cell."

She made a face. "The battery died. I forgot to recharge it last night."

"Well, they both sounded anxious to talk with you. I left the messages in your room. Do you want some dinner?"

"Nope. We got a burger on the way home. See you later, Dad." With a quick wave, she disappeared down the hall.

Karen smiled after her. "I'd say she enjoyed her visit."

"She's a bundle of energy, no question about that. I'm worn out."

Turning back, she took a closer look at him. He did look tired. There were dark smudges under his eyes, and grooves of weariness radiated from their corners. He'd lost weight too. His custom-tailored clothes, always impeccably fitted, hung too loose on his frame.

His breakup with Stephanie must be taking a serious toll.

He shoved his hands into his pockets. "How about having that cup of coffee we never got around to on my last visit?"

She folded her arms over her chest. "I don't see the point. We finished that discussion."

"This is a different subject. And it affects Kristen."

At his serious tone, Karen frowned and checked her watch. "I need to be at church in less than an hour for a meeting."

"We'll be done long before that."

A tête-à-tête with her ex hadn't been on her agenda, but if it involved Kristen . . .

"Okay. I'll put the pot on."

"Not here. Let's run down to the diner. You can go to church from there. I'd rather discuss this in private." He inclined his head toward Kristen's room.

A flutter of unease rippled through her. "What's wrong?"

"Let's talk about it over coffee."

She wanted to press, but the firm set of his mouth told her that would be fruitless.

"Okay. I'll meet you there."

In the ten minutes it took to gather up her purse, run a brush through her hair, and drive to the diner, her concern escalated. What could Michael have to tell her that affected Kristen? Her daughter had seemed happy and carefree when she arrived home—but had something worrisome happened during the father-daughter visit?

By the time she joined him and slid into the opposite side of the booth, she was in no mood for small talk. "What's this all about, Michael?"

"I had some bad news about a week ago." He pushed a mug of steaming coffee toward her and gripped his own. "I'm struggling with how to tell Kristen and thinking maybe we should do it together."

"What kind of news?"

"I have pancreatic cancer. Advanced and inoperable."

She stared at him, seconds ticking by in silence while she wrestled with his news, the buzz of conversation in the diner receding into the background.

Michael was dying?

It didn't compute.

"Is this . . . confirmed?"

"I got a second opinion."

She took a deep breath. Tried to process his announcement. "I'm sorry." Even as she uttered the words, they sounded lame.

"Yeah. Me too." He gave a brief, mirthless laugh. "So much for all those hours I spent at the gym, trying to stay healthy." He wiped a hand down his face. "But my main concern now is Kristen."

Kristen.

Karen's throat tightened. "She'll be devastated."

"That's why I wanted to talk to you about it first. See how you thought we should handle telling her."

"I . . . I don't know. I'll have to think about it."

"It can't wait too long, Karen. They're only giving me six months. At best."

She swallowed. "That fast?"

"Yes."

"There's no treatment?"

"Nothing that will extend my life by any appreciable amount. I'll stay independent for as long as I can, but I expect at the end I'll have to go to a hospice."

Hospice.

Michael.

That concept was almost harder to grasp. With his strict diet and exercise regime, she'd expected him to live into his eighties, as his own father had.

"That prognosis brings me to a favor I'd like to ask. I don't want an answer tonight. Pray for guidance, if you want to, but please consider it." He took a sip of coffee. Some of it sloshed out, and using both hands to steady the mug he set it carefully back on the table.

"I'll just cut to the chase. I have no real family to help me get through this, as you know. Just that distant cousin in California, and we don't keep in touch. So I need someone to see that things are done properly when I'm no longer able to make decisions on my own. Someone with good values, who can temper compassion with practicality." He paused. "Someone like you."

She gaped at him. After all that had happened between them, he'd ask her to take on a chore like this, with all its attendant responsibilities and demands?

What was he thinking?

Yet . . . how often had she talked about the importance of compassion to Kristen? Wouldn't helping the father her daughter loved in his greatest hour of need demonstrate a practical application of that virtue? And maybe her willingness to assist might help her daughter get through what was sure to be a profound trauma.

"I don't expect an answer tonight." Michael leaned forward. "All I ask is that you consider it. Please."

She wrapped her hands around her mug, letting the warmth seep into her cold fingers. "All right. I'll think it over."

The tension in his features slackened. "Thank you." He moved his mug aside and rested his hands on the table. "I also want you to know I've been thinking a lot about our last conversation—and about our marriage. You were right. I was the one who had a good thing. I'm sorry I never treated you as a partner. I'm also sorry I mocked your religion. In all honesty, I wish I had your faith now. It must be comforting to believe there's a higher power in control and a greater purpose than we can often discern to the events of our lives. I realize it's too little, too late, but I want you to know I'm truly sorry for all my mistakes."

"I appreciate that. And I'll let you know my answer in a day or two."

"Thank you." He glanced at his watch, took a final swallow of his coffee, and reached for the check. "You need to get to church. Go ahead. I'll flag the waitress down."

With a nod, Karen slid from the booth and exited the diner.

Reeling.

Michael was dying—and he wanted her to be there for him through all the minutia of his disease . . . and his death.

Selfish or not, her inclination was to refuse.

But she had to think about Kristen. While the divorce had been hard on her, Michael had remained part of her life. This separation would be final—and Kristen's world would once more be turned upside down. No matter her personal feelings, she had to factor in the effect of her decision on her daughter.

Because despite what she'd told Scott about learning to consider her own interests, this time Kristen came first.

Karen kept the news about Michael to herself until her Saturday coffee date with Val. And when she shared it, her sister's stunned expression mirrored her own reaction.

"But he's only . . . what? Fifty-one? That's way too young to die. I may not be Michael's biggest fan, but this is rotten."

"I know." The coffee grinder behind the counter echoed the churning in her stomach.

"Does Kristen know yet?"

"No. Michael and I talked on Thursday night about how to tell her. We decided to think about it for a few days."

"It'll be tough, no matter how you do it."

"Tough" was a perfect description for her next revelation too—but she needed to talk it through with someone. "He also asked me for a favor."

"He isn't pushing you to get back together, is he?" Val's eyes narrowed. "Sort of a dying man's wish and all that?"

"Not in the way you mean. But he's alone, and he asked me to take care of his affairs when he . . . after he can't do it for himself anymore."

Val snorted and shook her head. "He's got nerve, I'll give him that."

She gripped her cup tighter. "The thing is, I'm thinking of saying yes."

Her sister's eyes widened. "You can't be serious."

"Yes, I am."

"But why? After what he did to you, you don't owe him a thing."

"Maybe not, but Kristen loves him, and the next few months will be difficult enough for her. It might help if I put my animosity aside and give her an example of Christian love and charity in action. Let her know I've accepted her father's apology and forgiven him."

"Have you?"

"I've accepted his apology. I'm still working on the forgiveness part—but I'll get there."

For a few seconds, Val studied her. Then she shook her head. "All I can say is you're a far better person than I would be in the same circumstances."

"What would you do?"

"Tell the bum to get lost."

A smile flickered on her lips. "Don't hold anything back. Tell me how you *really* feel."

"Sorry. I don't mean to be heartless. But he doesn't deserve your compassion—or the sacrifices you'll have to make."

"We didn't either, when the Lord came to offer us salvation and redemption. He did it out of selfless love. That's the example I'm trying to follow."

"A hard argument to counter." Val leaned closer. "Listen, do what you need to, okay? And don't worry about what anyone else thinks. Talk to Reverend Richards about it, if you think that will help. He strikes me as a man who has his head on straight."

"He does—and that's not a bad idea." She sipped her drink. "And since we're on a church-related topic . . . I'm glad you started coming to services with us."

Val made a dismissive gesture. "I don't have anything else to do on Sunday mornings."

"Is that the only reason?"

Her sister swiped at a stray drop of caramel on the table. "There might be one or two others."

"Hmm." Karen leaned back and pretended to consider that. "David's in the congregation. Could he be one of them?"

"That wouldn't be a very noble reason to go to church, would it?"

"You're avoiding the question."

"Uh-huh."

Karen grinned. "Well, whatever the reason—or reasons—I know God is glad you've rejoined the fold."

"I'll probably return to my old ways once I'm back in Chicago."

"Oh, I don't know. You might be surprised. Maybe your visit to Washington will have a longer-lasting impact than you think."

A beat of silence passed between them, charged with some taut emotion Karen couldn't identify. It lasted only an instant before Val picked up her drink and redirected the conversation to their mother's progress, but Karen sensed her comment had touched a nerve.

Something was going on with her sister.

Margaret's illness might have been the catalyst for the return of the prodigal daughter, but was there more to Val's homecoming? After all, she'd disappeared several times without explanation and returned shaken. Cut off discussions about her love life. Started attending church again.

Why?

Karen hadn't a clue.

And unless their growing friendship took a quantum leap in the next couple of weeks, she had a feeling Val would return to Chicago leaving that mystery unsolved.

Beads of sweat formed on Karen's forehead as she crossed the lawn toward the church offices, and she swiped them away with her fingertips. Amazing. It was seven o'clock in the evening, and the sun had already dipped behind the tall trees, but the temperature still hovered somewhere between bake and broil.

She shook her head. It was going to be a long, hot August.

As she stepped under the overhang by the front door, a tiny warm breeze wafted her way. Better—but not much.

To her surprise, the door to the reception area opened and Reverend Richards stuck his head out.

"I spotted you crossing the lawn. Seeking refuge from the heat?"

"Returning the proof of the flier for the benefit. We need to get this printed and distributed to the participating churches ASAP." She waved a manila envelope at him.

"Then come in, by all means."

She entered and set it on the receptionist's desk. "I didn't expect to find anyone here on a Saturday night. I was just going to drop it through the mail slot."

"I thought I'd put a few finishing touches on tomorrow's sermon. Plus, the ladies' guild is meeting at our house tonight."

"Aha. I'm not the only refugee."

"Guilty as charged. How's your mom doing?"

"Improving every day."

"And Kristen?"

Recalling Val's suggestion from earlier in the day, she frowned.

"You look like a woman with something on her mind. Could you use a friendly ear?"

She sent him a small smile. "You have a sermon to polish."

"It's probably as good as it's going to get."

"Well . . . if you're sure you have the time."

He stepped back and motioned her in. "The ladies' guild meeting won't be over for two hours. I have plenty of time."

"In that case . . ." She took a seat in his adjacent office. "It's about Michael."

He claimed the chair beside her. "More problems?"

"Not the kind we've discussed before." Thank goodness she'd sought his guidance in the months before her separation. Since he was fully briefed, she could launch straight into the latest chapter, including Michael's apology and his request.

When she finished, the minister leaned forward and clasped his hands between his knees. "It sounds like you've already given this a lot of serious thought."

"I have. And I've prayed too. I realize his repentance may be driven by the fact that he needs me, but I have a sense his remorse is real. My conscience is prodding me to take the high road and do the charitable thing for Kristen's sake, if nothing else, but I'd like a second opinion."

"If you've already spoken to God, you don't need me."

"Your voice is easier to hear."

He smiled. "I've heard that line before. And I agree it can be difficult at times to discern God's voice—even for ministers." Then his expression grew more serious. "But you've done all the right things. You've prayed, given the request careful consideration, and come to a decision that feels right. I can't do anything for you that you haven't already done, except to say I admire your generous spirit and compassion, and that I think the Lord would be pleased by such an unselfish example of the charity and brotherly love he preached."

The knot in Karen's stomach loosened. "Thank you."

"Shall we join our hearts in prayer for a moment?"

"I'd like that."

He bowed his head, and she followed his lead. "Lord, we ask you to guide your daughter as she embarks on a difficult journey. Give her the grace and strength she'll need in the months ahead. Grant her wisdom and sound judgment as she faces hard decisions, and give her abundant blessings as she seeks to follow the example you set when you came to save—and to serve. Amen."

When Karen looked up, the minister touched her hand. "God go with you. I'll keep you in my prayers."

"Thank you."

And when she stepped out moments later to find the sky had transitioned from blue to gray, she suspected she would need every prayer said on her behalf.

21

"Val! Can I talk to you for a minute?"

At the summons, Val looked over her shoulder at Karen, who was still putting away her music in the choir section as the congregation dispersed.

"Sure. Give me a sec." She refocused on Kristen. "Pick a day and we'll have lunch before I go back to Chicago."

"Cool."

After giving her niece a hug, Val joined her sister. "What's up?"

"Reverend Richards asked me to review the program for the benefit." Karen waved a folded sheet of paper in front of her. "And I need to add your name if you're going to participate. Did you ever decide about the emcee thing?"

No. She'd been waiting for direction that had never come.

"Tell me again what I'd need to do." At best, the stall tactic would buy her sixty seconds.

Pointing out the items in the program as she spoke, Karen recited the duties. "You'd do the welcome and introduce the different entertainers listed here. There will also be a few closing remarks.

You know, thank-you-for-coming-and-we-appreciate-your-support kind of stuff. Very simple."

It did sound straightforward—and innocuous. Plus it was for a worthy cause. She should be able to handle it.

"Okay. Count me in." Leaning closer, she examined the lineup of entertainment, zeroing in on the listing for the church choir. "Look at that. 'Karen Butler, soloist.'"

Karen wrinkled her nose. "I may take that out. I want to keep my options open until the last minute. I'm still freaked out by the notion of singing in front of hundreds of people."

"Who's singing in front of hundreds of people?"

As Margaret came up beside them, Val took one look at Karen's dismayed face and jumped in. "Scott asked Karen to sing a solo at the benefit. We were checking out her name in the program proof."

Much to Val's surprise, her mother simply compressed her lips, as if she was physically curbing a derogatory comment.

She glanced at Karen, who raised her eyebrows. Margaret's restraint might be short-lived, but she was grateful her better nature had prevailed today. Karen didn't need anyone undermining her shaky confidence this close to the show.

As Margaret walked away to chat with some friends, Karen stepped closer. "At least she's trying. It kind of makes you think anything is possible, doesn't it?"

Val bent her head and rummaged through her purse for her keys.

If only that were true.

But her stay in Washington was drawing to a close, and short of a miracle, she had a feeling the liberating redemption she'd journeyed home to find would remain elusive after all.

A bowl of trifle in hand, Karen paused by the back door, heart aching.

Kristen sat hunched in an Adirondack chair, arms hugging her drawn-up knees, staring into the distance. In the two days since she and Michael had told Kristen the bad news, her daughter had ignored her friends, nibbled at her food, and lost her color. Karen hadn't seen her cry—but there'd been plenty of tears behind the closed door of her room, based on her puffy eyes.

She opened the sliding door. "Can I interest you in some dessert? I made that trifle you like from the recipe Val gave me."

Even in profile, her daughter's face was a study in misery. "I'm not hungry."

After a brief hesitation, Karen set the trifle on the counter and exited onto the deck. So far, Kristen hadn't accepted any of her overtures to talk—but she intended to keep making them.

"Do you mind if I sit with you for a few minutes? It's a nice evening."

A shrug was Kristen's only response.

Karen lowered herself into the matching chair beside her daughter and let her head rest against the back. The evening was cool—for August—and the muted drone of the cicadas provided a pleasant backdrop to the song of the birds as they prepared to roost for the night. A hawk circled overhead, soaring without effort in the cloudless sky, letting the wind lift it higher and higher. The quiet seeped into Karen's soul, offering a momentary respite from the current trauma.

"Steven says letting go was the hardest thing he ever had to do."

At Kristen's quiet comment, Karen turned her head. Her daughter was staring straight ahead, toward the common ground at the back of the property now darkened by end-of-day shadows. "Letting go of what?"

"His dreams. The use of his legs. A normal life. He thinks death is a lot like that for those left behind. That it's about letting go and learning to get on with your life even though nothing will ever be the same again."

A lump formed in Karen's throat. "I think he's right."

Kristen swiped at an errant tear with the back of her hand. "I don't know how to do that. How to let go. I don't want Dad to die." Her voice broke on the last word.

"I know, honey."

"Like, what was God thinking, anyway? He's only fifty-one!"

"Not everyone is given a long life. We just have to trust that this is part of God's plan."

"Yeah?" Defiance sharpened Kristen's features. "Well, I think it stinks—and I'm mad! I told that to God too."

"I'm sure he hears that a lot."

After a moment, the defiance melted away and her shoulders sagged. "It won't change anything, though."

"No, but it's okay to be upset."

"That's what Steven says. He told me he was mad in the beginning too—at everything and everybody."

"It's a normal reaction when life treats you in a way you think is unfair."

"But it *is* unfair."

"By our standards. But we all have to die someday. God just calls us at different times. I think your dad has accepted what's happening and is at peace with it. His biggest concern is leaving you behind. I think the thing that bothers him most is how upset you'll be by his death. He loves you very much."

"I love him too." Her forlorn words tugged at Karen's heart. "I wish there was some way I could help him."

"There is. You can be strong. Your dad needs to know you'll be okay. Try to help him understand that as much as you love him and as much as you'll miss him, you'll go on to have a full, happy life. That's what he wants for you."

A tear trickled down Kristen's cheek. "Sometimes I don't think I'll ever be happy again. It was bad enough when you guys got divorced, but this is worse. It's so . . . final."

Fighting back her own tears, Karen rose and moved to kneel in front of Kristen, taking both of her daughter's cold hands in her own. "I can promise you this. You will be happy again. And until you are, I'm going to be here for you. Anytime you want to talk or just need a hug, I'm available. We'll get through this together, okay?"

All at once, Kristen's lower lip began to quiver. Leaning forward, she threw her arms around Karen's neck.

"I don't know what I'd do without you." The words came out whispered and ragged.

Once more, tears clogged her throat as she stroked her daughter's long blonde hair.

Kristen held fast for another few seconds. Then she sniffled and backed up. "But . . . but what if s-something happens to you too?"

Today must be the day for hard questions.

Karen wanted to reassure her that she'd always be around—but she couldn't make that promise. As Kristen had already learned, life held no assurances. The world you knew could crumble overnight, with no warning.

She settled back on her heels and chose her words with care. "I hope I'm around for a lot of years. But no matter what happens, we always have to remember that even though things can change, and people do die, God's love never wavers. We're never really alone if we put our trust in him."

Kristen's silence told her that wasn't good enough. That at fifteen—with a tentative, tender faith that hadn't yet put down deep, sustaining roots—it was hard to understand the concept that there were different ways to be alone. And physical aloneness wasn't the worst of them, as her life with Michael had taught her. It was a lesson she hoped her daughter never had to learn.

Since words weren't providing the comfort Kristen needed, she simply pulled her into another hug and sent a silent prayer heavenward.

Please, Lord, I've promised Kristen we'll get through this together, but we need your guidance and strength. Stand with us and let us feel your loving presence as we make this final journey with Michael. Give us comfort and sustain us when we become overwhelmed. And after this time is past, please help Kristen heal and move on.

"Hey, pretty lady! This is a nice treat." Scott waved at Karen across the parking lot as he finished locking the church door.

She turned at his greeting, a flush of surprise—and pleasure, he hoped—pinking her cheeks.

"What are you doing here?" She angled toward him, the open car door between them.

"Steven and I squeezed in an extra lesson. We're trying to double up, with the benefit so close. What brings you to church on a Thursday?"

"I had to drop off the final program."

"Ah. The hand of fate at work." He closed his eyes and put his fingers to his temples, pretending to consult some unseen seer. "I see a trip to Mr. Frank's in your immediate future."

She smiled but shook her head. "I can't go today. Michael's coming over this afternoon to review some papers with me."

"Your ex?" Scott frowned and shoved his hands into his pockets. That sounded a little too cozy, considering what she'd told him about her marriage. "You two aren't . . . um . . . Sorry." He stopped. Raked his fingers through his hair. "It's none of my business."

"We aren't getting back together, if that's what you're wondering."

The tension in his shoulders melted away. "So what's going on?"

Distress darkened her eyes. "He's dying. Pancreatic cancer. He doesn't have any family, and he asked me to handle any decisions that need to be made when he's not able to do it himself."

Scott sorted through the double bombshell. The second one actually startled him more.

"You agreed to help him?"

"I think it's the best thing for Kristen. She's struggling with this already, and it would be worse if she thought her father had to deal with everything alone. He may not have been the best husband, nor always the most attentive dad, but she loves him. Besides, it's the charitable thing to do."

Expelling a long breath, he shook his head. "That's the most unselfish thing I've ever heard."

She gave him a wry look. "Not even close. I'm only doing this for Kristen. I'd have to scrape the bottom of my well of compassion to do it for Michael alone."

"That's more than understandable. How long does he have?"

"Six months, at best."

Or worst. Watching someone die had to be hard—even someone for whom you no longer harbored any special feelings.

"Are you sure you know what you're getting into?"

"No. I've never dealt with anything like this. And I know it won't be easy. I'll just have to do the best I can and muddle through."

Alone.

She left the word unspoken, but it echoed in his heart.

And he wanted her to know it didn't have to be that way.

Slowly, he reached over and laid his hand against her cheek. "In your place, I doubt I would be half as generous. And I don't envy you the task ahead. But I respect your decision, and I'm here if you need me to help. With anything."

Her eyelashes spiked with moisture, and she laid her hand over his. "Thank you."

At her touch, his pulse quickened and he cleared his throat. "You're welcome."

"Can I get a rain check on Mr. Frank's?" She gave him a shaky smile and removed her hand.

He missed its warmth at once.

"Anytime. I'll be around."

He wanted to linger. Wanted to reach out to her again and fold her in his arms this time.

Instead, he took a step back, lifted his hand in farewell, and walked toward his car.

When he looked back, she was still standing where he'd left her, one hand gripping the edge of her door, the other resting against the hollow of her throat. Looking as shook up as he was—and as needy. The yearning in her eyes told him she'd wanted that hug as much as he did.

With everything she had on her plate, though, she didn't need another complication in her life. Especially one as consuming and intense as romance.

Their day would come, however . . . he was sure of it.

But he had a feeling his self-discipline and patience were going to get a major workout in the meantime.

22

Karen moved to the front of the church and scanned the large group seated before her. The rehearsal with the four participating choirs and the solo performers had gone well—including her own song—and the event was sold out. Between ticket sales and ads for the program, Hope House would have more than enough funds to weather its financial crisis.

All the hard work had paid off.

She did one more sweep of the back of the church. Still no Val. Margaret's bridge club dinner must be running late—as usual. If her sister didn't finish her chauffeur duty soon, however, there'd be no time to run over her remarks.

Then again, Val was a pro. Even without a rehearsal, she'd do fine.

Karen moved behind the mike and smiled at the assembly. "I want to thank all of you for coming and for participating in this worthwhile effort. You did a great job tonight, and I know everyone will enjoy the program. Please be here by seven tomorrow and assemble in the fellowship room. I'll be around for a few more minutes tonight, if there are any questions. If not, break a leg tomorrow."

As she descended the steps from the stage, Melanie Thomas approached her. The director of Hope House was beaming.

"I'm overwhelmed! The outpouring of support has been unbelievable. I had no idea we'd end up with an event of this scale."

"It's amazing, isn't it?"

"I'll say." She pulled a sheet of paper from her purse. "I know this is last minute, but I received this yesterday, and I thought it might be powerful if the emcee read it at the end of the evening."

As Karen reached for the sheet, a glint of blonde hair at the back of the auditorium caught her eye.

"Speaking of the emcee, she just arrived. Will you excuse me for a minute?"

Karen headed toward the back, calling out to David as she passed the tech booth. "Could you hang around a little longer? Val's here, and I'd like to run through her comments and check the sound and light levels. It shouldn't take more than a few minutes."

"No problem. My neighbor is watching Victoria, and I told her I might be late."

With a wave of thanks, Karen continued toward her sister.

"Sorry about this." Val blew out a frustrated breath. "I had no idea Mom's quarterly bridge dinners dragged on till all hours." She scanned the emptying auditorium. "Looks like I missed the rehearsal."

"David's waiting around to set sound and lights for your part. Do you want to run through it once?"

"As long as I'm not holding anyone up. I read over the stuff. It shouldn't take long."

"That's what I figured. Start whenever you're ready."

With a nod, Val dropped her purse on a chair and walked toward the stage.

As she prepared to follow her sister, Karen caught sight of Scott approaching. She hadn't had a chance to talk with him after their choir sang, and while she thought she'd done okay, it would be nice to have that confirmed.

His heartening smile did the trick even before he spoke. "You were great."

"If I was, you deserve the credit. Without your support and coaching I would never have been able to stand up there and sing alone. But the real test will be tomorrow."

"I have every confidence in you."

"I wish I did."

He rested his fingers on her arm. "You'll be fine." He maintained contact a moment longer, then dropped his hand. "How's everything else?"

"Busy. And I don't expect the pace to lessen anytime soon. Once Val leaves next week, I'll have to pick up all the responsibilities for Mom again too."

"Remember my offer of help—for anything, anytime."

Gratitude filled her heart. What had she done to deserve such a caring, considerate man? "I will. Thank you."

Steven wheeled up behind them, and Scott turned. "Here's the other star of the evening."

The teen grimaced. "I made some mistakes."

"Only ones you and I would notice."

"You sounded great, Steven." Karen touched his arm as she added her reassurance. "It's nice to have a piano solo in the program."

Scott glanced at his watch, then back at her. "I promised Steven a ride home. Try to get some rest before the show."

"Not likely. I have a full day scheduled, including my last Saturday afternoon coffee with Val—and I'm not going to skip that." As her sister started to run through her comments, Karen motioned toward the stage. "Speaking of Val . . ."

"I know. Duty calls." Scott entwined her fingers with his and gave them an encouraging squeeze. "See you tomorrow."

She watched the two of them move toward the door, then rejoined Melanie in front as Val began breezing through her remarks.

"What did you think?" Melanie motioned to the sheet of paper in Karen's hand.

"Sorry. I haven't had a chance to read it yet." She dropped into the empty chair beside the Hope House director and skimmed through the typewritten document. "Wow! You're right. This is powerful stuff. It would be a great wrap-up for the evening. Where did you get it?"

"From the director of a similar program in Kansas City. It was sent to them by a former client who ended up choosing another option. She wanted the staff to know she was sorry she'd given in to the pressure to end her pregnancy, and she sent along a donation to support their work."

"I'll ask Val to read through it as soon as she finishes."

Setting the sheet in her lap, she listened as her sister ran through the emcee remarks. As she'd expected, Val's poise and confidence would put a polish on the evening.

And with her professional training, she'd be able to do justice to the compelling testimonial Melanie had brought with her.

Val closed her folder, shaded her eyes, and looked out at Karen. "How was that?"

"Perfect. The consummate pro." Karen rose and walked toward the stage. "The director of Hope House thought it might be effective if you read this at the end of the evening, as part of your closing remarks. Sorry to dump it on you cold, but she just gave it to me. Could you give it a try? We'll write a short intro for it before tomorrow night."

"Sure." Val took the sheet Karen handed her and moved back behind the microphone. This whole emcee gig was going a lot more smoothly than she'd anticipated. "We've got one more brief piece, David."

"No problem." His voice echoed from the back. "I won't turn anything off until you're finished."

Val set the paper on the podium, glanced at the heading—and stopped breathing.

"A Letter to My Unborn Child."

Seconds ticked by as she stared at the words. What was this all about? She was only supposed to say hi, good-bye, and do a few intros. No one had said a thing about reading a personal document like this.

"Val? Whenever you're ready."

At Karen's prompt, she sucked in a breath. Fought for control.

Pretend it's a script. Pretend this is a play, with no basis in reality and no connection to your life. Stay objective. Be professional. You're an actress. This is just another role.

Summoning up every vestige of her training, she began to read.

"My dearest child: I wish I could tell you all the things that are in my heart today. To cuddle you gently in my arms, to whisper in your ear, to stroke your soft, silky hair and feel the steady beat of your heart as I hold you close to my breast.

"But that is never to be. You are gone now, and all that remains is regret and guilt and pain. Not a day goes by that you are far from my thoughts. Each morning, I awaken to the vain hope that the empty place in my heart will be filled once more. And each evening, I go to bed with a prayer on my lips for mercy and forgiveness."

Her voice caught on the last word, and she cleared her throat. "Today is especially hard. It's the fourth anniversary of your due date, and I'm wondering what we would have done to celebrate your birthday, had I not robbed you of the gift of life our Creator gave you. I'd have baked a cake, of course, with five candles. Four for your age, and one to grow on. There would have been presents to open too, wrapped in colorful paper and decorated with shiny bows.

"After that, the two of us would have gone on a picnic. Chased a butterfly or two. Picked some flowers. Lain on our backs in the grass and looked for cloud pictures. Simple things. But precious things. Things I would have remembered all my life as I watched you grow into a fine young man or woman and as you began to make your own unique contributions to the world."

As she finished, Val gripped the edges of the podium. She'd made it through—but she felt as if someone had delved into her heart and written down the emotions and thoughts she'd carried there for nearly eighteen years.

"Val? There's more on the back."

More?

Please, God, no!

Fingers shaking, Val turned the page over. The words blurred, and she had to blink several times before they came into focus.

She couldn't do this.

"Val?"

Another prompt from her sister.

She gritted her teeth.

Just do it! Keep going! You'll be better prepared tomorrow. You're only having trouble now because this is unexpected.

In a halting cadence, she started to read again.

"But there were never any birthday parties. Or candles. Especially ones to grow on. I took away the future God had planned for you. I stole your life almost before it began. But not quite. Even though I couldn't see you or hold you or stroke your cheek, you were with me, nestled near my heart, growing and developing and waiting for the birth day that never came.

"Oh, my dear child, I'm so sorry. If I had it to do over again, I'd . . ."

Her voice broke, and the words blurred again as silent tears spilled out of her eyes.

She made one more valiant effort to regain control—but it was no use. Her heart felt like it was being ripped in two, and she was out of pep talks.

Jerking back from the mike, she stumbled toward the steps that led down from the stage. She tripped on the first one but somehow regained her balance and clambered down, blinded by the tears streaming unchecked down her cheeks.

She had to get out of here.

Fast.

She was halfway across the auditorium when Karen grabbed her arm.

"Val, what is it? What's wrong?"

She lurched to a stop. "I . . . I can't do this."

Pulling her arm free, she turned to flee . . . only to find David blocking her escape route.

"What's going on?" He sent Karen an alarmed look, then turned his attention back to her and gripped her shoulders. "Val, what is it?"

"I . . . I don't feel well." She shrugged free of his touch. "I need to go home."

"I'll take you."

"No!" She shook her head and eyed the door. "I'll be fine."

And with that lie vibrating in the air, she pulled away from David and ran from the building.

David dimmed his car lights and pulled to a stop in the park by the river. Not the one where he and Victoria had shared their lunch with Val the day she'd emerged, shaken, from the woods. Instead, she'd led him to the main park in town. The one with benches close to the river's edge.

Too close, considering that was where she was headed.

After Val's frantic flight from the rehearsal, he hadn't needed Karen's panicked plea to convince him to follow her. You didn't desert someone you cared about in their darkest hour.

Killing the engine, he turned off the dome light and opened his door as she approached the water, prepared to bolt from the car at the slightest indication she was going to do anything but sit on a bench. And she might, given the anguish and utter desolation and desperation he'd glimpsed in her eyes.

To his relief, she dropped onto a bench, shoulders hunched, head bowed. But he kept his door open, just in case. Besides, he intended to join her soon.

First, though, he needed a few minutes to sort through his own emotions.

Gripping the wheel, he faced the truth.

Val had had an abortion.

The woman who was stealing his heart had found herself in trouble and taken the easy way out. Chosen convenience over conscience.

The stark, ugly reality twisted his gut.

There was no way he could condone her choice, no matter how much he'd come to care for her. It went against everything he believed about the sanctity of life.

Yet as another image of eyes filled with abject misery and pain and soul-stirring regret flashed through his mind, he reconsidered.

Maybe her way hadn't been so easy after all.

Maybe it had extracted its pound of flesh in unremitting torment and guilt and grief.

Suddenly Val stood, and a surge of adrenaline shot through him. When she took a step toward the river, he vaulted from the car, sprinting toward her until he was grasping distance away.

"Val?" He tried for a calm tone, but her name came out hoarse and uneven.

She jerked toward him, her whole body trembling. Her eyes were less wild and frenetic now, the earlier agitation replaced by bleak emptiness and dull resignation, but her mascara-streaked cheeks were pale as death.

David held out his hand. "Sit with me a while."

She looked at his outstretched hand but didn't move.

"Come on, Val."

"You don't want to . . . to sit with me." Her response came out in a broken whisper.

"Yes, I do."

She shook her head, and the wretched sadness on her face pierced him. "Trust me. You don't. It would be better if you left and forgot all about me."

He kept his hand extended. "Forgetting about you isn't an option. And I can't walk away when someone I care about is hurting. Take my hand. Please."

She regarded his outstretched hand. Hesitated.

Please, Lord, let her trust me on this. Give her the courage to share what's in her heart, and give me the courage to listen without reproach—and to put judgment in your hands.

Slowly, tentatively, she reached out to him.

Twining his fingers with hers, he led her to the bench. As they sat, he switched hands and draped his arm around her hunched shoulders.

Several minutes passed, the silence broken only by the distant, plaintive whistle of a train.

When at last she spoke, she kept her gaze on the restless river below. "I guess you're wondering what that was all about tonight."

He stroked his thumb over the back of her hand. "You had an abortion." He did his best to banish censure from his tone. "A long time ago, I suspect."

She squeezed her eyes shut, but a tear slipped out and rolled down her cheek.

David wiped the trail of moisture away with a gentle finger.

"If you figured it out, why did you follow me?"

"I care about you."

"In spite of what I did?"

It was a simple question—but the answer was complicated.

"If you're asking me whether I approve of abortion, the answer is no. My position on that was formed long ago, after my five-year-old sister died of leukemia. I was eight, and I can still remember how devastated we all were. My parents wanted more children, but none ever came. They looked into adopting, but the cost was out of reach for our blue-collar family. Yet more than a million babies are aborted each year in this country."

He swallowed past the bad taste that statistic always left in his mouth. "Anyway, as I got older, I became active in the pro-life movement. I still do whatever I can to protect the unborn. That's why I agreed to help with the Hope House benefit."

She tried to pull her hand away, but he held fast.

"Val, look at me."

"I can't."

"Please."

Her throat worked as she swallowed, and slowly she turned her head.

"I care about you. A lot." He let that sink in for a moment before he continued. "Because of that, I want to be honest. The truth is, I'll never change my opinion about abortion. But people are human. They make mistakes. They yield to pressure. It's not my place to judge anyone's actions. What you did is between you and God. All I know is you paid a high price for the decision you made. I can see it in your regret and your pain and your sorrow."

A flicker of hope ignited in her eyes. "Does that mean . . . you don't hate me?"

"Not even close."

She searched his face. "I never e-expected this. Do you want . . ." Her breath hitched, and she tried again. "Do you want to hear what happened?"

"Very much—if you want to share it."

With a nod, she once more looked toward the dark river.

He listened in silence as she relayed her story in a halting voice. It played out as he expected.

Near the end, she dropped her voice. He had to lean close to hear her final words.

"I still have the ultrasound printout, showing a perfect baby. My son or daughter, who would have been seventeen this year. The same age I was when I . . . took that tiny life."

He stroked the back of her hand with his thumb as the pieces began to fall into place. "That's why you came back this summer, isn't it? To try and make peace with what happened."

"That was part of the reason."

She told him all the steps she'd taken—the visits to the river, the health center, the back-alley clinic.

No wonder her eyes had often seemed haunted. She'd been living a nightmare. Facing the demons of her past.

Alone.

"That took a lot of guts, Val."

"No." Her response was immediate, her tone firm. "Everything I did was motivated more by desperation than courage. But nothing worked. I even tried going back to church. That was a bust too." She choked back a sob. "At least someone healed this summer. Mom's doing great."

"Maybe you need to give yourself more time."

"I've had eighteen years." Her shoulders crumpled. "This trip was my last hope. I guess I'll just have to live alone with the guilt, like I always have."

All at once, the truth hit David like a punch in the midsection.

Val didn't think she deserved a husband. Or children. She was atoning for her mistake by consigning herself to a solitary life, depriving herself of the very things her heart most desired. That explained the sadness behind the yearning in her eyes when she looked at him and Victoria. She wouldn't commit to staying in Washington, to checking out the teaching job, because she was serving a self-inflicted life sentence. Her decision had nothing to do with her career being more important to her than creating a family.

David stroked her cheek, wishing he could ease her pain. "Whatever happened to forgiveness?"

At his quiet question, she looked at him and furrowed her brow. "What do you mean?"

"Maybe you've suffered enough for your choice. Maybe it's time to forgive yourself—and let God forgive you as well."

She was shaking her head before he finished speaking. "I don't deserve forgiveness."

"Forgiveness isn't about merit. It's about repentance and God's unconditional love."

Her expression grew skeptical. "I don't know if I believe in unconditional love."

He locked gazes with her, letting her see what was in his heart. "Believe in it. It might be rare, but it's real. May I make a suggestion?"

She gulped in some air. Swiped at a stray tear. Nodded.

"Why don't you talk to Reverend Richards?"

"I doubt that will help at this point." Her voice broke on the last word.

He angled his body toward her and took both her hands in his. "I wish you'd give it a try. Because, to be honest, I want you to find redemption, to be able to move on with your life, as much as you do. For selfish reasons." He gave her a moment to process that. "Besides, running back to Chicago isn't going to solve anything. And that teaching job at the high school is still open."

Watching her face, he held his breath and prayed she'd have the courage to take this one last step.

Finally, she gave a slow nod. "All right. I'll talk to Reverend Richards."

Thank you, God!

"I don't think you'll be sorry." He checked his watch, wishing for this one evening he didn't have any other obligations. But his daughter needed him too. "I have to pick up Victoria. Will you be okay driving?"

"Yes."

Would she?

Maybe. Her voice was stronger now, and she seemed steadier. She could probably handle the trip home.

But she didn't have to make it alone.

"I'll follow you."

"You don't have to do that. I'll be fine."

"Humor me, okay? I'll sleep better if I know you're safe and sound. Besides, I promised your sister I'd make sure you were all right, and I can't do that if I don't see you pull into your driveway."

He rose and extended his hand. She took it.

They walked in silence to her car, and once there he followed his heart. Drawing her into his arms, he wrapped her in a gentle, comforting embrace.

For a full minute they stayed that way, her cheek nestled on his shoulder, his chin resting on her soft hair. She felt good in his arms. As if she was meant to be there. For always.

And when she at last stepped back and he returned to his car, he resolved that *always* was a goal worth pursuing.

Whatever it took.

23

"Good morning, Val. Would you like some coffee?" Reverend Richards lifted his own mug in invitation as he entered his office.

Val dredged up an answering smile. "No, thanks. I've already exceeded my caffeine allotment for the day."

He took the seat beside her. "I should cut back myself, but I got into the caffeine habit in my previous corporate life and haven't been able to shake it."

That was news. "You worked in the real world?"

"I prefer to think of this"—he swept his hand over his office—"as the real world. Or the one that matters most, anyway."

Heat crept up her neck. *Way to go, Val. Real diplomatic.* "Sorry. That question didn't come out quite right."

He chuckled. "No problem. I get that comment a lot, and it's a setup I can't resist. But to answer your question, I came to ministry later than most. I was just ordained a couple of years ago."

A minister who'd had experience with the challenges and temptations of the secular world.

Maybe talking to him wouldn't be as difficult as she'd expected.

"So what can I do for you today?" He set his coffee on a side table and gave her his full attention.

Crossing her legs, she knotted her hands in her lap. "I'll be going back to Chicago soon, and I have a few . . . issues . . . I haven't been able to resolve on my own."

When she hesitated, he tipped his head. "Your mother's health can't be one of them. She seems to be doing much better."

"She is. She's recovered 99 percent of the function on her left side. David says it's quite remarkable. David's her therapist."

"Yes. David Phelps. A very nice gentleman. And his daughter is charming. They've been a wonderful addition to our congregation. I'm glad to see you've joined us too. Your mother inferred once that you'd been away from God for a while. May I assume your return is related to the unresolved issues you mentioned?"

"Yes—but it hasn't helped."

"Well, church attendance is a good thing, of course. But our physical presence alone doesn't have much meaning if we just sit there and wait for God to talk to us. Have you tried talking to him?"

"Yes. With my very pathetic praying skills."

"The Lord listens for sincerity, not technical proficiency. A good prayer is like a conversation with a dear friend, where we share what's in our heart with openness and trust."

"But a conversation involves two people, and if God is speaking back to me, I'm not hearing it."

"We do have to listen in a different way—and with diligence. Often his voice is nothing more than a whisper in our soul."

"Then I guess my hearing skills need some work too." Val sighed. "Since I can't seem to hear his voice, I hoped you might be able to offer me some guidance or insight."

"I'll do my best."

He waited patiently as she fiddled with the strap on her purse, not rushing her or asking a lot of questions, letting her set the pace. The man had excellent people skills. No wonder the congregation loved him.

But she could only delay so long, and stalling wasn't going to make it any less difficult in the end. She might as well spit it out.

"I guess you know I agreed to be the emcee for the benefit tonight."

"Yes. Everyone is very appreciative."

"The thing is . . . I'm thinking about pulling out."

She twisted her fingers together and braced for censure. Surprise. Irritation. The very things she deserved for suggesting she might renege at the last minute.

Instead, his tone remained conversational. "Why is that?"

Her knuckles whitened, and she forced herself to loosen her fingers. "I had a problem last night, with a final piece they want me to read at the end of the evening. It was a last-minute addition."

"The letter to the unborn baby."

She frowned. "You know about that?"

"Yes. The director of Hope House faxed it to me yesterday so I could approve its inclusion. It's very powerful and moving. I imagine it would be difficult to read out loud."

"Very. Especially for me." Val forced herself to maintain eye contact despite the temptation to drop her head in shame. "Because I could have written it."

His eyes softened. "I'm sorry."

That wasn't the reaction she'd expected.

Pressure built in her throat. "I am too."

The minister leaned forward, his expression compassionate and kind as he clasped his hands. "Tell me about it."

And so she did. Sparing nothing. Cutting herself no slack. Taking full responsibility for her actions.

"Even my motives for coming home this summer weren't that altruistic." She rubbed her temple, where a headache had begun to throb. "I agreed to help with Mom, but I was also determined to find closure on this. I wanted to get rid of the guilt and the pain and the burden that's weighed me down all these years."

She explained all the steps she'd taken, ending with a discouraged sigh. "But nothing's helped. If anything, I feel worse than when

I came. Plus, now I have another complication." She sent him an apologetic glance. "You're really getting an earful, aren't you?"

He gave her a reassuring smile. "If I didn't want to listen to people's problems, I'd have stayed out of the ministry. What's the other complication?"

"David. He's asked me to stay and apply for the drama teacher position at the high school. He thinks maybe we . . . that a serious relationship could develop between us."

"What do you think?"

"I think that's possible."

"And the problem is . . . ?"

"I don't deserve a happy ending, and he doesn't need a wife with unresolved issues."

The minister leaned back in his chair. "Let's tackle the unresolved issues first. I think what you've been seeking all these years is forgiveness. Absolution. And that only comes from one place. We hear a lot in society today about people needing to forgive themselves, but that's not enough. Real forgiveness only comes from God—and your renewed church attendance tells me you're seeking it in the right place now. Let me ask you this. Given a second chance, would you make a different choice today?"

"In a heartbeat."

"Then all your pain and guilt haven't been wasted. You've grown and matured and become a better, more sensitive person as a result of what you've gone through. And when we approach the Lord as true penitents who acknowledge the wrong we've done, he welcomes us and forgives us."

"That's what David said."

"I knew he was a smart man. But beyond forgiveness, God also gives us a second chance. Not always a chance to correct an earlier mistake, but to learn from it and move on. To embrace the future he offers us, to live fully rather than waste the opportunities he presents to us because we feel we're not worthy of them. Which brings me to the happy ending you spoke of."

"I've always believed happy endings are for other people. Or only in storybooks."

He leaned forward again, his posture intent. "I assure you they do happen in real life. I see them every day. The truth is, if we allowed ourselves only what we deserve, most of us would spend our lives in sackcloth and ashes. We're human. We all make mistakes."

"Some worse than others."

"True. Yet God loves us despite our flaws. That's why he sent his Son to show us the power of redemptive love. And his best hope for us is a happy ending—in eternity *and* here on earth. He doesn't want us to spend our lives punishing ourselves. He wants us to lay our mistakes and shortcomings before him and know he always stands ready to support us, to help us, and—if necessary—to forgive us. He cares for us as he wants us to care for others. One of the ways we can live out that example of caring is through a beautiful marriage. It seems to me he may be calling you to that vocation."

As Val looked into the man's earnest face, his conviction an almost tangible thing, she took a few moments to process what he'd said.

A few more to grasp the message of hope he had given her.

A few beyond that to accept it.

But when she did, when she embraced it and let it resonate deep in her soul, something extraordinary happened.

The crushing guilt she'd borne for nearly eighteen years melted away, leaving in its place sweet release. Liberation. Freedom.

Even her breathing seemed less labored.

Her vision misted, and she reached out to clasp the minister's hands. "Thank you."

His smile was like a balm on her battered heart. "I'm not the one you need to thank. I'm just the messenger. Shall we take a few minutes to speak to the source of that message?"

At her nod, he bowed his head. "Lord, we thank you for your abundant kindness and generosity, and for your gift of forgiveness. Help us always to know your healing grace, to walk secure in the knowledge that you are always beside us, even when we least deserve your love. Give us the strength to do our best to follow your teachings and to live according to your example. Steady us when we falter. Speak to us when we need guidance. And let us always remember the beautiful words from Matthew, so we never become disheartened or feel alone: 'Come to me, all you who labor and are burdened, and I will give you rest.'

"Today, Lord, we ask your special blessing and favor on Val as she prepares to let go of yesterday and move toward the tomorrow you have planned for her. Help her always to know your abiding love and care, and grant her a future filled with hope. Amen."

As the prayer concluded, Val took a deep, cleansing breath, relishing the sense of peace that had replaced the anguish in her soul. For the first time since her tragic mistake, the future held the promise of happiness—and she was anxious to begin that journey.

But before she took her first step into tomorrow, she had a couple of things she needed to do today.

"My treat, in honor of our last Saturday afternoon coffee." Karen opened her wallet and handed her credit card to the clerk behind the counter.

"You don't have to do that." Val continued to dig for her own wallet.

Karen restrained her with a touch on the arm. "Indulge me, okay? I'm just glad you didn't cancel out on me."

After a brief hesitation, Val capitulated. "Okay. Thanks." Picking up her frappuccino, she gestured toward a private corner table. "How about over there?"

"Fine with me."

As she followed her sister across the crowded coffee shop, Karen gave her an assessing scan. Not bad, considering last night's emotional breakdown and her shaky voice on the phone this morning. She did appear tired—but it was more like the weariness of a marathon runner crossing the finish line. As if she'd conquered a formidable challenge.

And after last night, Karen had a pretty good idea what that challenge was.

Val settled into a chair at the café table, and Karen perched on the edge of the one across from her. Her sister wanted to talk; she could sense it. And she wanted to be there for her.

But she was also afraid.

What if this conversation jeopardized the fragile, new relationship they'd painstakingly built over the summer? The one she'd begun to assume would continue to grow and flourish, giving her the sister she'd never really had?

Ignoring the elephant in the room, however, wasn't going to make it go away. If Val wanted to confess, she had to listen. That's what sisters—and friends—did.

Taking a deep breath, she broke the lengthening silence. "Saturdays won't be the same after you leave."

"It may not be our last coffee date after all." Val played with her straw. "I'm thinking about staying in Washington."

Karen did a double take. That wasn't what she'd expected. "Are you serious?"

"Yes." Val gave her a smile that seemed forced. "I thought you'd be happy to have a helping hand with Mom on a more permanent basis."

"You're staying because of Mom?" Also not what she'd expected. Nor did she think that was the main reason Val was considering such a radical change.

"Partly. But more because of you and Kristen and David and Victoria." She tightened her grip on her plastic cup. The frappuccino overflowed and puddled on the table, and she scrubbed at the wayward liquid with her napkin.

Wadding the soiled paper into her fist, she continued in a more subdued voice. "I'm also staying because I'm tired of running away."

Here it comes.

Karen braced herself. "What do you mean?"

"That's the real reason I left Washington. It reminded me too much of my mistakes." She moved her drink aside and gripped her hands together on the table. "Do you remember much about the summer I was seventeen, and my senior year in high school?"

"No. I was dating Michael, and everything but my so-called romance is a blur for those months. Besides, I was putting in a lot of hours at my job at the Y. I don't remember seeing you very much. You were either working at the diner or running around with that group you hung out with, and by the next spring, I was married. Why?"

"Something happened during those months that changed my life forever. It's why I broke down at the rehearsal. Why I've been running all these years."

So the suspicions that had kept her tossing most of the night were true.

And the moment she'd been dreading was here.

With an effort, Karen kept her expression impassive. "Are you telling me you had an abortion?"

"Yes." The admission came out in a whisper. "And not a day has passed since that I haven't regretted it."

After watching Val's remorse play out in living color last night, Karen believed that. And while her sister's choice twisted her stomach, her heart contracted with sympathy for the eighteen years of guilt and regret and self-recrimination Val had endured.

"Do you want to tell me about it?"

"Yes. If we're going to be friends, I don't want there to be secrets between us. But I'll understand if you can't accept what I have to say."

Karen listened as Val shared her story, up to and including her session with Reverend Richards this morning. She did her best to keep an open mind—and an open heart. Prayed for understanding and compassion. Reminded herself that judgment was God's, not hers.

“So now you know.” Val wiped away the beads of sweat that had formed on her cup. “I finally have the sense of closure I came home to find, and I’m ready to move on with my life. Odd as it may sound, moving on may include moving back to Washington.”

Reaching out, Karen took her hand and gave it a squeeze. “I can’t even imagine how awful it must have been for you to keep that secret hidden away all these years.”

Val searched her face. “Then you don’t hate me for what I did?”

Hate? Never. But she’d been afraid Val’s choices, which went against everything she believed in, might drive a wedge between them. God had answered her prayers, however, blessing her with the empathy and grace she needed to handle this with the compassion her faith taught.

“Not even close.”

“That’s exactly what David said last night.”

“I knew he was a good man.” Karen leaned back in her chair. “And speaking of David, you mentioned that he and Victoria were among the reasons you were staying . . . ?”

“I didn’t think that would get by you.” A whisper of a smile tugged at Val’s lips. “He asked me to apply for the drama teacher position at the high school. He thinks the two of us could . . . get serious.”

“What do you think?”

“I agree with him.”

Karen smiled. “I’m happy for you, Val.”

“Thanks. And now I have a favor to ask. There’s one more thing I need to do, and I’d like you and David to come with me.”

As Val explained her request, Karen felt the pressure of tears build behind her eyes. When her sister finished, she reached for her hand and gave it an encouraging squeeze. “Count me in.”

Val blinked and squeezed back. “Thank you.”

They sat that way for a long moment, hands—and hearts—linked, and then Karen checked her watch. “I hate to break this up, but we still need to shop and get ready for the benefit.”

"You're right." Val picked up her half-melted drink, fished in her purse, and pulled out a piece of paper. "Since Mom thinks I'm leaving, she made a list of the dishes she wants me to fix for dinner next week. Get this. Ratatouille is at the top. Can you believe it?"

Karen shook her head. "Who said miracles don't happen?"

A soft smile lifted the corners of Val's lips. "I'll never be a doubter again."

As far as Karen could tell, the benefit was a rousing success. Hope House was now in the black. Steven had given a stunning performance. She'd been pleased with her solo. And Val had read the letter at the end with such feeling and passion there wasn't a dry eye in the house.

As Karen was accepting accolades after the final curtain, Val, Kristen, and Margaret joined the group of well-wishers. They waited until the crowd dispersed before stepping forward.

"That was epic, Mom!" Kristen gave her an enthusiastic hug.

"I concur," Val seconded.

Her mother peered at her over the top of her glasses. "Well, you certainly surprised me."

Coming from Margaret, that was the equivalent of a Grammy. Karen stepped forward to hug her stiff shoulders. "Thanks, Mom."

"I'll add my congratulations too." Scott gave her a slow, admiring smile as he joined them.

Val's gaze shifted to Scott, then back to her. "Will you be riding home with us?"

"No."

"Yes."

At their simultaneous—and conflicting—responses, Karen glanced at Scott.

"I'll take that as a no." Val commandeered Margaret's arm. "Come on, ladies. If three's company, five is definitely a crowd."

As Val led them away, Karen propped her hands on her hips and called after them. "Hey! How am I supposed to get home?"

"At your service." Scott gave a mock bow. "But first we need to celebrate your debut."

"What did you have in mind?"

"Mr. Frank's?"

Perfect. Much safer than the romantic place by the river. "Sold."

"Let me grab my music and I'll meet you by the exit."

She started toward the back of the auditorium, accepting more praise along the way, but her gaze kept drifting toward Scott. And even though the compliments were heartwarming, she knew they were only partly responsible for the glow in her heart.

Frozen custard in hand, Scott homed in on a bench being vacated by an elderly couple. "Quick! Let's run for it!" He grabbed her hand and dashed toward the seat, beating out a teenage pair by seconds and dropping his keys in the process.

With a laugh, Karen sat beside him. "You learned the Mr. Frank's drill pretty fast, I see."

"What's that saying about he who hesitates?"

He reached for his keys, and the breath caught in Karen's throat. As he straightened up, she touched his hand. "You've got almost full dexterity back! When did that happen?"

He checked out her fingers resting against his, and when he lifted his head, an ember sparked to life in his eyes. "It's been a gradual thing."

For a long moment he looked at her, and Karen's heart missed a beat.

So much for thinking Mr. Frank's was safe.

He leaned toward her, his attention now focused on her mouth, his intention clear.

She wanted the kiss as much as he did—but not yet.

Mustering her resolve, she pressed a hand against his chest . . . and tried to ignore the pounding of his heart against her fingers.

"Scott . . . I can't. This isn't the time. I have so many plates spinning right now—if I try to add one more I'm afraid the whole lot will come crashing down. And I don't want to risk that."

He sucked in a breath. Backed off. Jabbed at his custard. "Sorry. I have difficulty reining in my impulses around you." He gave her a rueful smile. "Anyway, now you know how I feel."

Dare she risk revealing her own feelings? What if he belittled her sentimentality, as Michael had?

But he wasn't Michael. Not by a long shot.

Maybe it was time to follow Val's example and free herself from the chains of her past.

She took a deep breath, gathered up her courage, and gave voice to what was in her heart. "I feel the same way. You're a very special man, and I give thanks every day that you're part of my life."

Tenderness softened his features, and he reached out a tentative hand to touch her face. "Does that mean after . . . down the road . . . you'd be willing to explore a relationship?"

"Yes. And when that time comes, I plan to give you the full attention you deserve."

"Then I guess I'll have to work on my patience. Not my strong suit, as I've admitted before, but I'll do my best." He leaned back and swirled his spoon through his custard, creating peaks and valleys. "You know, I may never quite grasp why you agreed to help your ex-husband after everything he did to you, but I admire the strength of your principles and your commitment to keeping your promises. Not to mention your caring and compassionate heart. And you know what? A woman with those qualities is worth waiting for."

Swallowing past the lump in her throat, she took his hand. "Thank you."

"I'm the one who's thankful. Now let's talk about the benefit."

They moved on to lighter, more impersonal topics as they finished their custard and he drove her home. And when he walked her to the door, he said good-bye with a simple squeeze of her fingers—though based on the banked fire in his eyes, he wanted more. Yet he respected her wishes, practicing the patience he claimed he didn't have.

And as she watched him drive away, gratitude overflowed in her heart for this soon-to-end summer so filled with unexpected gifts. She'd reconnected with a sister long lost to her. Solidified her bond with her daughter. Taken the initiative to advance her career. Her relationship with her mother had improved. And she'd been blessed with a second chance at love.

All at once, Val's comment this morning about miracles replayed in her mind. Unlike her sister, she'd always believed in them, though she'd never experienced one.

But in these past few months, she'd witnessed many firsthand. In Val. In Scott. In herself. And somehow she knew that in the years to come, she would always think of that word in connection with this summer of grace, when so many lives had changed for the better.

24

Val stood on the bluff overlooking the river, the gentle breeze soft on her face. The expansive view was just as she remembered it from her many visits during that last year before she went away to college.

In the far distance, the broad river narrowed to a silver thread. The patchwork fields were shades of gold and green in these waning days of summer, and the noonday sun—warm without being overbearing—illuminated the scene with a brilliant light.

Now, as then, the height and panoramic vista uplifted her. By offering a clear view to the distant horizon, this spot had always seemed to speak of hope. And tomorrow. And God.

So it was a fitting place to take the final step on her journey to the past—and the first step into her future.

She looked at Karen, who stood on her left holding a single yellow rose. Her sister's eyes reflected love and support and encouragement, and she telegraphed a silent thank-you back with her own.

On her other side, David held a small trowel. Kindness and goodness radiated from him, and she felt the sting of tears.

Thank you, Lord, for sending this wonderful man into my life.

Thank you, too, for all the blessings you've given me this summer. Please be with me now as I close this chapter of my past.

Val stroked the simple cardboard tube in her hands. It had taken her almost eighteen years to remove it from its dark hiding place. To expose it to the sunlight. To face her mistakes and find the healing redemption she had long sought.

But now she could put it to rest forever.

At Val's nod, David went down on one knee and dug into the rich earth, creating a small trench four inches wide, twelve inches long, and six inches deep. When he finished, he rose and stepped aside.

For a long moment, she stood there cradling the tube. Then she closed her eyes and spoke in the silence of her heart.

My dear child, please forgive me. Please know that not one day has passed that I haven't thought of you and loved you and regretted the life I stole from you. I now leave my one physical link to you in this beautiful place, high on a hill, where the gentle rains can fall on it and the golden sun can warm it. But I will never forget you. You will always be in my heart. And I promise that when we meet in heaven, I will hold you close, as I never had the chance to do on this earth. I will whisper the words of love that are written in my heart and belong only to you. But in the meantime, I commend you to God's loving care. Good-bye, my little one.

A tear trickled down her cheek as she knelt beside the small trench. She placed the tube inside and carefully scooped the dirt on top. After she patted it down, Karen handed her the rose, and Val set it on top of the tiny mound.

She knelt there alone for another minute, her head bowed. But when at last she started to rise, she felt hands on both sides lifting her, supporting her. Then Karen and David enfolded her in their arms.

No words were spoken.

None needed to be.

The very presence of these two special people said everything.

As they returned to the car, David and Karen kept their arms linked with hers. And though it was unseen, Val keenly felt another presence as well. One that surrounded her . . . consoling her, forgiving her, filling her with hope.

And as she walked away from yesterday, she was filled with a quiet certainty that this presence would remain with her for all her tomorrows.

"You've had quite a week."

Val opened her eyes. From her prone position on the ground, the intense blue of the sky filled her field of vision . . . until David's face moved into view as he leaned close to brush a strand of hair off her forehead with a gentle, lingering touch.

"Yes, I have." She reached for his hand as he sat back on the checkered cloth he'd brought for their picnic. His firm fingers entwined with hers, and as he gave a gentle squeeze, she released a soft, contented sigh.

"Is that from exhaustion or happiness?"

"Both. I think I could sleep for a month. Think about all I did in the past seven days. I interviewed at the high school here. I resigned from my job in Chicago. I closed up my condo and put all my furniture and personal stuff in storage. I moved back to Washington."

He leaned back on his elbows beside her. "You're making me tired just listening to that litany."

"Think how I feel. I did all the work."

"But it was worth it, wasn't it?"

"Yeah. More than."

He turned on his side and propped himself up with one elbow to trace the contour of her chin with a tender, whisper-soft touch. "I missed you, Val."

Her heart skipped a beat. "I missed you too."

He checked the nearby playground where Victoria was swinging, then leaned close and brushed his lips over hers in a sweet, simple kiss that left her yearning for more.

Backing off, he hovered a few inches away from her face. "Don't look at me like that or I might have to kiss you again."

At the sudden, rough timbre of his voice, she gave him a teasing smile and played with a button on his shirt. "Is that a promise?"

Grabbing her hand, he folded her fingers in his own and adopted a stern tone. "Stop that. My willpower is already stretched way too thin."

"In that case, I'll be good."

His eyes darkened. "Oh, I have no doubt of that."

A jolt of electricity shot through her. Sizzled.

Okay. Enough of this.

She pulled her hand free and nodded toward Victoria. "We have a chaperone, remember?"

"Yeah. Thanks for reminding me." He sat up and leaned back against his palms, one ankle crossed over the other. "So . . . tell me how you're settling in. You okay about living with Margaret?"

Following his lead, she sat up as well and crossed her legs. "It's okay for a while. She's dropped a few broad hints that it could be a permanent arrangement, but I made it very clear the situation was temporary. As soon as I find an apartment, I'm out of there. I'm used to being on my own."

"Not too used to it, I hope. Because I have some other plans in mind."

Her heart skidded to a stop. Raced on. "We haven't known each other long enough for this discussion."

"It doesn't always take a lot of time to know that a relationship is meant to be."

She plucked a clover, lifting it to her nose to inhale the fresh, sweet fragrance. "Maybe. But I've made other mistakes by being too rash. This time I want to be absolutely certain."

"I understand that. And I don't intend to push. You need to sort out your new life, and the two of us have some logistics to work through. But I want to be very upfront about my own feelings and intentions." He took both her hands in his, never breaking eye contact. "The fact is, I've fallen in love with you. I didn't expect to. Or necessarily want to in the beginning. Yet it happened, and I'm not sorry. I'll give you however long you need, but someday, when you're ready, I'd like you to be my wife."

Her pulse began to hammer as she stared at him. "Is . . . is that a proposal?"

"No." His reply was prompt—and firm. "You're not ready, and I don't intend to rush you into a decision. I just want you to know where I'm coming from. And that someday, I hope in the not-too-distant future, I do plan to propose."

"Daddy! Val! Come see what I found!"

It took several seconds for Victoria's summons to register—and several more for David's words to sink in.

The man who had helped her transform her life wanted her to be part of his—for always.

It didn't get any better than this.

"We'll be right there." As David called out a response, he rose and held out his hand. Val took it without hesitation, and in one lithe movement he pulled her to her feet.

As they joined his daughter a few moments later, David lowered himself to her level.

"Is that a cocoon, Daddy?" She pointed toward a small object attached to one of the branches of a bush.

"Yes, it is."

The little girl turned to Val. "Daddy said this is where butterflies come from. Did you know that?"

"Yes, I did." Val dropped down beside her.

"Can I wait here and watch it come out?"

"It won't happen that fast, sweetheart." David inspected the cocoon.

She studied it too. "How long will it take?"

"Every type of moth and butterfly is different. Some are ready to come out in a couple of weeks. Some stay in all winter and don't come out until the spring."

"You mean it might still be there at Christmas?"

"Maybe. If the butterfly comes out too soon, its wings won't be strong. And when it tries to fly, it will fall and get hurt. You wouldn't want that to happen, would you?"

"No."

"We'll check it again on our next visit, okay?"

"Okay." She turned to Val with a hopeful expression. "Will you come with us too?"

"Yes, sweetie. I'll come." Val smoothed back a stray strand of Victoria's hair, then directed her gaze toward David. "And I have a feeling this butterfly might be ready to fly long before Christmas."

"Like an early Christmas present, right, Daddy?"

David gave his daughter a hug, but his smile was all for Val. "Yes, honey. And it would be the best Christmas present of all."

Epilogue

—— Four Months Later ——

"They make a nice couple, don't they?"

At Scott's comment, Karen shifted around to watch Val and David walk hand in hand to the wedding cake on display in the center of the small banquet room. Val was glowing, and David had eyes for no one but his bride. "Yes, they do."

"I like the symbolism of having a wedding on New Year's Eve."

"I do too. Especially for Val. She's on the brink of a new life in so many ways."

"It's great that she connected at the high school."

"I know. The students love her, and I guess the administration does too. I wasn't sure they'd go for the job-share thing she and that other teacher cooked up, but I think she's as good at sales as she is at acting. With David adjusting his schedule too, they won't have much need for day care."

"Family first. I admire their priorities."

"So do I."

Several successive flashes went off as the newlyweds cut into their wedding cake, and Karen clapped along with the other guests.

As the applause died down, she turned to Scott. "Would you like some cake?"

He reached for her hand. "To be honest, I'd prefer some time alone with you."

She squeezed his fingers. "That can be arranged."

With Michael now gone, her life, too, was on the brink of a new beginning. One she hoped would include this man in a much more significant way—as soon as possible. "Have I told you lately how much I appreciate all the Chinese takeout and errand-running and gymnastics-practice chauffeuring you did when I had to work late or deal with paperwork for Michael?"

"You've mentioned it a few dozen times, I think."

"But you know what? I'm even more grateful for all the times you held my hand and offered encouragement after a really rough day. For listening to my angst over Kristen's issues and my own struggles with anger and forgiveness. And most of all, for never pushing me to take our relationship to the next level while Michael was alive. I wouldn't have gotten through this whole thing without you."

"Yes, you would. You're a strong woman."

"I'm not sure I'm that strong."

"I am." He leaned closer, and the embers in his eyes—the ones he'd kept banked all these months—suddenly burst into flame. "And as for thanks, I can think of one way you—"

"Here you are, Karen." Margaret bore down on them, interrupting in her usual imperious tone. "Val wants to take a family picture before they cut the rest of the cake. Come along. People are ready for dessert, and we don't want to delay things."

Without waiting for a reply, she marched off toward the bride and groom.

Karen gave an exasperated sigh. "Talk about rotten timing. Leave it to Mom."

A soft chuckle sounded close to her ear, Scott's breath warm against her skin. "Go ahead. Duty calls. I'll wait."

She shook her head. "You've done more than your share of that in recent months. I'll be back as fast as I can."

Keeping an eye on Scott, Karen joined her family. Smiled as the photographer took photo after photo. Hurried back to the man she loved the instant she could escape.

He rose as she approached, taking the hand she extended. "That didn't take long."

"We rushed. Kristen was as anxious to rejoin Steven as I was to get back to you. Nobody should need the matron of honor for a few minutes."

"What do you say we find someplace a little more private?"

"Sounds good to me."

He led her out of the dining room and glanced down the hall toward the lobby of the private club. A cozy fire crackled in the hearth, and a small, vacant settee stood across from it.

"That has our name on it." He headed toward it with a purposeful stride.

As they took their seats, he angled toward her, resting an arm across the top of the back. "This beats fighting for a bench at Mr. Frank's any day."

"Ah, but that has its charms too. I remember one particular visit when we had to squeeze together on a sap-covered bench."

"I remember that too. Sap has had a fond place in my heart ever since."

She gave a soft laugh and scooted closer to him. "I do agree it's hard to beat snuggling up in front of a crackling fire on a cold winter night." She checked her watch. "Almost midnight. What a nice way to ring in the new year."

"Speaking of new years—and new beginnings—I have an announcement." Scott didn't change his posture or expression, but all at once a quiver of excitement stirred the air. "I have another new job."

Frowning, she tilted her head to look up at him. "But you already have several. Music director at church. Sax player with a jazz group. A full roster of students for private lessons. What more can you take on?"

"How about the St. Louis Symphony Orchestra?"

She sent him a puzzled look. "What do you mean?"

"My classical training was on the clarinet, so while you were otherwise occupied this fall I dusted off those skills and auditioned in November. An opening came up two weeks ago, and they offered me the job."

Her eyes widened. "But . . . that's a world-class orchestra!"

He sent her a look of mock indignation. "Are you saying I'm not good enough?"

She nudged him with her elbow. "You know better. I'm in awe of your talent on the sax, and I'm sure you're every bit as good on the clarinet. But why didn't you tell me about all this?"

"It might never have amounted to anything. Besides, you've had a few other things on your mind."

"Nothing that should have taken precedence over this! Scott, this is so . . . incredible . . . fabulous . . . wonderful . . . I can't find enough superlatives to tell you how happy I am for you!"

He gave her a slow smile. "There are other ways to express joy." Confirming they were alone with a quick scan of the lobby, he pulled her into his arms. "I've waited a long time for this moment. So get ready."

"I'm more than ready." She was reaching for him even before she finished her whispered reassurance. Throughout Michael's last weeks, Scott had practiced the patience he'd claimed he didn't possess, never pressuring her to give him time she didn't have, settling for no more than a few stolen lip brushes that had offered a tantalizing hint of the passion he kept on a tight tether.

But now, at last, it was time.

And Scott's kiss was everything she'd dreamed of.

Tender, yet ardent. All-consuming. And filled with promise.

When at last—and with obvious reluctance—he pulled back, she could utter only one word. "Wow!"

"My sentiments exactly." His voice wasn't quite steady. Nor was the hand that touched her face. "I have something else to tell you too. The symphony will be going on a three-week European tour in April. I hoped you might join me at the end, in Paris. I can't think of a better place for a belated honeymoon, can you?"

Her lungs stopped working. "Are you . . . is that a proposal?"

"What do you think?" His tender, intimate smile erased any doubts.

"You want to get married in April?" She savored the words even as she tried to take them in.

"No. I said *belated* honeymoon. As far as I'm concerned, the sooner the better for the wedding." He took her hands, and she could feel the slight tremor running through them. "After your last experience of marriage, I know you deserve a prince this time around. Unfortunately, I seem to have misplaced my crown. In all honesty, I'm not the best bargain around. I make mistakes, I'm not always patient, and I have a temper that can get the better of me.

"But I do have some good qualities. I believe in honoring promises. I believe love is a gift to be treasured and cherished all the days of our lives. I believe in keeping my priorities straight. And I believe God brought us together for a reason. I think I know why, and I hope you feel the same way. Because I love you with all my heart. And I always will."

With a trembling hand, Karen reached out to touch Scott's face, to assure herself he was real and not some fairy-tale fantasy she'd conjured up. But when he caught her hand in his, then turned it over and pressed his lips to her palm before he let her place it against his cheek, the lingering tingle of his kiss and the slightly rough texture of his five o'clock shadow beneath her fingertips was tactile proof he was very real.

A grandfather clock began to chime behind her, the sonorous bong ringing in the new year—and reminding her how quickly the seasons of life slipped by.

But this first day of the new year marked the start of a new season. A better season.

She and Scott had done their share of weeping.

This was their time to laugh—and to love.

She leaned closer to him, until she was only a whisper away. "I do feel the same way. I love you with all my heart too. Maybe I'm being sentimental, but I always thought a Valentine's Day wedding would be wonderful. That would also give Kristen some time to get used to the idea—though she already thinks you're terrific, so it should be a smooth transition. Is that too long to wait?"

The flame in his eyes put the blazing fire in the grate a few feet away to shame. "I think I can manage six weeks. Especially knowing I have a lifetime ahead with you." He stroked her cheek, then let his fingers play in her hair. "Now I think we need to seal this engagement properly."

As he leaned toward her, Karen caught a movement in her peripheral vision. Val had started down the hall but stopped when she saw the cozy duo on the settee. For a brief second, their gazes connected. Val smiled, and in her eyes, Karen saw joy and approval and love. With a thumbs-up, the bride blended back into the shadows and retraced her steps.

Then Scott's lips gently settled over hers. And just before she lost herself in his arms, in the fleeting instant before his kiss swept her away, Karen gave thanks for the blessings that graced her life.

And for that certain summer when four lives had intersected to create a tapestry of love.

Author's Note

For readers who know me only through my suspense novels, *That Certain Summer* may seem like quite a departure. But in truth, it isn't.

For one thing, I've been writing modern-day (contemporary) romance novels for years—long before I delved into suspense . . . though this story is bigger and more complex than my previous contemporary books.

In addition, no matter the genre, what interests me most when I write a book are the people on the pages. Whether it's a high-stakes, edge-of-the-seat suspense novel or a contemporary romance, I want to understand the forces that shaped both the characters and the choices they make—even when I don't agree with those choices. And I want to take readers along on that journey.

For that reason, in every book I try to create intriguing, complex people. People who exhibit courage and honor and principles, who trust in God and walk the talk. People who've lost their way. People who've made mistakes. People who repent—and people who don't. Whether it's a suspense novel or a book like *That Certain Summer*, the genre I choose is simply a vehicle for delving into the minds—and hearts—of my characters as I put them in challenging situations that test their mettle.

And the truth is, every time I meet a new character and embark on a voyage of discovery with them, I learn something new about what makes people tick and how our relationships influence every choice we make.

In the end, while I strive to write entertaining books that keep people up late at night eager to see what happens next, my main goal is to pull readers into the lives of my characters. To make them turn the last page thinking, *Those people were real. I felt for them. And I'm sorry to say good-bye.*

I hope *That Certain Summer* did that for you—and thank you for joining me on this journey.

Irene Hannon is a bestselling, award-winning author who took the publishing world by storm at the tender age of ten with a sparkling piece of fiction that received national attention.

Okay . . . maybe that's a slight exaggeration. But she *was* one of the honorees in a complete-the-story contest conducted by a national children's magazine. And she likes to think of that as her "official" fiction-writing debut!

Since then, she has written more than forty contemporary romance and romantic suspense novels. Irene has twice won the RITA Award—the "Oscar" of romantic fiction—and her books have been honored with a Carol award, a National Readers' Choice award, a Retailers Choice award, a HOLT medallion, a Daphne du Maurier award, and two Reviewers' Choice awards from *RT Book Reviews* magazine. In 2011, *Booklist* named *Deadly Pursuit* one of the Top 10 Inspirational Fiction titles of the year.

Irene, who holds a BA in psychology and an MA in journalism, juggled two careers for many years until she gave up her executive corporate communications position with a Fortune 500 company to write full time. She is happy to say she has no regrets. As she points out, leaving behind the rush-hour commute, corporate politics, and a relentless BlackBerry that never slept was no sacrifice.

A trained vocalist, Irene has sung the leading role in numerous community theater productions and is also a soloist at her church.

When not otherwise occupied, she loves to cook, garden, and

take long walks. She and her husband also enjoy traveling, Saturday mornings at their favorite coffee shop, and spending time with family. They make their home in Missouri.

To learn more about Irene and her books, visit www.irenehannon.com.

Enjoy some SUSPENSE with your ROMANCE?
Here's an excerpt from Irene's latest bestselling romantic suspense novel!

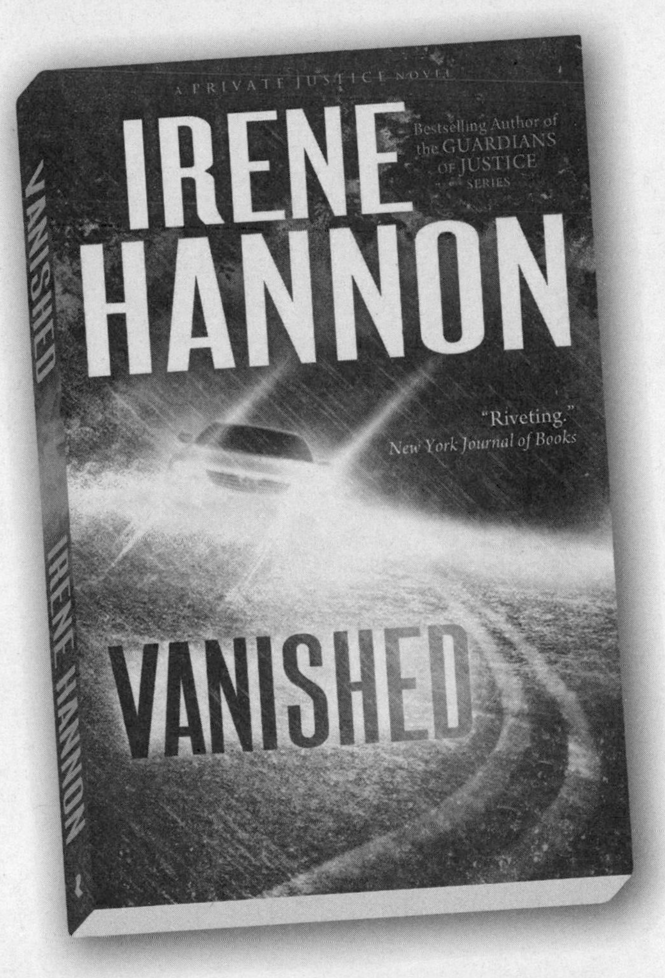

"An excellent suggestion for readers who enjoy Mary Higgins Clark's subtly chilling brand of suspense."
—*Booklist*

a division of Baker Publishing Group
www.RevellBooks.com

Available Wherever Books Are Sold
Also Available in Ebook Format

1

What a lousy night to get lost.

Moira Harrison peered through the April rain slashing across her windshield. Even at full speed, the wipers were no match for the torrential onslaught. The faint line bisecting the narrow strip of pavement—the only thing keeping her on the road and out of the ditch filled with churning runoff immediately to her right—faded in and out with alarming frequency.

Tightening her grip on the wheel with one hand, she cranked up the defroster with the other. Fogged-up windows were the last thing she needed. As it was, the high-intensity xenon headlights of her trusty Camry were barely denting the dense darkness of the woods-rimmed rural Missouri road. Nor were they penetrating the shrouding downpour.

So much for the premium she'd paid to upgrade from standard halogen.

She spared a quick look left and right. No light from house or farm broke the desolate blackness. Nor were there any road signs to indicate her location. Maybe a St. Louis–area native would be better able to wend his or her way back to civilization than a newcomer like her, but she doubted it. Dark, winding rural routes were confusing. Period. Especially in the rain.

With a sigh, Moira refocused on the road. If she'd known Highway 94 was prone to flooding and subject to sudden closure, she'd never have risked subjecting herself to this poorly marked detour by lingering for dinner in Augusta after she finished her interview.

Instead, she'd have headed straight back to the rented condo she now called home and spent her Friday evening safe and warm, cuddled up with a mug of soothing peppermint tea, organizing her notes. She might even have started on a first draft of the feature article. It wouldn't hurt to impress her new boss with an early turn-in.

A bolt of lightning sliced through the sky, and she cringed as a bone-jarring boom of thunder rolled through the car.

That had been close.

Too close.

She had to get away from all these trees.

Increasing her pressure on the gas pedal, she kept her attention fixed on the road as she groped on the passenger seat for her purse. Maybe her distance glasses were crammed into a corner and she'd missed them the first time she'd checked.

Five seconds later, hopes dashed, she gave up the search. The glasses must still be in the purse she'd taken to the movie theater last weekend. That was about the only time she ever used them—except behind the wheel on rainy nights.

It figured.

The zipper on her purse snagged as she tried to close it, and Moira snuck a quick glance at the passenger seat. Too dark to see. She'd have to deal with it later.

Releasing the purse, she lifted her gaze—and sucked in a sharp breath.

Front and center, caught in the beam of her headlights, was a frantically waving person.

Directly in the path of the car.

Less than fifty feet away.

Lungs locking, Moira squeezed the wheel and jammed the brake to the floor.

Screeching in protest, the car fishtailed as it slid toward the figure with no noticeable reduction in speed.

Stop! Please stop!

Moira screamed the silent plea in her head as she yanked the wheel hard to the left.

Instead of changing direction, however, the car began to skid sideways on the slick pavement.

But in the instant before the beams of the headlights swung away from the road—and away from the figure standing in her path—one image seared itself across her brain.

Glazed, terror-filled eyes.

Then the person was gone, vanished in the darkness, as the vehicle spun out of control.

Moira braced herself.

And prayed.

But when she felt a solid thump against the side of the car, she knew her prayers hadn't been answered.

She'd hit the terrified person who'd been trying to flag her down.

The bottom fell out of her stomach as the car continued to careen across the road. Onto the shoulder. Into the woods. One bone-jarring bounce after another.

It didn't stop until the side smashed into a tree, slamming her temple against the window of the door to the accompaniment of crumpling metal.

Then everything went silent.

For a full thirty seconds, Moira remained motionless, hands locked on the wheel, every muscle taut, heart hammering. Her head pounded in rhythm to the beat of rain against the metal roof, and she drew a shuddering breath. Blinked. The car had stopped spinning, but the world around her hadn't.

She closed her eyes. Continued to breathe. In. Out. In. Out.

When she at last risked another peek, the scene had steadied.

Better.

Peeling her fingers off the wheel, she took a quick inventory. Her arms and legs moved, and nothing except her head hurt. As far as she could tell, she hadn't sustained any serious injuries.

But she knew the person she'd hit hadn't been as lucky—a person who might very well be lying in the middle of the road right now.

In the path of an oncoming car.

Her pulse stuttered, and she fought against a crescendo of panic as she tried to kick-start her brain. To think through the fuzziness.

Okay. First priority—call 911. After that, she'd see what she could do to help the person she'd hit while she waited for the pros to arrive.

Plan in place, she groped for her purse. But the seat beside her was empty. Hadn't her purse been there moments before?

With a herculean effort, she coerced the left side of her brain to engage.

The floor.

Her purse must have fallen to the floor while the car was spinning.

Hands shaking, she fumbled with the clasp on her seat belt. It took three jabs at the button before it released. Once free of the constraint, she leaned sideways and reached toward the floor—just as the driver-side door creaked open.

With a gasp, she jerked upright. A black-shrouded figure stood in the shadows, out of range of her dome light.

Her heart began to bang against her rib cage again as a cold mist seeped into the car.

"I saw the accident. Are you all right, miss?"

The voice was deep. Male. And the only clue to his gender. The monk-like hood of his slicker kept most of his features in shadows.

But she didn't care who he was. Help had arrived.

Thank you, God!

"Yes. I . . . I think so. I banged my head against the window, and I'm a little dizzy. But . . . I hit someone on the road. I need to call 911. And I need to help the other person."

The man leaned a bit closer, and she glimpsed the outline of a square jaw. "You've got a nasty bump on your temple. Moving around isn't a good idea until the paramedics check you out. I'll help the person you hit." He tipped his head and looked across her. "Is that blood on the passenger seat?"

As Moira shifted sideways to look, she felt a jab in her thigh. "Ow!"

"Watch the broken glass. Lean a little to the right." The man restrained her with one hand on her upper arm as she complied. "Hold on a second while I brush off the seat."

He was silent for a moment, and she shivered as the wind shifted and the rain began to pummel her through the open door, soaking through her sweater.

"Okay. I think I got most of it."

He released her, and she collapsed back against the seat. As he retracted his hand, she caught a quick glimpse of his gold Claddagh wedding ring. The same kind her dad wore.

Somehow that comforted her.

"Stay put." He melted back into the shadows, beyond the range of the dome light. "I'll call 911 and check on the other person. Give me a few minutes."

With that, he closed the door.

Alone again in the dark car, Moira tried to keep him in sight. But within seconds he disappeared into the rain.

As the minutes ticked by and the full impact of what had happened began to register, her shivering intensified and her stomach churned.

She could have been killed.

And she might have killed or seriously injured someone else.

Wrapping her arms around herself, Moira closed her eyes as a wave of dizziness swept over her.

At least help had arrived.

With that thought to sustain her, she let the darkness close in.

MEET IRENE HANNON
at www.IreneHannon.com

Learn news, sign up for her mailing list,
AND MORE!
Find her on

Coming Summer 2014 . . .

Who could guess that a little girl's simple, heartfelt letter would touch so many lives—or reap so many blessings?

Watch for this new contemporary romance from bestselling author

Irene Hannon!

"Hannon captures your attention at page one and doesn't let it go until long after you've finished the book!"

—*Suspense Magazine*

Don't Miss Any of the GUARDIANS *of* JUSTICE series

Revell
a division of Baker Publishing Group
www.RevellBooks.com

Available Wherever Books Are Sold
Also Available in Ebook Format

Don't Miss Irene Hannon's Bestselling
HEROES OF QUANTICO series

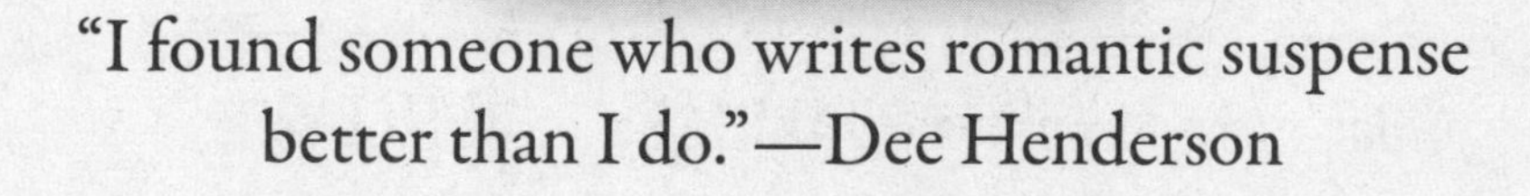

a division of Baker Publishing Group
www.RevellBooks.com

Available Wherever Books Are Sold
Also Available in Ebook Format